HARD CURRENCY

INSPECTOR PORFIRY ROSTNIKOV MYSTERIES
BY STUART M. KAMINSKY

*Death of a Dissident**
Black Knight in Red Square
*Red Chameleon**
*A Fine Red Rain**
*A Cold Red Sunrise**
*The Man Who Walked Like a Bear**
*Rostnikov's Vacation**
*Death of a Russian Priest**

OTHER MYSTERIES BY STUART M. KAMINSKY

Down for the Count
Exercise in Terror
The Fala Factor
He Done Her Wrong
High Midnight
The Howard Hughes Affair
The Man Who Shot Lewis Vance
Murder on the Yellow Brick Road
Never Cross a Vampire
Poor Butterfly
Think Fast Mr. Peters
Buried Caesars
*Lieberman's Folly**

*Published by Ivy Books

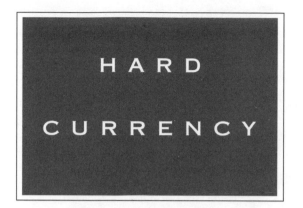

HARD CURRENCY

STUART M. KAMINSKY

FAWCETT COLUMBINE • NEW YORK

A Fawcett Columbine Book
Published by Ballantine Books

Copyright © 1995 by Stuart M. Kaminsky

LIBRARY OF CONGRESS CATALOGING-IN-PUBLICATION DATA

Kaminsky, Stuart M.
Hard currency / Stuart M. Kaminsky.
p. cm.
ISBN 0-449-90725-2
1. Rostnikov, Porfiry Petrovich (Fictitious character)—Fiction. 2. Police—Russia—
Moscow—Fiction. 3. Russians—Cuba—Fiction. 4. Moscow (Russia)—Fiction.
I.Title.
PS3561.A43H37 1995
813'.54—dc20   94-28273
CIP

Manufactured in the United States of America
First Edition: February 1995
10   9   8   7   6   5   4   3   2   1

To Jeff Rice
with thanks for
his friendship and advice.

HARD CURRENCY

Two Cubans lost in the jungle were kidnapped and tied to stakes while their native captors circled them shouting, "Ocha, Una, Ocha, Una."

Suddenly the native leader approached the first Cuban and shouted, "Ocha, Una?"

"Ocha," the Cuban guessed, and the entire tribe raped him.

Then the native leader turned to the second Cuban and shouted, "Ocha, Una?"

"Una," said the second Cuban.

"Good," said one of the natives. "First, Ocha. Then, Una."

—A joke currently popular in Havana

ONE

Iliana Ivanova adjusted her backpack, looked down Rusakov-
skaya Street, and went over her plan for robbing the bald-
headed businessman who waited next to her for the bus.

It was a warm May afternoon, and there was no one else at
the bus stop on Rusakovskaya Street but Iliana and the man,
who wore glasses and carried an ancient briefcase. The man did
his best to avoid eye contact with the girl. He shifted his briefcase from hand to hand, looked at his watch, examined the
clear late-morning sky, and looked down the broad street trying
to conjure up a bus.

Most Muscovites who were working were already at their
jobs. Those who had no jobs were hustling the streets, standing
in lines for food, brooding in their apartments, or going mad in
the parks. Sokolniki Park was directly behind the bus stop. That
was where Iliana Ivanova, who was known to herself and her
friends as the Yellow Angel, planned to take the man. The park
was vast—a fifteen-hundred-acre forest of ancient trees and
clearings with restaurants and cafés, which were hardly ever
open now.

The Yellow Angel was only a bit nervous. She had pulled off the same plan almost two dozen times since leaving Tbilisi six months ago, and not once—well, not counting the fat Armenian in Grozny—had any victim shown the slightest suspicion. The reasons were obvious. The Yellow Angel was almost nineteen but she looked no more than sixteen. She was thin with large breasts, a clear-skinned face with pink cheeks, and shoulder-length naturally blond hair. Her brown eyes were large and sincere. Dressed in jeans and a clean shirt, she looked like a schoolgirl, an impression she emphasized by the large book she always carried under her arm. The book was something about economics. She had tried to read it once when she was sick and recuperating in the shack of a widower outside of Petrov, before she came to Moscow and found Anatoli. The widower who had taken her in was probably fifty. Iliana had played the virgin for him, hating his farm smell, the coarseness of his palms, the little brown mole next to his nose.

She had managed to keep the man out of her bed for all but two nights by feigning sickness. When she left, Iliana had sorely wanted to smash his stupid potato face, but she contented herself with simply stealing what she could carry.

Tbilisi had been fine for most of her life. When she was fourteen, Iliana had moved out of the apartment on Chavchavadze Avenue she shared with her parents and younger brother. She had moved in with a dull-witted nineteen-year-old boy who worked in the Vlodima glove factory in Miskheta and gave her whatever she wanted that he could afford, which was very little. In return, she gave him a baby. Three weeks after the baby had come the Yellow Angel took the baby to her mother, who welcomed it and slammed the door on her daughter.

Iliana worked in Tbilisi with a gang called the Golden Lepers. Then the Soviet Union came apart, Georgia declared independence, people were shooting and killing each other on the streets. Less than a day's drive away in Azerbaijan and Armenia, there was even more fighting and killing. Some of the Golden Lepers joined the battle without knowing what it was about, and two of them died shouting support for Gorbachev's old buddy Shevardnadze. Most of the Lepers, including Iliana, took advantage of the chaos to loot and rob.

She had done well. As bait for Golden Leper robberies, she simply joined in when she had lured a victim into an alleyway or behind the Iveria Hotel or into the bushes near the fountain in Victory Park.

Then Illya had been caught—fleeing with a stolen wallet, he had run into the arms of a soldier. Then Illya talked, quickly, about all the Golden Lepers, including Iliana, to whom he had proclaimed eternal love unto death.

And so Iliana had gone to her mother's house, insisted on kissing her son good-bye, and then headed out of Tbilisi, into the countryside and toward the north. Since then, she had been required to take on the sole responsibility for luring and robbing her victims, which sometimes made her a bit nervous, but she also had no one to share with, which pleased her. All her victims had been eager to believe she was a beautiful, semi-innocent child they had been fortunate enough to encounter at a moment of her greatest financial need. The man at the bus stop would be no different.

What she didn't like about Moscow was that it could be cold, very cold. Warm winds blew across the south slopes of the Caucasus Mountains from the Black Sea to the west or from the Caspian Sea to the east. It seldom snowed in Tbilisi, and when it did, the snow barely clung to the streets. Here, in Moscow, winter had been brutal. Six months ago, Iliana would have been determined to head someplace warmer when the winter came again, but now she had a family, people who respected and appreciated her.

Cars sped by them toward the heart of Moscow. The Yellow Angel was only vaguely aware of them, though a police car would have registered immediately. She watched the bald businessman, who finally had no choice but to make eye contact, if only for an instant. Iliana smiled sweetly and did not flinch. In spite of the chill air, she let her coat open innocently as she shifted the book to her other hand. Beneath the cloth coat she wore a white skirt and a knit sweater. The man adjusted his glasses and looked away in the direction from which the bus should have appeared.

"Late," said Iliana with a smile of resignation.

The businessman made a grunting sound and checked his watch.

The man was a bit larger than Anatoli, and definitely heavier, but he did not look like a man who knew or welcomed violence. Iliana's fingers played with the smooth handle of the knife in her pocket. It was a folding fishing knife, which she always made a point of opening slowly in front of her victims. It was encouraging to watch them suck in air or freeze like frightened weasels when the blade clicked. This one would be no different. It wasn't that she would ever use the knife. Threatening to cry rape was more effective, since that was the direction the victims' thoughts had probably been running.

"I'm going to be late for the Polytechnic," she said with a deep sigh. "I'm already late."

"So am I," said the man, looking at his watch again.

"Late for school?" asked Iliana.

"No," the man said. With a slight laugh he turned to the girl and adjusted his glasses. "Late for work. The hospital. I'm a doctor. Not far from the Polytechnic."

"I don't think the bus is coming," she said, shaking her head. "Strikes. No fuel. No parts. The Czechs, Bulgarians, even the other Commonwealth countries treat Russia like . . ."

She shook her head in disgust.

The bald man grunted again and shook his head in agreement.

"My name is Katerina," Iliana said, tossing her hair back and holding out her hand.

The man glanced around to see if anyone was watching and stepped forward to shake the girl's warm hand.

"You have strong hands," he said, stepping back again.

"Training," she said. "I want to be a cosmonaut, but the way things are . . ."

"There will be cosmonauts again," the bald man said. "Even women cosmonauts. They'll sell advertising space to Coca-Cola and keep sending rockets to burn up in the sun. Only now the Americans will pay for it. They will send pretty girls up so they can sell their pictures to American and French magazines."

Iliana laughed.

"There is a *tahksee* stand on the other side of the park," Iliana said. "Maybe we could share a ride. You said you work near the Polytech?"

The bald man looked at Iliana now and adjusted his glasses yet again. Then he looked forlornly once more down Rusakov-skaya.

"You have money for a cab?" the man asked.

Iliana shifted her backpack and pulled a worn wallet from the front pocket of her coat. She opened it to reveal bills, not too many, but enough to show the man she could pay. There were more rubles, some deutsche marks, French francs, and six American dollars in her backpack, but she kept them hidden from her victims, who might well have wondered where a schoolgirl got so much money.

"My father told me to take a cab if the bus didn't come," she said, returning the wallet to her pocket. "If I miss another day, they'll throw me out. Girls are barely tolerated at the Poly-tech."

The bald man ran his tongue over his teeth and made a decision.

"All right," he said.

"Good," said the girl. "Let's hurry."

"I can't run," said the man. "My heart."

"We'll walk," said Iliana, moving into step next to the man. "Your name is . . . ?"

It was always good to know the name of the victim, in order to use it—to threaten to tear it away from the one who bore it, to make him think that she would scream it to the police, the newspapers, the man's wife, mother, or lover.

"Yevgeny Odom, Dr. Yevgeny Odom," the man said, looking straight ahead and moving briskly.

"Here, we go this way," Iliana said cheerfully, patting the knife in her pocket.

"I know," Yevgeny Odom said.

"You live close by?" asked Iliana as they entered the park on the gray concrete path.

Odom grunted.

They were still too close to the street for the Yellow Angel to make her move. She had learned from experience in . . . what was the town? No matter. She had learned to be patient, to be sure no one could see or hear, to pick the right hour. Late morning was perfect. The only ones who might stumble onto her committing a crime would be some old *babushka* with a child or a gray grandfather with arthritic knees.

Odom stopped.

"Tired already?" she said, looking back down the path.

A little farther. She had to get this soft one with the bad heart a little farther into the park. She could get him behind some bushes with a sexual suggestion, make him go to his knees, show him the blade so that he would be happy to turn over his watch and his money. It would be fast. She would warn him that if she were caught she would deny the robbery, claim that she had run from the bald man when he made sexual advances, thrown her behind the bushes, demanded that she do obscene things. She would also take the man's shoes and stuff them into her backpack.

Iliana knew enough about the police to be sure that her claims of sexual assault would not be believed, but her carefully selected victims would not know this, and she was sure that they would prefer to take the loss, hide their shame, and go along with their lives, which were difficult enough without dealing with underpaid and surly policemen.

"Why are you stopping?" asked Iliana.

"I live there," Odom said, pointing over the tops of the trees toward a group of apartment buildings. "I have a car. We can drive. I don't think I can make it to the cab stop."

"You have a . . ."

"There's no place to park where I work, and it costs too much for gas." Odom was panting. "My manifold is . . ."

"Fine," said the Yellow Angel with a soft smile. To get to the apartments they would have to leave the path and go into the trees. "I'll pay for gas."

Odom nodded and started off the path and onto the grass. "This way," he said.

She followed him and was pleased that he was leading her into a dark copse of birch trees. The birds were noisy. The path was well behind them.

"Stop," she said and stepped in front of the man.

"What?" asked Odom, trying to catch his breath.

"This is far enough," she said, dropping the backpack and the economics book to the ground.

The man blinked, then looked around as if to see whether anyone else might have stumbled into this secluded spot to witness the girl's strange behavior.

"You're a prostitute, aren't you?" the man panted.

Iliana shook her head slowly as she removed the knife from her pocket, careful to keep a few feet between her and the frightened man. Everything was going perfectly.

Crows—huge, fat, gray-black, and ugly, perhaps two or three—went wild in a tree above them. Neither man nor girl looked up.

"What are you doing?" asked Odom, holding his briefcase in front of him like a shield and taking a step back.

"Not what I am doing," said Iliana. "What you are doing. You are giving me your wallet and your watch. Now, quick."

She lifted her knife toward Odom's face. The man took another step backward and almost tripped.

"Quick," she whispered, looking toward the path beyond the trees.

Odom was sweating through his gray suit now. He pulled out his wallet, handed it to Iliana, who pocketed it in her coat, and then removed his watch and handed it over.

"The briefcase," said Iliana. "There are valuables in it."

"I . . . yes," said Odom.

"Open it," she said, holding the point of the knife inches from Odom's nose.

Odom gulped, and Iliana, her heart pounding, tried not to laugh. The man looked like a cartoon character. He removed his glasses and placed them in his coat pocket. This seemed funny to Iliana. She would enjoy telling this whole adventure to Anatoli and the others as soon as she could.

As Odom opened his briefcase, Iliana said, "Just dump it out and drop it. Then take off your shoes."

The man stopped with his hand inside the briefcase. He looked at the girl.

"Now, Kola," the man said. "You are free."

"What?" asked Iliana. "What is it? What do you have? Hurry up," she commanded, shifting nervously from foot to foot.

"Only this," said the bald man. He leaped at her with a black metallic blur.

Iliana did not understand what happened next. It was a rush

of heat and pain. Something snapped in her wrist as the black object hit her, and she dropped the knife.

She screamed in pain and stumbled backward. The bald man had dropped his briefcase and was advancing on her in a half crouch. He was smiling horribly and making a rough sound like a hungry dog.

"No, wait, stop," Iliana cried, holding up her unbroken arm to protect herself. The raging man in the gray suit was pounding her with his fists.

Iliana went to the ground and tried to curl into a ball.

"Please," she said, and the blows ceased. "I'm not a thief. I'm hungry. I wasn't going to hurt you. I've never done anything like this before, nothing, ever. My god, you broke my arm. But it will be fine, fine. I'll tell you what. Let's go behind the bushes. I'll take off my clothes."

She struggled with her unbroken arm to pull down her sweater. The pain was screaming with electricity.

She breathed heavily, tasted dry leaves in her mouth, opened her eye to see a blue-green beetle calmly munching on a blade of grass.

The bald man was panting wildly now as he again raised the metal bar.

"Don't hit my face," she pleaded, looking up at the man from her knees. It was like she was praying.

"I won't hit your face," Odom said, breathing deeply.

"I've never done anything like this be—"

"I don't care," said Odom. "Be quiet. Shh."

Iliana looked up. The bald man had the fingers of his left hand to his lips. In his right hand was the black thing, which Iliana could now see was a piece of metal pipe. There was blood on the pipe. Her blood.

"My father . . ." Iliana tried.

"Quiet," said the man, leaning down over her and whispering. "Sh. Sh. Yevgeny is sleeping."

Iliana went quiet, spat out something, a leaf, a piece of grass, the beetle.

"You don't go to the Polytechnic. You're a runaway," the man said.

"Yes," Iliana said.

"How old are you?"

"Fifteen," she lied.

"You made it very easy for him," the bald man said. "You were not very smart. Do you know what park you are in?"

"No, I . . ."

"Sokolniki Park, the park of the falconers. The Czar's huntsmen trained their falcons here. They swooped down on command, snatched birds in flight, and brought them back to their masters."

"I've never . . ." Iliana began and then stopped.

"You are going to do what I tell you," the man said. "You will do it exactly as I say, with enthusiasm and a perfect imitation of good cheer. You understand?"

"Yes," said Iliana.

The pipe suddenly swooped down, making the sound of the rushing wind through its hollow center. It came down across her back as she tried to turn away. The pain was hot and wet. She screamed.

"No screaming," said the man. "No screaming or you die."

Iliana bit into her cheek to stifle her scream. She wished for the gunfire in the streets of Tbilisi, prayed that Anatoli or one of the others had followed her, vowed that if she lived through this she would never again work alone, never.

"No screams," she said softly.

"Good," said the man. "Then we begin."

Porfiry Petrovich Rostnikov disliked airplanes in general and Aeroflot flights in particular. He had heard from Prokofyev, who headed military security at Sheremetyevo International Airport, how Aeroflot was now being mismanaged by both the government and private investors. They had resorted to metallic cannibalism—plundering dead planes for parts—to keep the dwindling fleet flying.

There was a runway covered with weeds and hidden from most travelers that served as the graveyard of the flying dinosaurs of the former Soviet Union.

Prokofyev had offered to show the archaeological site to Rostnikov when next he flew, but the detective had chosen to leave the heap of rusting corpses and broken wings to his imagination.

There were many reasons beyond the decay of Aeroflot that caused Rostnikov's general distrust of machines that flew. A primary factor was his concern that, on the slightest whim, the plane might grow weary, shed a wing, or decide that a small bolt that held the engine together should suddenly be spat out.

The behavior of animals was unpredictable within parameters that made Rostnikov comfortable. The behavior of machines, which could be predicted, struck him as no more to be counted on than the goodwill of a dancing bear. The purring of an engine and the purring of a cat were not signs of contentment but of potential irrationality.

These things had been on his mind when Rostnikov's superior, Colonel Snitkonoy, known to all as the Gray Wolfhound, had seen him off at the airport.

They had spoken in the VIP lounge, a dark empty room with a bar that sold vodka and tasteless chips for hard currency. Elena Timofeyeva had sat in the vast, stale-smelling waiting room next to the VIP lounge as the Wolfhound had paced and gone over both Rostnikov's assignment and the problems of the Special Investigation Office that were Rostnikov's responsibility.

The Gray Wolfhound was a man designed to command re-

spect. Always immaculately uniformed, with fair, well-cut fea-
tures, blue eyes, and a mane of perfect white hair, the Wolfhound through wars, coups, and attempted coups had not only
survived but prospered. Those in government and on Petrovka
Street, however, had long considered the Wolfhound a joke
whose function was to make glowing speeches and to escort
middle-level foreign visitors on tours.

But the work of Porfiry Petrovich and his assistants, who had
been demoted to the Wolfhound's staff, had been given credit
for preventing the assassination of the president. The Wolfhound had become a hero, and his ceremonial office, small
though it was, was now being given increasingly delicate cases.

Some of these assignments came from those in the government who feared that the loyalty of more traditional depart-
ments could not be counted on in case of a sudden change in
the government. Other difficult cases came from those who
hoped that the man and his staff would fail and others loyal to
the past would replace them.

"Delicacy," the Wolfhound had said to Rostnikov, who sat in
a particularly uncomfortable purple VIP chair looking up at the
standing colonel. "The Cuban government does not wish to
prosecute a Russian citizen for murder without the assurance
that our government will not interfere."

Rostnikov nodded dutifully, though the colonel had made
this point at least four times in the past two days.

"Make no mistake"—the colonel pointed solemnly at Porfiry
Petrovich—"the Cubans still rely upon our goodwill and we
upon theirs. A time may come soon when our government will
be in a position to resume meaningful trade with Cuba."

Rostnikov nodded as Colonel Snitkonoy clasped both hands
behind his back.

"In addition, there are members of the People's Congress
who have taken particular interest in this case. I have been told
that there is concern that if it is not concluded with dispatch,

certain radical elements, Pamyat, Stalinists, looking for a cause—in this case the conviction of a Russian citizen of murder in Cuba—will make an issue, demand his release, attack the government. And, I tell you this in confidence, there is concern that members of both the Congress and the KGB may be encouraging such a reaction. And so you are, as quickly as possible, to review the investigation of the Cuban police, confirm their findings, and return as quickly as possible."

"What if he is innocent?" Rostnikov asked.

"That would greatly complicate the situation," said the colonel. "But . . . you have seen the reports."

Rostnikov nodded again.

"And?"

Rostnikov shrugged.

"Inspector Rostnikov," the Wolfhound said with a weary sigh. "There are sensitivities here."

"I will be sensitive to sensitivities," said Rostnikov. "But . . ."

Colonel Snitkonoy shook his head.

"But what? Find what you will find, Inspector. Do what you must do. But it would be best if the man is guilty and the Cuban government has done an outstanding job of criminal investigation."

"Let us hope then that this Russian citizen is guilty of murder," said Rostnikov.

"I do not find irony engaging or instructional," said the colonel, looking toward the door of the lounge. The bartender and a few passengers were being kept out of the lounge by two uniformed officers under the colonel's orders.

"I will do my best to refrain from irony," Rostnikov said. "And the Kazakhstani minister?"

"Deputy Inspector Karpo can do the paperwork," the colonel said. "The man died of a heart attack. Unfortunately . . ."

". . . well timed," said Rostnikov.

The Wolfhound remained silent for an impressive ten seconds

before speaking slowly, earnestly, as he had spoken to the paper mill workers in Estonia before the collapse of the Union, as he had spoken to his troops in Czechoslovakia, as he had always spoken when sincerity had been called for to insure victory.

"Our nation is in jeopardy, Inspector Rostnikov. Our office is closely watched. If we are to serve our nation in this difficult period, we must strive for complete victory in our investigations."

"An Englishman once said that those who most often achieve victory are those who are most convinced that they are right. . . ." said Rostnikov.

Before the colonel could finish his first wary nod of agreement, Rostnikov continued.

". . . at the very moment when the only sane response is doubt."

"I am enlightened," said the Wolfhound wearily. "Enlightened."

"I will do my job, Colonel," said Rostnikov.

"I know," said the Wolfhound. "But if you could do this one with a little less curiosity and zeal than you normally display, our future may be a bit more secure. Curiosity is not required in this situation."

"I understand," said Rostnikov.

"There is a long and twisted road between understanding and action, Porfiry Petrovich," said the colonel. "Have I ever attempted to temper or thwart your investigations?"

"No," Rostnikov admitted.

"Have I supported your findings and those of our staff when I have believed them?"

"Yes."

"Have I not allowed our office, at your request, to assume responsibility for the investigation of the . . . how do they say it in America?"

"Serial killer," Rostnikov said.

"Ah, yes, serial killer. Serial killer." Colonel Snitkonoy tested the sound and seemed to find it acceptable. "The risk of failure is great."

"But the rewards of success are many," said Rostnikov.

"I grow weary of your epigrams, Porfiry Petrovich. You are reading too many American novels."

"Perhaps," said Rostnikov.

"Then there is nothing more to say," said the colonel.

And nothing more had been said. The colonel shook Rostnikov's hand and departed, and Rostnikov painfully and slowly rose from the chair in which his crippled leg had gone stiff and rebellious with pain. The leg had been mangled by a Nazi tank in the battle of Rostov when Porfiry Petrovich was a boy soldier. A determined, half-crazed, and shell-shocked doctor had saved the leg, though any dermatologist or brain surgeon could have seen that the leg demanded amputation. And so, for more than thirty-five years, Rostnikov had dragged his left leg as if it were a ball and chain.

Now, cramped in a small seat of an Aeroflot plane on its way to Havana, Rostnikov put aside the American mystery novel he had been reading and tried once more to find a position that would not cause him extreme pain. He failed. He glanced at his deputy inspector, Elena Timofeyeva, who had spent the first twelve hours of the flight to Cuba going over her Spanish language book, taking notes, and occasionally closing her eyes. The flight was only scheduled for twelve hours and ten minutes. There were still "several hours" to go till landing in Havana, according to the stewardess, who answered any questions— whether about arrival time, or about food, or drink, or the lack of paper in the toilet—with a depth of surliness usually encountered only in government food store clerks.

The flight had started badly. When Rostnikov had offered Elena the window seat, a one-minute struggle involving feminism, power, and confession had ensued.

"I will be quite comfortable on the aisle," she had said as people squeezed past them down the narrow aisle.

"I prefer the aisle," Rostnikov responded, pressing himself against the arm of the seat.

She gave him a look of grudging acceptance, suggesting that he was yet another man going through the motions of being polite and domineering.

"I would tell Emil Karpo the same thing," Rostnikov said as she eased into her seat. "I prefer the aisle. I like to be able to move about."

She had nodded, not believing him but recognizing the authority of the inspector who had given her the honor of going with him to Cuba. Her eyes met his and said, "This is to be a trip in which I am patronized. I can see it in our first exchange."

Elena did not feel completely comfortable in her new position as the only female in the Special Investigation Office of the MVD. She wanted, and made it known that she wanted, no special treatment. She worked hard, put in extra hours, tried to cooperate with the men in the office even when they were wrong. She was rewarded by being ignored or patronized.

Elena was a pretty, slightly plump young woman of almost thirty-one. She had clear skin, blue eyes, and remarkably even large, white teeth. Her dark hair was straight, cut efficiently short. Though confident of her skills, she was aware that she had been given her position largely through the influence of her aunt, Anna, with whom she lived in Moscow. Anna Timofeyeva had been Deputy Procurator General for all of Moscow, and Rostnikov had been her principal investigator till Anna's heart attack and forced retirement. Following a series of clashes with the KGB, Rostnikov had been transferred to the Office of Special Affairs, a dead-end ceremonial closet run by Colonel Snitkonoy.

Rostnikov and the investigators he had brought with him from the Procurator General's office, Sasha Tkach and Emil Karpo, were then singled out by the KGB for several impossible investigations, investigations designed to embarrass the Wolfhound and his staff. But Rostnikov had managed to escape embarrassment in each of these investigations, and, when the Soviet Union and Gorbachev had collapsed, the Special Affairs Office, having no political power or identity, emerged as one of the few untainted investigative offices in Russia.

As he stood in the aisle of the Aeroflot plane observing his young aide, Porfiry Petrovich wondered if he had made the right choice in selecting Elena Timofeyeva to accompany him to Cuba. In fact, he had had no choice. Karpo could not be pulled from the serial murders and the death of the Kazakhstani minister. Tkach had made it clear that he did not want to leave Moscow. Besides, Elena could speak Spanish.

"Elena Timofeyeva," Rostnikov said softly, letting his eyes meet those of the portly dark man in the row behind them who was paying unabashed attention, "I do not enjoy airplanes. I do not like to look out of windows and be reminded of space, time, and the frailties of human technology, particularly Soviet technology. I prefer to lose myself in books and sleep when it will come. I also like to wander the aisles to keep my leg from going stiff. It would be a favor to me if you take the window seat. Therefore, in this case, it is not I who would be doing you a favor but you who would be doing me one."

With disbelief and reluctance, Elena consented, and Porfiry Petrovich sank gratefully into his too-narrow seat, wondering how he had become a policeman when in fact he had the heart of a priest.

But Porfiry Petrovich Rostnikov, named by his father for Dostoyevsky's prosecutor in *Crime and Punishment,* knew he had been fated to be a policeman from the moment of his birth.

Though his parents never urged him to pursue such a career, the literary designation represented a destiny that had been planted in his soul, something which Russians were now permitted once more to possess.

There were a few other Russians and an oasis or two of Ukrainians, Estonians, and Lithuanians on the flight. Rostnikov had checked the boarding list with airport security. All of the passengers looked reasonably uncomfortable. Only the Cubans, or those Rostnikov assumed were Cubans, seemed to take the long flight, terrible food, and metallic noises of impending doom in stride.

Rostnikov had brought four American paperback mysteries, two 87th Precinct novels by his favorite, Ed McBain, and one each by Donald Westlake and Susan Dunlap. He had never read a mystery by a woman, so he read the Dunlap first and enjoyed it. When he finished the Dunlap novel halfway through the flight of agony, he elected to read one of the McBains, a novel he had read before called *Kiss*.

It was then that they flew into turbulence that bounced the plane and made the wings rattle. Rostnikov put down his book and looked at the madmen and madwomen who surrounded him, seemingly unconcerned that they were flying over the dark ocean in a massive metal can operated by the airline with the worst safety record in the history of aviation.

He clutched his tattered paperback to his chest with hands of steel, felt the metal buckle of the seat dig into his stomach with each bounce, and thought of his wife.

Sarah, in spite of a few relapses, was recovering well from surgery almost a year ago. She was working again, at the music shop, and she seemed to have more energy than before. Porfiry Petrovich was sure the increased energy was a result of the two little girls. Ludmilla, ten, and Elmira, six, were the granddaughters of a woman who had been convicted of murdering the manager of State Store #31 during a spontaneous food riot. Rostnikov and Sarah had taken the girls in. Though quiet and frightened, Ludmilla and Elmira also seemed to be intelligent, and they wanted very much to please.

Rostnikov's son, Iosef, now firmly established in Moscow after four years in the army, was working in the theater, talking about becoming a policeman, and visiting his parents' apartment to help amuse his "little sisters."

They, his family, were safe, if a bit hungry, in Moscow. But the tossing of the plane still made him uneasy, and he felt the need to talk.

"Elena," he said. "You are working on your Spanish?"

She closed the book in front of her and turned to him.

"No," she said. "I was going over the reports."

"Share with me your endeavors," said Rostnikov, folding his arms and trying to ignore a particularly sudden and violent drop of altitude that drew a gasp from someone at the rear of the plane.

"I am going over the copy of the file of Igor Shemenkov," said Elena.

"You must have memorized it by now," said Rostnikov.

"Some of it," she confirmed.

"When I was a boy, before the war, we had to memorize Gorky and Lenin and Marx," said Rostnikov.

"Yes," said Elena politely.

"I'll tell you a secret," said Rostnikov in a whisper. "Lenin and Marx were a mystery yet I remember long passages. Gorky was intriguing but I remember nothing of his work."

Elena nodded.

"This strikes you as pointless conversation," said Rostnikov. A man in a gray uniform hurried down the aisle toward the back of the plane either in frantic need of the rest room or to check on some new horrible sound that foretold the implosion of the airplane. "But I assure you it is not."

"You are my superior and it is essential that I give you my full attention."

"Your sense of responsibility gives me comfort, Elena."

"I am pleased that it does."

"When I think I am going to die in an airplane, I grow surly and sarcastic," said Rostnikov. "I was being sarcastic."

"So was I," Elena replied.

In spite of his concern about the worried man who had run down the aisle, Rostnikov smiled. Elena returned the smile.

"A test, Elena Timofeyeva," said Rostnikov. "Are you ready?"

"A test?"

"We are being accompanied by a member of State Security," he said.

"KGB," she answered.

Inexperienced as she was, she did not look about the cabin at the mostly masculine faces. Instead she continued to look directly at Rostnikov.

"The new collegium is still dominated by the leftovers of the Communist party," he explained. "They protect the apparatus of the KGB while giving its branches new names, new uniforms, new public faces. You know all this?"

"I know all this," said Elena.

"The Office of Special Affairs is a small but irritating fleck in the single eye in the center of their collective forehead," he said. "But since they have but one eye . . ."

"Cyclops," she said. "Mythology."

"They wish to remove us," he said. The plane rocked madly.

"I understand," she said. "My aunt has given me her views on this historical direction. May I say something, Inspector Rostnikov?"

Something had changed in her voice and Rostnikov gave her his full attention. She shifted in her seat to face him and seemed undecided for an instant. Then, with a small intake of air, she said, "I feel very awkward being on this assignment. I wish to do well. I will do well, but I feel too . . ."

"Formal?" he asked.

"Perhaps," she agreed. "But I don't know, awkward, concerned that I will say the wrong thing. I do not want this awkwardness to interfere with my efficiency."

"The KGB agent," he said gently. "Which one?"

Still she did not look around the cabin.

"One of two," she whispered. "The thin man on the aisle four rows back or the woman in front of us, the one who keeps trying to listen to us over the noise. She is doing her best to keep from showing her frustration."

"Good," said Rostnikov. "Which one?"

"Perhaps both," she said.

"One," he repeated, shifting his left leg. He decided he would have to stand up again soon in spite of the bobbing airplane, to bring the leg back to some semblance of painful life.

"The man," Elena concluded.

"Reasons?" asked Rostnikov.

"He did not look at either of us when he went past to his seat," she said. "Every other passenger gave us some kind of glance. We are an odd pair. He worked too hard at not noticing."

"Perhaps he is preoccupied," said Rostnikov.

"He finds some reason to turn away or engage in conversation each time I go to the rest room," she continued. "He does not want to make eye contact."

"Conclusion?" Rostnikov said, grasping the railings of his chair with white-knuckled despair.

"He does not want to be remembered," Elena said, her words coming in rattling leaps as the plane jerked up and down.

"But he draws attention to himself with his studied indifference," said Rostnikov. "I'm afraid we did not merit a star of the KGB staff. The man's unenviable task will be to stay close to us without our knowing he is there. The less we see of him the less likely he is to be remembered. It is a hopeless task. We will probably end up feeling sorry for him and inviting him to have coffee with us. I am looking forward to Cuban coffee. I understand it is very good. The man following us is Povlevich or Powelish," said Rostnikov. "Karpo would know the date of his birth and which of his teeth is most in need of dental attention. It is enough that I know he works for a man named Klamkin, also known as the Frog. Klamkin reports to a Colonel Lunacharski, who covets the office of our Gray Wolfhound."

"I see," said Elena seriously.

"We live in a world of unnecessary complexity," Rostnikov said as he rose. "It is the curse of being Russian. We don't believe that the mad world is sufficiently mad so we create even greater madness and then point to the chaos we have created as proof of our theory."

"We have a tragic history," Elena said.

"The greatest comedy is tragedy," he said. "Do you know who said that?"

"Lenin?"

The plane suddenly stopped rocking and began a smooth, steady rise.

"Gogol," he answered, and began to make his way down the aisle to the distant rest room.

As Rostnikov limped past him, the KGB man lazily and naturally turned his head away and closed his eyes.

TWO

"**I** was just walking my dog," the old man said, pointing at his dog. "I walk Petya every morning. Here. There. Everywhere. I'm a veteran."

They were standing next to a thick tree in Sokolniki Park. The bark of the tree was peeling with age or some blight. Tkach didn't know which, but he did notice that the tree was dying. As he had conducted the interview, Sasha had turned the old man, whose knees buckled with arthritis, away from the police laboratory crew and Emil Karpo, who were going over the area and examining the mutilated body of the girl.

"Citizen Blanshevski," Sasha said. "Did you see anyone in the park this morning? Any people you usually see? People you have never seen before?"

"Comrade," said Blanshevski. "I prefer to be called Comrade. I don't mind saying I am a veteran. My brother died fighting the Germans." The old man spat. "Whenever I think of the Germans, I spit. I have given my life to the Party. You should know that. So call me Comrade or I have nothing to say."

Sasha gently bit his lower lip. He said nothing for a moment. For the three weeks since his thirtieth birthday he had, with the help of his wife, Maya, managed to pull himself from the thick pool of self-pitying misery in which he had been immersed for months.

Thirty was not as bad as he had feared, and there had been a great compensation. Their second child had come, a boy whom they named for Sasha's father, Ilya, much to the joy of Sasha's mother, Lydia, who was still temporarily living with Sasha, Maya, and their two-year-old, Pulcharia. Ilya was healthy, and he slept reasonably well. Maya had begun to get her figure back and with it the health that had seemed to ebb away in pregnancy.

Sasha felt that he was looking like himself once more. The mirror showed him a face that looked no more than twenty-three. He was, he knew, reasonably good-looking if a bit thin. His straight blond hair tended to fall over his eyes and he had to throw his head back to clear his vision. There was a large space between his front upper teeth, which seemed to bring out the maternal instinct in many women, and this had gotten Sasha into trouble on more than a single occasion.

But now things were looking better. Elena Timofeyeva, with whom he had been teamed for almost four months, had gone to Cuba with Rostnikov. Elena's cheerful sense of the future had been almost unbearable. Sasha preferred, at least for now, the company of Emil Karpo. At his worst moments of depression, Sasha knew that he was a dynamo of good cheer compared to the man known throughout the MVD as the Vampire.

"Comrade Blanshevski," Sasha Tkach tried again, "did you see . . . ?"

"A man," Blanshevski said, adjusting the blue cap on his head. "Petya, wait. The police don't want your crap around here. Dog is really my wife's." Blanshevski leaned toward Sasha; he whispered now in case his wife might be hiding in the tree. "Hate the dog. Hate it. I'm a prisoner of the dog. The Nazis . . ." He spat again. "The Nazis couldn't have tortured me more if they had captured me. If I believed in God, I would pray for the dog to die."

"Then why don't you kill it?" Sasha whispered back.

The old man looked down at the whimpering little dog and shook his head.

"Can't," said Blanshevski. "I'm not a violent man. Besides, I'm used to him."

Something shuffled where the search was taking place, and Tkach found himself looking over the old man's shoulder. Karpo was kneeling next to the body. The amount of blood was . . .

"You saw a man," Tkach said.

"I saw Comrade Aloyon, who sits on the bench way over there and reads the paper when it's warm, cold, hot, who cares," said the old man. "I saw the woman with the fat baby. I don't know her name. See her maybe twice, three times every week. Saw her even before the baby. Never even said hello. She's always in a rush. Me, I'm not in a rush. Where have I to go? I walk a dog I don't like in the morning. I have some tea or something for lunch. I look at my wife and out the window. I . . ."

"A man," Tkach said. "You saw a man."

"Businessman," said Blanshevski. "I forgot. I shave. I shave twice a day. I strop my own straight razor. Skin is still smooth. Almost nothing left of the blade. I try to keep busy but . . ."

He shrugged and looked at Sasha for sympathy. Sasha shrugged back thinking that a month ago, before his thirtieth birthday, he would probably have considered strangling the old man.

"Businessman," said Sasha.

"Maybe forty, fifty," said Blanshevski. "Bald, glasses. Carried a briefcase. Gray suit. Looked a little like that one on the television. The game show where they spin that wheel. I'll think of it. Oleg something."

"Where did you see him?"

"There," he said, pointing. "Petya has to do his stuff."

"He can do it here," said Sasha. "We're far enough away."

"I don't want them to think it's evidence," said the man. "I heard they can do things. Go through a toilet and get DRA."

"DNA," Tkach corrected.

"Because of this damned dog, I could get involved here," said the man.

"You are not a suspect, Comrade Blanshevski. You are a witness. The bald man."

"It's all right, Petya," Blanshevski said, and Petya bleated with gratitude and relieved himself. "The man came out of the park and got in a car. I was this close to him. Not like you and me. Like we are to the dead girl. I've seen people torn like that. The war. You're too young to remember the war."

"What kind of car?"

Over the man's shoulder Tkach saw Karpo get up, look around, and begin to move toward them.

"I don't know. A little car. Dark. I don't know kinds of cars. I've never had a car. A car is a car. Tin, wheels, things that go wrong. Inefficient. My daughter's husband has a car. I don't know what kind. They told me."

Karpo was now next to them. Blanshevski looked up at him nervously.

"Could you recognize him if you saw him again?"

"He's my daughter's husband. You think I'm a fossil."

"Not your daughter's husband. The bald man."

"I know. I know that's who you meant. I was . . . I don't know. A bald man. My eyes are not perfect. Watch where you're standing."

The last was directed at Karpo, who looked down to avoid Petya's dropping.

"Bald?" said Karpo.

The old man nodded uncomfortably.

"How big was he? My size? Inspector Tkach's?"

"Not as tall as you," said Blanshevski, reaching down to pick up the dog, who was whimpering again. "More weight. Not heavy really, but . . . more weight."

Karpo reached into the pocket of his black suit, removed a notebook with a dark cover, and pulled out a drawing. He handed the drawing to the old man.

Tkach knew the drawing well. He watched the old man's face as he put the dog down and squinted at the drawing.

"This man has hair," said the old man, pointing at the hair of the man in the drawing.

"I know," said Karpo.

"No glasses," the man said, shaking his head. "No glasses and hair. It's not a photograph."

"I am aware of that," said Karpo.

"Still . . ." Blanshevski said. "It could be the man. I can't be sure."

Karpo took the drawing back and put it into his notebook.

"I have Comrade Blanshevski's address," said Tkach.

"You can go home," Karpo said to the old man.

"Remember Petya just . . ."

"I remember," Tkach assured him.

The old man adjusted his cap once more and looked back at the bloody body. He seemed about to say something but changed his mind when he looked at Karpo's pale face and unblinking eyes. Then he scurried away.

When the man and dog were out of earshot, Tkach said, "You think it's him again?"

"The liver is missing. So is the right eye. The victim is young. We'll wait for the laboratory report."

During the past five years, forty people, all young men and women, had been found dead in parks and wooded areas rang-ing from central Moscow to Istra, over thirty kilometers outside the city. Almost half of the murders had taken place during the day. In fact, the only pattern anyone had been able to find in the killings was that the killer alternated the times, daytime for a month, then nighttime for a month, with the exception of September of the past two years, when the killings seemed to be randomly divided between day and night. Almost all the murders had involved sexual violation and mutilation.

In spite of the great number of almost certainly related murders, until recently only a few in the MVD and KGB had known of the crimes. When they were listed in the files they had not been officially linked until the new power of the Special Affairs Office had permitted Karpo to go into the restricted files of the Procurator's Office. When he reviewed the files, he found that some of them had been removed by direct order of the Minister of the Interior, but there was enough to track down and enough to begin a profile. Less than two days after Karpo had shown interest in the files of the serial killer, the existence of what was certainly the single worst killer in Russia since Joseph Stalin suddenly became common knowledge. Other criminal investigation branches were only too willing to allow the Special Affairs Office to take over. Journalists from other countries, obviously tipped by Russians who were afraid to ask for themselves, had begun to push and prod, to write of cover-ups, and to hint at even greater horror than the great horror itself.

Rostnikov had concluded that it was the enormity of the horror that had kept the killings a secret until now. In the midst of political turmoil, coups, ethnic riots, and gang warfare, no one wanted to accept the fact that a monster was loose in Moscow, killing, mutilating, and cannibalizing. A KGB defector named Mishionoko had told the Italian newspaper *La Republica* of the monster in 1989 but no one had taken him seriously. Now it was widely believed that every unsolved killing in Russia was being blamed on the monster so that when a suitable scapegoat was found dozens of political murders could be suddenly and conveniently solved.

Tkach moved past Karpo and walked toward the body, passing one of the three men who were on their knees going through the leaves and grass. Though the body was blood-soaked, twisted, and mutilated there was something about it that seemed familiar to Sasha.

Twenty yards away, one of the grass searchers stood up.

"Here," he said. "Knife. No blood."

Karpo moved toward where the man was pointing. Tkach kept looking at the body. Suddenly he knew what was disturbing him and he shuddered. In spite of its distance from human form, the young woman's body bore a clear resemblance to Sasha's little daughter, Pulcharia. The corpse with the bloody black hole where an eye had been could have been his daughter.

"I remember," a voice came through the trees.

Sasha forced himself to turn from the body, willing himself not to shake. Karpo stood next to the investigator hovering over the knife. Everyone had stopped at the sound of the voice.

"I remember," Blanshevski repeated as he came through the trees. "The car. The bald man's car. It had a sticker on the bumper. One of those stickers, you know. It said something about blood."

The old man stopped and looked at the policemen.

" 'Give blood,' it said. I'm sure. 'Give blood.' It was white with red letters. 'Give blood.' "

No one spoke and the old man's eyes turned to the dog in his arms. He stroked the dog and repeated, "I'm sure."

One of the lab technicians whose name Karpo did not know motioned to the deputy inspector.

"I'm sure," the old man repeated yet again as Karpo and Sasha approached the body and the kneeling technician.

The technician lifted a pale bare leg of the dead girl and twisted it so that the bottom of her foot faced Karpo.

"A tattoo," the man said. "On the bottom of the foot. I think it's a hammer."

"It's a gun," said Karpo.

"Capones," said Sasha with a sigh.

Behind them the old man said, "Yes, Petya, I am absolutely sure."

They landed in Havana in darkness. Rostnikov had tried to sleep on the plane for the final few hours when the turbulence had stopped, but each time he dozed he had the sensation of falling and nausea. He woke up to the groaning of the plane, the sound of his own rapid breathing, and the aching of his withered leg.

He was happy to land and anxious to get to a bath where he could read for half an hour before settling into a bed. He planned to sleep for at least a solid day.

The airport in Havana was smaller than Rostnikov had imagined. In fact, it was small by any international standard and far from the vast empty echoing of the Sheremetyevo in Moscow.

Their luggage, one bag each, was lined up and waiting as they entered the terminal. A line was forming for each item to be checked on metal platforms. The stone-faced customs clerks reminded Rostnikov of pathologists about to examine the stomachs of the recently dead, certain they would find nothing they had not encountered before.

The thin KGB man, four people ahead of them, was doing his best to focus on the contents of his leather suitcase, which had been opened on the table before him.

Suddenly a large man in a faded but neatly ironed blue uniform approached, smiled at Elena Timofeyeva, and said in slightly accented Russian, "You don't have to wait in line. Please follow me."

Without waiting for a reply, the man picked up their luggage, turned, and walked slowly through the crowd. Rostnikov nodded to Elena and followed the man, who nodded at the weary customs inspector who was violating the packed undergarments of the thin KGB man.

The uniformed man with their luggage pushed open a double door marked "Oficiales Solamente" and reached back to hold it open so Elena and Rostnikov could follow.

"Am I moving too quickly?" the man asked as they entered an almost empty waiting area about the size of a tennis court.

"We are fine," said Rostnikov.

"Yes," said Elena.

"As you wish," said the man. "This way. I have a car."

Three children, the oldest no more than five, were playing on the chrome-and-plastic seats of the waiting room. A heavy woman in a pink flower-print dress watched the children, trying not to doze off.

"Air-conditioning is off again in the airport," said the big man, looking back at them. "I don't know if it is intentional to save power or a parts breakdown."

He strode onto the sidewalk in front of the airport. Three Russian-made buses were lined up, their doors open, their drivers talking to each other. Two cars also stood at the sidewalk. One was a recent-vintage white Lada with blue lights mounted on its roof and the other an old rust-and-blue American Chevrolet. The large man went to the Lada and opened its trunk.

He threw Rostnikov's and Elena's cases into the trunk, slammed it shut, and turned to Rostnikov with a smile. He held out his hand.

"I am Major Sanchez, Havana Police."

Rostnikov took the man's hand.

"Your Russian is perfect."

"You flatter me," said Sanchez, taking Elena's hand. "I spent four years in your country. My wife is Russian."

33

Elena withdrew her hand from his.

Sanchez's hair was dark, thin, and receding. His skin was light brown and his teeth remarkably white. His forearms and neck were powerfully muscled.

"You have children?" Rostnikov asked.

"Confused children," said Sanchez. "They speak Russian and Spanish and think in a combination of the two that creates interesting juxtapositions. Shall we go?" Sanchez moved to the passenger side and opened both the front and rear doors. "I suggest you open the windows."

Rostnikov got in the front seat and Elena into the rear as Sanchez moved briskly to the driver's side and got in.

"You speak no Spanish?" Sanchez asked.

"None," said Rostnikov, trying unsuccessfully to maneuver his leg into a position that was not terribly painful.

"Pero usted habla Español muy bien, yo pienso," Sanchez said to Elena, looking at her in his rearview mirror.

Elena looked toward Rostnikov, who was watching the traffic as Sanchez drove slowly out of the parking lot.

"Ah, I see," said Sanchez in Russian. "You were hoping to keep your knowledge of our language a secret. Well, I wish you luck."

"Where are we going?" Elena asked.

"Hotel," said Sanchez. "There are many empty apartments in the Russian embassy. The place is almost abandoned, an echoing sterile mausoleum crying out for history or ghosts. You would be bored. There's an apartment building for Russians and Bulgarians, the Sierra Maestra on First Street, right on the water, but it's noisy and most of your people who are still there are a sullen lot, waiting to be called back to whatever country they've now become members of. Am I talking too much?"

They flashed down a broad street almost empty of cars. Beyond the rows of houses set back against the trees there were spots of light, suggesting a sleepy village more than a major city.

"No," said Rostnikov.

"You have questions?" said Sanchez.

"What were you doing in Moscow?" asked Rostnikov, still looking out of the window, his eyelids heavy.

Sanchez laughed.

"I was studying literature and languages," he said. "At Moscow University. That's where I met my wife. I was in the army. It was expected by my family that I would come back from your country and become a general, a leader of our nation."

"But . . . ?" asked Rostnikov.

Sanchez shrugged.

"I lacked ambition," he said. "To be ambitious in Cuba is to risk the enmity of others who are ambitious. It is difficult enough to survive without creating enemies."

"But you are a major," said Elena.

"At my age and with my education, I should be at least a colonel," said Sanchez.

"So," said Rostnikov, "we are not to take your assignment to us as a sign of great respect for our mission."

Sanchez laughed again.

"Precisely," he said, looking at Elena in the mirror. "Before Yeltsin you would have merited at least a colonel. Now you get an unambitious, overage major. There. On the right. That used to be a Catholic girls' school. Then it was a school for your people. Now it is empty."

Rostnikov caught a glimpse of the two-story white house with brown trim and barred windows.

"We would like to see Shemenkov in the morning," Rostnikov said.

"When you wish," said Sanchez. "I am at your service."

Rostnikov smelled the sea. Past Sanchez he could see moonlight on the water as they crossed a small bridge.

"From this point on, the Malecon," explained Sanchez. "Walkway along the sea. Runs the length of the city. You'll be at the El Presidente, a short walk to the old stadium, where there's a complete workout facility. I'll bring you there tomorrow."

Rostnikov did not bother to ask how Sanchez knew of his weight-lifting habits. The man obviously delighted in surprises, and Rostnikov had no reason to deny this pleasure to his host.

"That is most kind of you," said Rostnikov.

"It is both my duty and my pleasure to be gracious," said Sanchez. "It is also my curse to be honest, so I tell you that he did it."

"He?" asked Elena from the darkness of the back seat.

"Shemenkov," said Rostnikov.

"I have a copy of the report in the trunk," said Sanchez. "In Russian. More detailed than the one we sent to Moscow. We have discovered more. Your engineer is guilty. There were three witnesses. I suggest you talk to him, interview the witness, see Havana, sit by the pool for a few days, relax, allow me to entertain you, and go home."

Sanchez's eyes met Elena's in the rearview mirror. She had started to turn away when the Lada came to a sudden halt that threw her awkwardly forward. Rostnikov kept himself from cracking his head into the windshield by pushing against the dashboard.

"Are you all right?" asked Sanchez.

"Yes," said Elena, sitting back.

Rostnikov nodded and looked out the window at the swiftly moving motorcade of five dark cars that had cut them off and caused Sanchez's sudden stop. Men wearing fatigue uniforms and carrying weapons looked out of the windows of the cars. In the middle car, the back seat window facing the Lada rolled down and a man with a flowing gray beard looked out, his eyes finding and meeting those of Rostnikov. The two men looked at each other for the beat of a heart and then the window slowly closed as the caravan moved forward and out of sight down a dark street.

36

"Fidel," said Sanchez. "He has a house not far from here. No one is supposed to know where it is, but . . . He has houses everywhere."

Sanchez drove two blocks along a divided boulevard with empty pedestals on the median strip.

"This is the Avenue of the Presidents. Each of those pedestals held the statue of a Cuban president. They were all torn down after the revolution."

"We have some fresh empty pedestals in Moscow," said Rostnikov, as Sanchez turned down a narrow street of three-story homes, made a right, and then another right to pull up in front of a hotel. Three taxis and a bus were parked in front of the hotel and a few people were seated on white plastic chairs beyond a low stone balustrade.

"The food is adequate, the rooms sufficient, the plumbing bad, and the toilet paper scarce," said Sanchez. "One of the better hotels in Havana."

"We appreciate your choice of accommodations," said Rostnikov.

"There was another reason for putting you into this hotel," said Sanchez, his smile now gone. "Maria Fernandez worked here. But your countryman had the minimal good taste to murder her in an apartment on the other side of the city. Your Russian stabbed her fourteen times, including three rather deep thrusts in the right eye. I have managed through persuasion and what little influence I have to get you the very room where Señorita Fernandez sometimes entertained visitors from a variety of countries dealing in hard currency. *Señorita Timofeyeva, usted tiene la cuadra próxima, tres ciento quarenta y cinco.*"

"*Muchas gracias,*" Elena responded as Sanchez got out of the car.

"You speak Spanish like an American," he said, opening the door for her as Rostnikov struggled out of the passenger side.

37

"I learned in New York," she said.

Across the top of the Lada, Rostnikov watched as Sanchez held on to Elena's hand, smiled, and said, "I have always had an attraction to Russian women."

"You must learn to control it," she answered, removing her hand. "In the long run it will lead you to disaster."

"*Qué lástima*," he said with a sigh.

"*Sin verguenza, es verdad*," she said.

While Sanchez moved to the trunk of the car and opened it, Rostnikov surveyed what appeared to be a giant rat on one of the three stone steps leading up to the patio in front of the hotel. A second look told him that it was a small, diseased dog.

"Many dogs in the city," said Sanchez, handing Rostnikov his suitcase. "Not much food. You have hard currency?"

"No," said Rostnikov. "Only rubles."

"Worth nothing," said Sanchez, handing Elena her suitcase. "I'll get you Canadian dollars in the morning. They'll take them at the restaurant, and the café, and the shop near the pool."

He slammed the trunk shut and held out his hand toward the hotel entrance.

"There are American movies on the television every night," he said, leading the way. "New movies. We don't pay the Americans. What can they do, sue us?"

The lobby of the El Presidente resembled the lobby of a small hotel in Yalta in which Rostnikov had stayed less than a year before. The furniture was imitation eighteenth-century French, and the walls were papered. The lobby was bright, and a handful of people were at a small bar in the far corner laughing and talking in German.

There were two clerks at the desk, both in blue uniforms. One was a young woman with red hair, the other a young man with blond hair and blue eyes. Neither spoke Russian.

"They speak some English," Sanchez said in English. "I understand your English is very respectable, Inspector."

"It has been adequate in the past," Rostnikov replied in English.

Sanchez smiled once more, handed each of them a key he had received from the blond desk clerk, and said, "The elevators are right there. Slow, but . . ."

"We shall be comfortable," said Rostnikov.

"Shall I meet you in the restaurant for breakfast?" Sanchez asked.

"Late lunch would be better," replied Rostnikov.

"Perhaps . . . ?" Sanchez said, turning to Elena.

"Late lunch will be fine," she said.

Sanchez shrugged and handed Rostnikov a brown folder stuffed with paper. Rostnikov took it, shook his host's hand, and said, "Two o'clock in the restaurant."

"As you wish," Sanchez said. "Welcome to Havana and have a good night's sleep. The television movie tonight is *Scent of a Woman*. Al Pacino. Magnificent performance."

"We appreciate your hospitality, Major Sanchez, and your movie review," said Rostnikov.

In the mirror over the check-in desk Elena watched the door of the hotel open and the thin KGB man from the airplane enter. The thin man paid no attention to the Cuban in the blue uniform and no attention to Rostnikov or Elena. He crossed the lobby, suitcase in hand, and moved immediately toward the bar.

"May you have an interesting visit," said Sanchez, catching Elena's eye. *"Buenas noches."*

THREE

The man who said "Pardon me" as he accidentally jostled a fat woman standing next to him on the bus was tall, erect, and athletic-looking in his American jeans, yellow pullover shirt, and denim jacket. He had a full head of dark hair and wore blue contact lenses, which he had paid for dearly at the medical center where he worked six hours a week to supplement his salary.

The red-and-white bus lurched along the section of Lenin Prospekt that had once been called the Kaluga Road. Moscow's first hospitals had been built along this stretch of road when it was still mud and brick.

Though he was only a few miles from Sokolniki Park, where he had murdered Iliana Ivanova early this morning, Yevgeny Odom was not the least bit worried that he might be recognized by any of the people he had encountered near the bus stop or in the park.

He had been careful, as always. Before he had driven the car back to the little parking lot across from the medical center, he had driven to the crumbling barn on his uncle's abandoned little farm where, using the tools he had hidden, he rolled back the mileage on the odometer, carefully calculating and subtracting the additional five kilometers it would take to get back to the parking lot. Then he added just enough gas to get the gauge back to where it was when he took the car. He was as confident of his ability to manipulate the Volga as he was of his ability to return the vehicle before its owner, a nurse who worked the day shift, would notice it was gone. He had spent nine weeks looking out the window near his table at the clinic, watching the woman arrive, watching her leave. The woman never came out during the day, never.

The bus stopped in front of the ornamental park that held the former Neskuchny Castle, the home of the now dying Soviet Academy of Sciences. As the apartment buildings around the academy were vacated by scientists fleeing to other countries, former Communist party hacks with no education were getting ruble-rich renting the apartments to those who could afford them, including those who pooled their resources or resorted to crime to get the money.

He would never use the car again. He was almost certain that no one had seen him in the park and no one had seen him get in to or out of the car. Nonetheless, he would never use it again. Nor would he ever again be the bald, bespectacled businessman. The bald man had not been one of his most satisfying creations, but it was getting to be quite a challenge to come up with new identities after almost forty killings.

Yevgeny smelled the bodies pressed against him and looked out the window as the bus crossed Gagarin Square and entered the Southwestern District. Yevgeny lived there, in one of the large interconnecting housing areas beyond the Lenin Hills on the site of the former village of Cheryomushki.

The bus was now a five-minute walk from where it had all begun a dozen years before. He had been on the edge of despair, looking forward to a life of no meaning, a job without prospects, a dreary one-room apartment, and a few nights a week out with Boris or Ripkin, getting drunk and talking about women and the hell of Boris's marriage.

The first murder had been an accident. It had been in December. He had been waiting for a bus, much like the one he was now on. It was night. He had been just a bit drunk, dreading the return to his apartment, when she moved to his side. He could remember her in perfect detail, far better than he could remember any of them since, including the girl this morning. She had been as thin as his mother and she wore too much makeup. Her name, she said, was Dmitria and she smelled of artificial flowers. Had she been a whore he would simply have dismissed her, but there was something about her that made it clear to him that approaching him had been difficult for her. Still, he had not been excited till she asked him if he could lend her a ruble or two, even some kopecks, to get home. She had, she said, just come from the park in front of the university where there had been a gathering of students and young people mourning the anniversary of the death of the Beatle, John Lennon. She claimed that she had miscalculated when she went to the commemoration, and she promised to return the money.

He didn't know why, but he immediately said that he would be happy to drive her home, that his name was Illya Ripkin, that he was an Olympic ski trainer. The sense of excitement had been amazing. It had been the most dangerous of all the murders since all the subsequent ones were carefully planned. He took her in the darkness of a windowless dead-end alleyway behind the Riga Railway Station. The creature within him had gone mad with the smell of blood and lust, and for the first time, Yevgeny had let it free. It had leaped at the frightened girl, who screamed, scratched and clawed with dirty fingernails as the animal fed from a hunger that had been suppressed for forty years. It was the most vivid night of his life, more vivid even than the night he had sat up waiting at his mother's bed-side for her to die, watching her spit blood and babble of some-one named Yuri whom she called her only love.

Now there were two parts of Yevgeny Odom. The pleasant man with the ready smile donned disguises and found victims who would satisfy the beast caged within him, the beast he nur-tured, soothed, then set free.

When he was a child, he loved to go to his uncle's farm, the farm where he had taken the car. When there had been rain, a pond of mud formed in the thick weeds behind the barn.

Yevgeny would slip into the mud and the mud would take him lovingly. He had fallen in love with the mud, had felt it seep under his pants and tug at his penis and testicles. Dmitria and the others had been like the mud pond, only better, much better.

Yevgeny decided as he looked out the window that he would visit his father very soon. Yevgeny's mother was long dead. His father lived far outside the city, in a home for retired railway and Metro workers. He would bring his father a gift, one of the mementos he had taken from a victim. The African boy's neck charm. No, his father wouldn't like that. The pocketknife of the boy who said he was from Kiev. White horn handle. Yes, that would be perfect.

Yevgeny worked his way toward the exit door and eased him-self out when the bus came to a stop. The night air was crisp and cool, and he was anxious to get to his apartment. There was so much to get done. Since he had discovered and ac-knowledged his need, he had spent one hour each day prepar-ing his body—push-ups, sit-ups, hundreds of them turning his body hard. Running in place for hours in his bare feet till he was drenched, depleted, exhausted, and ready. He called the beast Kola, his own nickname as a child. Kola was his secret child, a child who needed protection. It was Yevgeny's mission to devote himself to that protection.

Yevgeny read everything he could find on serial murderers. He had taught himself to read English and French, since most of what was available on the subject was in these two languages. From his reading he learned what to do and what to avoid. There was no pattern to the killings he planned for Kola, neither in location nor in time. All that was similar was the method and the approximate age of the victims. He had no choice in that. Kola's satisfaction depended on it.

Now, as he walked boldly down the street, the shiver of anxiety he had felt exactly four times in the past few weeks scratched sharply down his back, followed by the urge to find someone he could tell what he had done, someone who would appreciate the commitment and difficulty and need.

Old Mrs. Allyamakaya, who lived just below him, was sitting in front of the apartment building with a woman who could almost have been her twin. Both women looked up as he approached.

"Dobriy vyehcher," he said.

"Good evening," Mrs. Allyamakaya said with a toothless grin.

"The night is beautiful," he said, looking to the sky.

This was evidently something she and her friend had not considered before, so they looked upward.

"Beautiful," Mrs. Allyamakaya's friend said.

"Here," he said, reaching into his bag. "I have three peaches. Too ripe to save. They must all be eaten tonight. One for each of us."

He handed a peach to each of the women and they beamed at him gratefully.

"We live in troubled times," he said with a deep sigh. "Very troubled times. But we must be grateful for the opportunity to enjoy the taste of a peach."

"All times in Russia have been troubled," said Mrs. Allyamakaya, gumming her peach. Juice dribbled down her chin.

"Good night, little mothers," he said, stepping past them. "I suggest you not stay out too long. There's a chill in the night air out of the north."

"Thank you for the peach, *Tovarich* Odom," Mrs. Allyamakaya's friend said.

"Yes," said Mrs. Allyamakaya as he disappeared into the building.

"God bless that young man," said Mrs. Allyamakaya's friend, wiping her hand on her dress.

"May there be more like him in the future," said Mrs. Allyamakaya. "If Russia is to survive and prosper, it will be through the work of young people like him."

Cuba is dotted by small police stations with perhaps two or three cells in each. Each station is headed by a major with a single gold star in the middle of his blue baseball cap. Station operations are run by a captain or lieutenant. There is also a plainclothes lieutenant whose job it is to know the district and to direct investigations if a crime occurs.

The sun was bright and the streets of Havana hot, but not as hot as Moscow on a humid summer afternoon. A pair of small boys ran past the Guanaba Police Station on their way to the little park a block away. If the old man who tended the park was feeling well enough, the gate would be open and the boys could find friends to fight or play with.

One of the boys looked up at one of the windows of the small white two-story building and met the eyes of Major Fernando Sanchez. Sanchez looked through the boy into the center of the earth and the boy's face went pale as he hurried on.

Behind Sanchez were Rostnikov, Elena Timofeyeva, and Igor Shemenkov, all seated in wicker chairs circled around a small white wicker table. A folder filled with thin sheets of paper sat on the wicker table. The room had blue curtains. There was a small desk with a black leather chair and photographs of young uniformed Fidel Castro and Che Guevara on the wall. An air conditioner with a green potted plant atop it hummed in the window through which Sanchez, his back to the trio, looked out onto a wide, busy street of children.

"You know I never wanted to come to this country," said Igor Shemenkov in a low voice, first to Rostnikov and then, once more, to Elena Timofeyeva. He sighed deeply and waited for a response to his declaration.

Rostnikov saw a man in blue pants and a formerly white guayabera shirt that had yellowed with age and careless washing. He saw a man of about forty with a dark, rough face and alert eyes. Shemenkov was losing his hair, but Rostnikov thought the man's brooding roughness and his open sincerity might be a very appealing combination to women. He looked at Elena, who held a notebook at the ready.

Elena was attentive and a bit tired. She looked strong, clean, and pretty. He detected nothing that would suggest anything but a professional interest in the man across from her. He watched her eyes stray from the notebook for an instant to the back of the Cuban policeman at the window. Then she looked back at the blank pages before her.

"Unfortunately," said Rostnikov, "a distaste for the scene of the crime is not a defense."

"I'm not trying to say . . ." Shemenkov began, and then turned to Elena.

"I worked. I did not complain. I learned the language. You know how many Soviet advisers bothered to learn Spanish?"

"All of them," said Elena. "It is required."

Shemenkov smiled and shook his head. He looked at the back of Major Sanchez and ran his rough palm over his head to hold down the last thin strands of his hair.

"Have you ever taken a language course for foreign advisers?" Shemenkov said. "I'm not talking about the military courses, the diplomats' courses. I'm talking about the few weeks of phrases and badgering we got. One in ten. Yes, one in ten learn to speak Spanish."

He held up a single finger so they could count it and pointed it at himself.

"Your family is from Minsk?" asked Rostnikov.

"Yes."

"I've been to Minsk twice," said Rostnikov. "I have two cousins there. One is a fireman. The other works in the office of a radio manufacturer. The fireman's wife has three kidneys."

"That is unusual," said Shemenkov. He looked at Elena for some clue to the puzzling conversation of the policeman with the bad leg.

"Perhaps," said Rostnikov.

"Is it good or bad?" asked Shemenkov.

"Three kidneys? She has infections in one of the kidneys. My cousin wonders if it is the last kidney, the one she doesn't need."

"I see," said Shemenkov, though he saw nothing.

"A band at our hotel played music most of the night for the German tourists," said Rostnikov. "The Presidente. You know it?"

"Yes," said Shemenkov cautiously.

"I am in the room of Maria Fernandez," Rostnikov said. "You know it?"

"Yes."

"My window and that of Elena Timofeyeva face the pool. We had little sleep. I would like to be home in my own bed surrounded by people who speak Russian. Tonight I would like to see my wife and the two girls who are living with us, also possibly talk to my son. I do not travel well."

"I'm sorry," said Shemenkov.

"Thank you," said Rostnikov. "You claim that you did not kill Maria Fernandez."

"I did not kill her," Shemenkov said evenly. "We had a little quarrel, yes. But she was fine when I left the room."

"Witnesses," said Rostnikov, looking down at the folder on the table between them.

"Lies," said Shemenkov, putting his hands, palms down, on the wicker table and looking at both of them.

"Why would they lie, Igor Shemenkov?" asked Rostnikov.

"Jealousy," the man said.

"Jealousy? What were they jealous of?"

"I had Maria," he said. "Victoria says I killed her. I know she says this. But I did not. Victoria hates me."

"Why does she hate you?" asked Rostnikov.

"Victoria is . . . was in love with Maria," he said.

"So?"

"In love," Shemenkov repeated, leaning toward Rostnikov and speaking slowly. "Like lust, sex."

"I am familiar with the passion," said Rostnikov.

"Maria was in love with me and I with her," Igor said.

"You have a wife and two children in Minsk," said Rostnikov. "That is not meant as criticism, only as a possible reason why you might not want the continued attention of—"

"I planned to divorce my wife and marry Maria," he said. "I loved Maria. I would not kill her. I would not pinch a hair on her head, though I know the hairs of the head have no feeling. It was enough for me that the hair was Maria's."

The sound that Sanchez made at the window reminded Rostnikov of the groaning of the toilet pipes in his apartment in Moscow.

"I would not harm Maria," Shemenkov insisted, looking at Sanchez, who turned around and shook his head. "I swear to you on the memory of my mother, the honor of my father, the virginity of my sister."

"When did you last see your sister?" asked Sanchez as he

moved away from the window, folded his arms, and stood with his feet slightly apart.

"My sister?"

"Tell them what happened," said Sanchez. "Your words."

Shemenkov shook his head, bit his lips, and looked at Elena.

"Believe me," he pleaded. "I didn't kill Maria."

"It doesn't matter if I believe you," she said.

"It matters to me," Shemenkov said. He hit himself in the chest with an open right hand. "There is no justice in this country. Not for Russians. Not anymore. They laugh at us. Look at him." He pointed to Sanchez. "He laughs at me."

Rostnikov looked at Sanchez. The major did not appear to be amused.

"I don't mean he is laughing openly, like a Russian," Shemenkov explained earnestly. "It is inside. They've learned to laugh inside. Castro laughs at us to this day. They took our money, our technology, sent fools like me to help them, and they gave us nothing. We thought we were in charge, but they used us."

Shemenkov started to rise, but Sanchez motioned for him to sit. Shemenkov looked to Rostnikov and Elena for support, saw none, and sat.

"What has this to do with the murder of Maria Fernandez?" asked Rostnikov.

"Background," explained Shemenkov. "For forty years they took everything and now they want to let us know that we were the fools. They want to . . . The witnesses against me. All Cubans. All Cubans. Deny that."

Sanchez shook his head and looked at Rostnikov.

"Tell us what happened, Igor Shemenkov. The night of the death of Maria Fernandez."

"A Minint conspiracy," said Shemenkov.

"Minint?" asked Elena.

"Ministry of the Interior," explained Sanchez, looking at his watch and folding his arms.

Rostnikov shifted his weight, thought for an instant of his wife. This morning in Moscow she had sent the girls to school and gone off to work. He forced himself to look at the creature across from him. Shemenkov sighed and then went on.

"Or maybe the *Santería*. There was a *Santería*, the son of a priest or whatever they call them. He bothered Maria, and he threatened me. Or—"

Shemenkov stopped abruptly and sat back.

"I didn't do it," Shemenkov repeated. He pressed the palm of his right hand against his forehead.

"Then don't tell us what you didn't do. Tell us what you did," said Rostnikov.

"I dressed," said Shemenkov, looking at Elena. "I put on my blue shirt with the buttons and . . ."

"How many buttons?" asked Sanchez.

"How many . . . ? Why do you need to know how many buttons on my shirt?" asked the confused Shemenkov.

"I need to know it as much as Inspector Rostnikov needs to know what color your shirt was or that you got dressed."

"I'm sorry," said Shemenkov. "Maria and I had dinner at the Maracas Club. Is that all right?"

Rostnikov nodded, and Sanchez went to sit in the leather chair behind the desk.

"Does he have to be here?" asked Shemenkov, nodding at Sanchez.

"The room is wired for sound," said Rostnikov. "There is a microphone in the telephone."

"And one in the table in front of you," Elena added.

"It is more convenient," Rostnikov continued, "if Major Sanchez is here so that we can avoid the embarrassment later of pretending that we do not know that he knows what we are saying."

"I do not understand the police," said Shemenkov.

"And that is one of the few advantages we have," said Rostnikov. "You went to dinner at the Maracas. Please do not tell us what you ate."

"All right," cried Shemenkov, running both hands through his wispy hair. "All right. We ate, went to the apartment of Carlos Carerra, had some rum, oranges, crackers. Victoria came, drank too much, said stupid things. Carerra's wife, Angelica, told her to leave. They screamed. Hair pulling. Maria and Carlos got them apart."

"And you sat watching?" Rostnikov prompted.

"I do not hold rum well," said Shemenkov. "It is a weakness. They had no vodka."

"Go on."

"I . . . I said some things about Victoria. Perhaps they were a bit . . ."

"A bit?"

"I called her a drooling lesbian freak."

"Ah," said Rostnikov.

"Carlos and Angelica got Victoria into the hall. Maria and I could hear them screaming down the stairs. Then, Maria started in on me. She accused me of being without sensitivity. Remember what I said about her hair? Were those the words of an insensitive man?"

"Dios mío," groaned Sanchez. He put his hands over his eyes and swiveled half a turn away in his chair.

"She scratched my face," Shemenkov said. "She had a temper. But I loved her. She loved me. She had life. She made me feel alive. Are you married?"

"Yes," said Rostnikov.

"Well, see. You know. Hasn't your wife scratched your face? Screamed? Thrown things?"

"No," said Rostnikov.

"My wife has scratched, thrown things, kicked holes in the wall," said Sanchez with a deep sigh. "You have a point here?"

"Don't you see? I had been dead for years before Maria, no life, nothing to look forward to. And she was right. I was insensitive."

"You just said . . ." Elena began, but Rostnikov held up a hand to stop her as he nodded to Shemenkov.

"Go on," said Rostnikov.

"Go on? There is no 'on' to go to," said Shemenkov. "I went into the bathroom to clean my scratches. Maria said she wasn't through with me. I could hear her mumbling in the living room till I closed the door and turned the water on. When I came out . . ."

"How long were you in the bathroom?" asked Rostnikov.

"How long? I don't know. Not long. Not short. More short than long. I didn't want Maria to leave without me. I went out and there she was, on the green sofa, looks like a dead lizard, the sofa does. Covered with blood. I went to her, touched her, saw the knife, her open eyes. I felt . . . the panic of an animal. I howled. I wept. Then I heard someone behind me. I picked up the knife. I thought 'Robbers, *Santería*,' but it was them, Carlos, Angelica, Victoria too. Someone screamed. Someone hit me in the face. I don't know."

Shemenkov went silent, his eyes focused back in vague time and memory.

"The three witnesses say that they saw him kneeling over the dead woman with a knife in his hand," said Sanchez. "He turned on them and they thought he was going to attack. Victoria Oliveras kicked Shemenkov in the face."

"She broke my nose," wailed Igor Shemenkov. "Look, see here. If you'd have come last week you would have seen only a purple—"

"Your story," Sanchez prompted. "Remember? Carlos Carerra grabbed the knife. The two of them held our intense *amigo* here while Angelica called the police."

"You see?" said Shemenkov.

"See what?" asked Rostnikov.

"Injustice," said Shemenkov.

"Inspector Timofeyeva and I will go to the apartment," said Rostnikov. "We will look at it. We will, with the permission and cooperation of the police . . ."

Rostnikov looked to Sanchez, who nodded.

" . . . examine the apartment, talk to the witnesses."

"I am innocent," said Shemenkov emphatically.

"There is no rear entrance to the apartment," said Sanchez. "There is only one stairway out of the building. All three witnesses say that no one passed them going up or down the stairs."

"A neighbor," said Shemenkov.

Sanchez shook his head.

"There is one other apartment on that floor. There was no one home. The door was locked. That is the top floor."

"I did not do this," Shemenkov repeated. "If there were anything left to swear to, I would do it. No God. No Party. I swear on . . . on . . ."

"You loved her every hair," said Sanchez.

"Every hair," agreed Shemenkov. "I did not kill her."

"A crowd gathered almost immediately after the murder," Sanchez went on, a look of distant boredom on his face. "One woman, a flower vendor, was walking by outside. She said she heard a howl of pain from the window. She stopped and stood there till the police came. She says no one came out of the building."

"Hiding," said Shemenkov, looking hopefully at Elena. "The killer was hiding until . . ."

"Building was searched, up, down, everywhere. There is no other way out," countered Sanchez.

"A window?" said Shemenkov.

"First- and second-floor windows were locked from inside," Sanchez responded. "The apartment is on the top floor. There have been eleven break-ins in the neighborhood in the past month."

Shemenkov's eyes scanned the room looking for answers. There were none there.

Rostnikov leaned forward and touched the bewildered man's arm. Shemenkov tried to focus on the homely face before him but seemed unable to find him.

"Igor Shemenkov," said Rostnikov. "Do you have a diminutive, a name your friends and family call you?"

"No."

"He is called *Perets*," said Sanchez wearily. "Pepper." He looked at Elena.

Rostnikov nodded.

Shemenkov seemed to awaken just a bit from his stupor. He looked at Elena.

"It seems our Russian adviser has a temper," explained Sanchez. "That's how he got the name."

"I didn't . . ." Shemenkov began. Then he shook his head and placed his wide palm on his forehead, as if checking for a temperature.

"I have a hobby," said Shemenkov suddenly. "I make miniature animals from the shells of coconuts. With these hands. Would a man who does such a delicate thing murder like that?"

"I think you've hit upon a flawless defense," said Sanchez.

Rostnikov rose awkwardly, nodded to Elena to take the file, and stepped around the little table to help Shemenkov to his feet. Throughout the ten or so minutes of sitting, Rostnikov's leg had pulled at him like a spoiled child demanding attention. It was not quite pain, but a nagging dull shock, a demanding tightness. It was difficult to move.

"Rise, Shemenkov," he said, pulling the dazed Russian into a standing position. "Officer Timofeyeva and I, with the help of the Cuban police"—he looked again at Major Sanchez, who smiled cooperatively— "will conduct a complete investigation."

"You are in a hurry to go home," said Shemenkov. "Or you want a vacation here. You won't help me."

"Officer Timofeyeva and I will not leave Cuba until we know who murdered Maria Fernandez."

"That's all I ask," said Shemenkov, wearily holding out his hands.

Sanchez had walked to the door and opened it. A burly man in a blue uniform and a blue baseball cap entered the room. Sanchez nodded toward Shemenkov and the burly policeman stepped forward and touched his arm.

"Venga," the policeman said in a high voice that surprised Rostnikov.

Shemenkov was ushered out without another word. When the door was closed, Sanchez looked first at Elena, who had stood up, and then at Rostnikov.

"Forgive my intrusions," said Sanchez. "But we have many crimes—more each day as our people become more desperate. Not long ago we boasted that there was almost no murder, no violence in Cuba, but now . . . The man is guilty. If he were not Russian, he would have been tried and convicted."

"I would like Elena Timofeyeva to talk to Victoria Oliveras," said Rostnikov.

Sanchez nodded.

"She is in a women's prison not far in the countryside. I will have Señorita Timofeyeva taken there when you wish."

"And I would like to talk to Carlos and Angelica Carerra."

"They speak no Russian. I don't know if they speak English. I will be pleased to translate. Anything else?"

"Something to eat, perhaps?"

"I should have offered," said Sanchez, smiling at Elena. "You know he is guilty, your Russian."

"With certainty at the moment, I know only that I am tired and hungry," said Rostnikov.

FOUR

The door to Paulinin's basement laboratory in the Petrovka Police Station was unmarked and unnumbered. Dozens had mistaken it for a rest room. If the odors did not convince them of their error when they opened the door, the sights that greeted them made it instantly clear that they had blundered into madness.

Karpo entered Paulinin's sanctuary at ten on the night of the murder of Iliana Ivanova, whose name he did not yet know.

Karpo's distaste for the sprawling room had nothing to do with the odors nor the glass containers filled with greenish liquid and the remnants of body parts. It was the lack of order that displeased him.

In one corner stood a quartet of unpainted plaster statues of religious figures. In another corner, tucked under a table, was a box of empty bottles. The walls were lined with steel-topped tables covered with fragments of clocks, papers, parts of toys, and unnameable machinery.

Three long tables in the center of the room were also covered with stuff.

It was a room totally unlike Karpo's own small room, which was neat and clean, like the cell of a monk. A bed in one corner. One table with a drawer alongside the bed. An old, large chest of drawers that had belonged to his family and now, along with the narrow wooden closet at its side, held Karpo's few possessions. A small wooden desk. And ceiling-high bookshelves almost filled with identical black notebooks containing Karpo's carefully written and cross-referenced files of unsolved Moscow crimes going back thirty years.

Karpo looked across the clutter, past the headless bust of a dressmaker's dummy, at the man in the dirty blue smock. Paulinin looked back at him.

"I would like more time," Paulinin said.

He was a bespectacled, nearsighted monkey with an oversize head topped by wild gray-black hair.

"I can return when you wish," said Karpo.

"I didn't say I had nothing for you," said Paulinin. "I was stating a wish. I have things to show you. Come."

Karpo made his way around the lab tables, avoiding something shapeless and quivering in the shadows. Paulinin had moved to his desk against the wall.

"Sit," Paulinin ordered, pointing to the metal folding chair next to his desk.

Karpo lifted a pile of books from the chair, searched for someplace to put them, and settled for a spot on the floor between a metal coffeepot and what looked like a pants pressing machine. Then he sat.

Paulinin swept away some frayed notes on his desk, piled a few books onto an already precarious pile, and placed a notebook in front of him.

"I'll share a secret with you, Karpo," Paulinin said, pushing his glasses back on his nose with unscrubbed fingers. "I will share a secret and some tea."

Paulinin reached down to his left, came up with a pot and

two clear laboratory measuring cups. As he poured and served, Paulinin rambled.

"They are all butchers," he said. "Butchers. Only Liebinski has pride. Only Liebinski has the right to call himself a pathologist. And he is not that good. The others are a disaster, a disgrace. And no one cares. No one cares. I get a lung or a brain and it looks as if it has been handled by a street cleaner."

"There are times when it may have been," said Karpo.

Paulinin looked over the rim of his cup to see if the gaunt policeman might be making a joke at his expense. But there was no humor in the pale Tatar. It was one of the things Paulinin liked about the forbidding figure who sat across from him.

"Perhaps, but the incompetence of a trio of ill-trained men without pride in their work is not the secret. Your visiting foreign minister from Kazakhstan is the secret."

Paulinin put down his cup and opened a drawer. From the drawer he pulled a clear glass pot.

"The minister's liver," he said triumphantly. "Who do I trust with the minister's liver? Which fool? Which liar? Which incompetent? Which politician? Who would appreciate what I have discovered? Only you, Emil Karpo."

Karpo finished his tepid and tasteless tea. Was there an aftertaste of some bitter chemical in the cup?

"I appreciate your confidence."

"Before I moved down here," said Paulinin, looking around the lab, "I think I had a sense of humor. But now? I am too much in the company of ruptured spleens and infected brains. One loses one's sense of humor. I knew that. It is a loss I accept in exchange for the sanity of being left to work. We are considered eccentrics, you and I."

"It is not a choice I have made," said Karpo.

"But it is one you should savor. The minister. One of the butchers in the hospital pathology laboratory who works in a well-lighted surgery with stone drains and equipment that functions said the minister died of complications resulting from liver failure, that the man was an alcoholic, and had been killing himself with drink for decades. Look at this liver. Take it. Hold it. Remove it from the bottle if you like. What do you see?"

Karpo took the bottle. He did not choose to open it or take out the liver.

"Enlarged, discolored. That might be a result of how the liver has been treated and preserved since its removal."

"Good," said Paulinin. "More?"

"It is intact," said Karpo, turning the bottle. "With the exception of one anterior—"

"I removed that," interjected Paulinin impatiently. "I removed that. But you see the point. Bujanslov, who did the autopsy, based his conclusion on, at best, a small piece of tissue. Any madman can see this is not the liver of an alcoholic."

"And . . . ?" Karpo resisted the urge to look up at the clock, which he knew hung over the lab table across the room.

"Induced acute hepatitis," whispered Paulinin. "The minister's liver is saturated with the enzyme characteristic of the disease."

In the dim light in the corner, the unblinking Karpo would have been a frightening specter for most people. Paulinin simply smiled.

"So he died after an attack of acute hepatitis."

"Induced, I said. Induced. He was injected with a massive enzyme-and-alcohol overdose. Injected directly into his liver. His liver was induced to fail. He was murdered. I find no case on record of such a murder."

Paulinin rocked in his wooden chair, delighted, as Karpo put the jar containing the liver back on the desk. Paulinin looked at it as if it were a witch's crystal.

"How did the murderer get him to accept an injection?"

Paulinin reluctantly removed his gaze from the liver in the jar, pushed his chair back, and stood up.

"The body is a mess," he said, clasping his hands. "But I looked at it. Bujanslov is worse than a dolt, worse than an idiot. The minister had been sedated. The contents of his stomach . . . Botched job. Botched job. I even found the hole where the liver was injected. Spot near the vertebrae where the French and Americans go in for liver biopsies. Bujanslov the Butcher almost destroyed it in his need to make a hole the size of the Mir Hotel just to remove an inflamed liver."

"And you have a report?"

"No, you have a report," said Paulinin, placing the rough handwritten sheets in Karpo's hand.

"I will turn these over to the proper investigative office."

"I don't care," said Paulinin, sitting down again. "I am interested in science, not justice. I don't believe in justice. I don't care about it. I am, however, offended by incompetent murderers and pathologists."

"The victim in the park this morning," said Karpo.

"I've been busy with the minister's liver," Paulinin said with a wave of his hand, "but in respect for you I examined the body. It was a pleasure to see a body before the butchers got their rusty hatchets into it."

Karpo waited, report on the minister in hand. Paulinin looked down at the pile of scrawled notes on his desk and then looked up at Karpo.

"Beaten with a pipe," Paulinin said. "While she was kneeling. Blows didn't kill her. Eleven stab wounds did. The knife did not belong to the killer. It belonged to the victim. Traces on the knife of the material in her pocket."

Paulinin held up a hand and pinched his thumb and one finger together till they turned white.

"Traces so small they would fit between these fingers with a universe of room to spare. Even with these crude instruments I have found it. Even with the crude instruments that are rapidly turning me into a blind man."

"I'm sorry."

"I'm not complaining," said Paulinin. "I'm explaining my frustration with the impossible task I perform while butchers posture and preen in the sunlight."

"I appreciate your skill and dedication," said Karpo.

"I measured the wounds. Always difficult. Even. Close together. You want an informed conjecture?"

"Yes."

"Your killer was frenzied, out of control. He ripped out an eye, possibly while the victim was still alive."

"And?"

"And," Paulinin said, taking off his glasses and rubbing his nose, "he is right-handed. He is tall, as tall as you are. He is strong. He is not old but not very young, perhaps forty. He was carrying a briefcase or suitcase. Bits of imitation leather where he dropped it on the ground while he did his work. Had you not brought the grass in . . . who knows?"

Karpo had seen a slight indentation in the grass near the body.

"The victim?"

"Ah, the victim," said Paulinin, putting his glasses back on. "At least five years older than she looks. She had a baby within the last year. Pelvic expansion. And she has two tattoos, one of a small yellow angel on her left buttock and one of a gun on the sole of her left foot. I've seen that gun tattoo in the same place on four young people in the past two years."

"Capones," said Karpo. "A gang. Any more?"

"Much more," said Paulinin. "But it will take more time. Is it past lunch?"

"It is night," said Karpo.

"I have a tin of fish and some canned bread. Join me."

"The Yellow Angel's dead. Georgi says it was *Tahpor*."

Anatoli Xeromen already knew this much.

"How?" he asked.

The gangly young man with the pockmarked face and red Mohawk haircut answered, "Knife. Georgi said he stabbed her twenty times. Something like that. Then . . ."

"Then . . . ?" Anatoli prodded without looking up.

"He . . . Georgi says he fucked her, tore out her eye and something in her stomach, and ate . . ."

Anatoli Xeromen nodded to stop the report and sat upright in his high-backed wooden chair.

The two young men were alone in the Capones' war room in the Gray Blocks. The red-haired messenger had no choice but to stand patiently and watch as his boss's eyes moved back and forth as if he were reading an invisible message. The chair in which Anatoli sat was not particularly comfortable, but it was a throne from which Anatoli ruled. His throne room was a muted scream of stolen goods that Anatoli had decided to keep as furnishings. Mismatched, expensive rugs, some Persian and Turkish, several thick pastels from Sweden, and one from the United States, a Disney covered with scenes from *Peter Pan*.

The walls, painted bright yellow, were covered with perfectly aligned political posters extolling and attacking communism, Lenin, Stalin, and Gorbachev; movie posters of Marilyn Monroe, Harrison Ford, and Gene Tierney; posters of Renoir people in parks and cafés; posters of Moscow Circus performances. The furniture was every bit as eclectic: an eighteenth-century brocaded pink-and-purple sofa, plush leather armchairs, bean-bag chairs in Crayola colors, heavy wooden tables with claw feet, tables with white marble tops, and tables with thick glass tops mounted on gilded legs.

The room, which had once been a Communist party meeting

room for tenants, was on the main floor of one of six fat ten-story buildings in the town of Cherboltnik, fifteen miles west of Moscow. The clutch of buildings had begun to crumble and crack within a year after they had been completed in 1951. These six buildings were known officially as Moscow River Gardens, though they were outside of Moscow, nowhere near the river, and boasted only a garden of useless furniture, abandoned rusty car bodies, and debris that not even the resourceful residents could turn into anything useful. There was not a resident of the Moscow River Gardens who called the complex anything other than Gray Blocks.

Several hundred yards away, six identical buildings faced the Moscow River Gardens. These buildings, officially named the Gagarin Communal Residence, were known to everyone as Black Blocks.

Gray Blocks and Black Blocks had long been enemy king-doms for the young who lived in them. Each kingdom had its own army of the nearly illiterate, who battled each other, stole from each other, and even, on rare occasions, maimed and murdered each other. There was more fulfillment in that than there was in the world beyond the Outer Ring Highway.

Then, five years ago, a leader emerged from Gray Blocks, an unlikely leader, Anatoli Xeromen, who lived with his mother in one of the dark boxes within the concrete block. Anatoli was short and thin, his nose sharp and Romanian, his hair straight and of no distinct color, a situation he had remedied by dyeing it purple. Anatoli feared nothing and no one. Anatoli did not care whether he lived or died. And Anatoli was smart.

He had risen to leadership in Gray Blocks by his fearlessness and the fear of others, who wanted no block of concrete to fall on them when they least expected it. He had then united the two crumbling, dirty kingdoms with promises of revenge against the city of Moscow, promises of plunder and power.

The Capones had ridden into Moscow to terrorize Metro

passengers, pedestrians, and storekeepers. Their numbers increased, and Anatoli became a force in stolen goods and intimidation throughout the city. He had his own car, his own bodyguards, and the respect of petty criminals who wanted nothing to do with the Capones and their crazed leader who insisted that every member have a weapon of his or her choice tattooed on the sole of his or her foot. Betrayal of Anatoli or the Capones by any member was punishable by forfeiture of the leg on which the tattoo appeared.

Anatoli's mother, a firm believer in God, told all who would listen that she had been blessed with a son whom God had anointed for greatness. No one dared to contradict her.

Anatoli and the Capones did not hide. Visibility and fear were their commodities. Everyone knew the mark of the Capones, their punk English look, their hair. But now there was one who did not respect the Capones—*Tahpor*, the Ax, who had mutilated Yellow Angel and now spread fear among them. Anatoli already sensed a threat to his dynasty—that there might be an individual even more daring and dangerous than Anatoli Xeromen.

And then, too, he had liked Yellow Angel.

"You and Gino," he said to the young man with the red Mohawk, "go to the police. Ask for her. Say we want the body."

"What if they . . . ?" the young man said.

"They know she was one of us," said Anatoli. "The tattoo. Unless *Tahpor* . . . just do it. Ask for the one they call the Washtub."

The young man with the red hair could think of many reasons why he should not go to the police, but he voiced none of them. Anatoli had given him the name *Speechkee*, "Matches." His real name was Lev Zelinsky. He was seventeen years old and a Jew. Anatoli cared nothing about the backgrounds of the Capones. All he asked was loyalty, and in return for this he shared what they all extorted, bartered, and stole.

So instead of coming up with a reason to stay away from the police, Speechkee said, "In the morning."

Anatoli nodded and the young man with the red Mohawk hurried away.

Anatoli rose and looked at the poster of Gene Tierney. The poster was black-and-white, a reprint. He was sure that the eyes must really be gray. He was fascinated by this woman with the hint of a knowing smile. She must surely be dead by now, as dead as Yellow Angel. Gene Tierney smiled at him and kept her secret.

Tomorrow Anatoli would tell the Capones that they would have to find and punish *Tahpor*. There was no choice. Unless they found the killer of Yellow Angel, Anatoli's power over the gang would be undermined. Besides, he truly wanted to kill whoever had done this to Yellow Angel. He wanted to batter the killer's face with the heel of his boots.

Anatoli looked once more at Gene Tierney. It was late, and he had promised his mother he would come up to the apartment by midnight and have a hot chocolate with her. Anatoli left the war room.

Sasha Tkach carefully opened the door to his apartment. Since there were two locks now, entering quietly had become a feat that defied success, but he tried his best.

Sasha, shoes in hand, had a series of hopes. He hoped his wife and children were asleep in the bedroom. He hoped his mother was asleep in the living room, which he had to cross to get to the kitchen alcove where there might be something he could eat without waking anyone. Then, if he got that far, he hoped he could undress, put on clean shorts and an undershirt, and watch something on the little television in the corner, preferably a soccer match since he would not be able to turn on the sound.

These, he believed, were not unreasonable hopes for a police-man who had just put in a fourteen-hour shift dealing with murder and bureaucracy. Murder had been far easier to cope with.

Sasha missed his former partner, Zelach, who had recently re-turned to limited desk work after almost being killed as a result of Sasha's negligence. Karpo was reliable and professional, and he expected Tkach to be the same. Zelach was, putting it kindly, slow-witted, but with Zelach, there was no doubt that Sasha was in charge. His more recent partner, Elena Timofeyeva, was smart, efficient, ambitious, and, though he had more experience than she did, she was older than he and maddeningly confident.

When Elena was selected to accompany Porfiry Petrovich to Cuba, Sasha had been jealous. The prospect of private nights away from his family in a place where he heard there was still a reasonable supply of food was something to fight for, but the crucial issue had been a simple one. His French was nearly per-fect, but Sasha spoke no Spanish.

So, at the moment, he was asking very little, as he closed the door to the living room, turned the locks without letting them click noisily, and made his way carefully across the room.

Before he had taken five steps he knew something was wrong. When he took the sixth, he knew what it was. His mother was not snoring. Her snoring had necessitated moving himself, Maya, and the children into the bedroom. Perhaps, he thought hopefully, she is dead. If she is, I'll simply let her lie there and discover the body in the morning.

"Sasha," came his mother's familiar loud voice.

Lydia was nearly deaf and far too proud to admit it.

In the bedroom beyond the door, Maya or one of the chil-dren stirred.

Sasha stood still.

"I see you there," Lydia said. "What are you doing?"

Useless though it was, Sasha whispered loudly, "Shh, Mother. You'll wake—"

"Turn on the light," she ordered. As he obeyed he stepped on something hard.

Lydia was sitting up in bed ready for combat, her gray-black hair a wild nest, her small face pinched in the glare of sudden light.

"Are you hurt?" she asked.

Another sound from the bedroom.

"No, Mother. Maya and the children are—"

"Then why are you limping?"

"I just stepped on—"

"There's no point in lying. You're working with that Karpo. He is mad."

Lydia was convinced that each of her son's colleagues had some dangerous deficiency that would result in the maiming or death of her only child. The result of this conviction was that she was almost always angry with her son. The irony of this was that Sasha was convinced that he was a constant danger to those who worked with him. It was Sasha whose passions had betrayed him and almost gotten Zelach killed. It was Sasha whose depression had gotten him into a terrible and unnecessary fight in a bar while he and Elena Timofeyeva were conducting an investigation. Elena had not been hurt, but Sasha had suffered both broken ribs and painful bruises.

"I'm well, Mother," he said. "I just want to eat something and go to sleep. Let me turn out the light and—"

"What are you hiding?" Lydia asked suspiciously as the bedroom door opened. Sasha suddenly felt massively sorry for himself.

"Hiding? Nothing."

Maya stepped into the room wearing a giant T-shirt with the words "Comic Relief" printed on it in red letters. With her fingers she was brushing her long auburn hair away from her sleepy face.

Sasha shrugged as Maya reached back to close the bedroom door.

"He's been hurt," Lydia insisted.

"No," said Sasha.

"Come," called Maya, motioning to her husband.

Sasha dutifully took the five steps to the door. Maya turned to Lydia and said, "I'll deal with him."

Lydia was on her way to turn off the light when Sasha and Maya closed the door behind them.

"Hungry?"

"*Ya galohdyen. Ya oostahl,*" he whispered back. "I am hungry. I am tired."

"Tense?"

"Tense," he agreed.

She rubbed his cheek and chest while she unbuttoned his shirt.

"Let's go in the bathroom," she said.

They had been reduced to making infrequent love in the small bathroom. Sasha was excited, but the thought of the rusting toilet bolts and ceaseless dripping in the sink depressed him.

"Lydia is moving back to her apartment next week," Maya whispered so softly that he wasn't sure he had heard her correctly.

"Moving?" he repeated.

"Definitely," she said. "I am well enough to take care of the baby. She can come over after work a few hours and help with Pulcharia."

"She agreed to this?"

"She agreed."

"That is a miracle. Miracles should be celebrated," Sasha said. "Let's go in the bathroom."

At that moment Pulcharia said, "I want a drink." Ilya awoke and began crying, and Lydia rushed into the bedroom without knocking.

Much to his wife's relief, Sasha Tkach laughed.

After he had pulled the curtain on the single window in his one-room apartment, it took Yevgeny Odom twenty minutes to convert the space from a drab jumble of third-hand furniture into a war room that he was confident would earn the admiration and respect of Marshal Tutianovich himself had he been alive to see it.

On one wall of the small room hung the large chart that he had pulled from beneath his bed and carefully put in place. He had searched the Lucite surface carefully, as he always did, for signs of cracking or wear. There had been none, though a small patch in the lower right-hand corner would bear watching. He had checked his markers—red, black, and green with backups— and, satisfied, hung the black-and-white street map of Moscow on the opposite wall. It too was covered with Lucite and he checked it as carefully as he had the chart.

Was that a tiny crease, a shadow? He checked it again. It seemed to be all right.

He removed the ugly blue vase and the tablecloth from the metal tabletop and rolled the table from its place in the corner to the center of the room.

Next Yevgeny rolled a chair next to the table. The chair with its black metal arms and its woven green seat and back was his prize possession. He had spent a month's wages and part of his savings on the chair four years earlier.

Then Yevgeny sat in his chair and checked the books he had placed on the metal table to be sure they were lined up and ready for use.

Then, as he always did, he swiveled first to the chart and then to the map to be sure that they needed no adjustment. His perspective seated in the center of the planning room was different from his perspective standing.

The chart, in neatly ruled columns, listed each of Yevgeny's victims, along with age, approximate height, weight (again approximate), color of hair and eyes, description of clothing, place of birth, address (if known), place where he had killed them, details of the killing (weapon, number of wounds, etc.), date and time of killing, phase of the moon, the weather. Some of the information was missing, but not much. He had made it a matter of great importance to collect details from investigation of the victims' possessions. There had been several times when he had been forced to travel as far as Kiev to get information and one time when he had to pose as a policeman to get data from the neighbor of a young woman Kola had killed not far from the Slavyansky Bazaar on . . . what was the new name of the street? Yes, Nikolskaya. Madness. It had been Twenty-fifth of October Street all his life, and now they had changed all the street names. As if changing a name changed history.

Yevgeny checked his markers again to be sure they were moist and sharp. Then he looked at the charts.

The information was color coded. Personal information about each victim was in red. Information about the location of the attack was in green. Data about the weather, phases of the moon, the time and day in general, were in black. He could have coded further, but Yevgeny did not want the chart to look like some festive game.

The map was stark. He had drawn it himself from a street map he purchased at a tourist bookshop. He had done it first in pencil. He had read a book on scale drawing and another on charting before he had begun. When he had been satisfied with the map, he had painstakingly gone over every line with carefully applied India ink and he had changed the names of streets as anti-Communist fervor erupted.

The Moscow map carried small red circles at the precise location of each murder. Next to each circle was the date of the killing and the name of the victim.

Yevgeny had shaved, cold showered, and changed into his hand-washed slacks and drip-dry white shirt.

He was ready.

The room existed, as all war rooms do, to plan the defeat of the enemy. In Yevgeny's case, the enemy was any agency of the law that had been searching for him and for Kola.

The task was to provide his pursuers with no trail to follow. He was the lone submarine being pursued by a massive armada, but through wit and cunning he would elude them all.

To confuse them, Yevgeny would make them think there was a pattern. He would commit three consecutive attacks on the same day of the week, two or three exactly ten days apart, two in a row during full moons, every other attack in a park.

It was essential to keep checking, to be sure he had not accidentally or unconsciously fallen into a real pattern. Another concern was that some policeman would see a pattern where none existed and blunder onto his next attack by mistake.

He lacked one thing—someone with whom he could share his victories. He wasn't sure when this need . . . no, he was not prepared to call it a need . . . this wish to tell someone had begun. Some time after the African boy on . . . He looked up at his chart. The girl this morning had been young and pale. There had been a tattoo of a yellow angel on one of her buttocks. Kola had removed her liver and taken two or three bites. And the eye . . . This was the kind of young girl who might carry the virus, but Kola was not afraid of such things.

Yevgeny put his hands behind his head, examined the chart and then the map, considered, and then made a decision.

He had never committed an attack in a Metro station. There was a very good reason why he had not done so, but a Metro station would be perfect. In fact, he suddenly understood, a

Metro station was essential if the police were not to wonder at some point why he had avoided such an obvious place.

He would have to ride the lines and look at the stations that he already knew down to the last detail of each mural. He would have to look with a fresh professional eye, considering the best place and time. It would have to be done soon. He knew that. Kola wanted to get out. There had even been times, like this morning, when Kola had almost burst out before it was safe.

A thought rose in the mind of Yevgeny Odom, the thought that he might be going mad. Perhaps that was another reason to make contact with someone who might understand, someone who could confirm that he was not insane. It was a powerful thought, but he pushed it away. His mind filled instead with visions of Metro stations buried deep below the ground, the massive escalator system, so deep, the deepest of the stations such as Revolution Square and Mayavovsky Square.

He would get little sleep this night, but it would be a night worth living.

FIVE

Elena Timofeyeva sat in the empty cafeteria of the women's prison waiting for Victoria Oliveras. The stone tables and benches were gray and clean. The light from the narrow windows was bright, and the large photographs of Castro, Che Guevara, and Celia Sanchez that looked down at Elena were depressing.

The ride to the women's prison had taken about an hour, during which the driver of the ancient Buick and his partner, both un-uniformed men in their early thirties, had argued about whether they had enough gas and if the tires would make it.

They had been recruited by Major Sanchez to take Elena Timofeyeva. He had told them that they would be paid for their service to Cuba when they brought her back. The two men, Jaime and Abel, had accepted humbly and gratefully, but once in the car they had begun to complain.

It was also clear to Elena as they drove down narrow roads past African-style thatched huts and through small towns where apparently windowless little homes were jammed next to each other that the two men had no idea she could understand their language.

On several occasions during the journey, the young men had discussed her sexually. She had looked out of the window as they gave her high marks for body and face and low marks for potential passion. But, ultimately, they seemed more interested in the possibility of the Buick's actually completing the journey.

And then, when they had reached the prison, the men had asked for money so they could go to a nearby small town to get something to eat.

Elena had let them mime and speak loudly in simple Spanish, repeating the word *pesos* and pointing to their mouths.

While they were going through this a woman in a light khaki uniform appeared. There was a star on her collar and above the right pocket of her blouse a white-on-black patch saying "Minesterio del Interior."

"Can I help?" asked the woman in Russian.

"No, gracias, pienso que yo puedo de harcerle," Elena answered in Spanish, certain that Jaime and Abel could hear her.

Then Elena gave them some Cuban pesos and told them to return in two hours.

When they drove off, the woman in uniform identified herself as Lieutenant Colonel Lopez, director of the City of Havana Women's Prison. She was a tall, slender mulatto with a handsome, weary face. Her skin was clear and her manner efficient, which had suited Elena.

Elena had been expected and the order had come down for her to have a complete tour of the prison before meeting Victoria Oliveras.

"Victoria is working," Lieutenant Colonel Lopez said. "She will be available in one hour. Meanwhile, I have been instructed to show you our prison."

The tour had been as efficient as Lieutenant Colonel Lopez's manner and it was evident to Elena from the start that what she was seeing was a showcase, a model prison maintained for foreigners. She knew because the Soviet Union had also maintained such prisons and she had visited both the showcases and the much more numerous and punitive remnants of the past.

The "work with internment" prison itself consisted of three two-story buildings, one building for the guards, most of whom were women, and the two cell blocks. Beyond the gates of the prison and the fifteen-foot-high metal fence was lush, green jungle through which Elena had been driven for the last five miles of the journey.

Elena was told by the lieutenant colonel that though the building had been built in the 1960s for nine hundred women, there were only four hundred now inside. Their sentences ranged from one month to twenty years for nonviolent felonies such as petty theft, drug sales, and economic crime.

The tour had taken Elena through fluorescent-lit corridors. She was shown large cells for four to six women, each cell individually coordinated in identical bedspreads and pillows with matching pillowcases. It looked better than any Moscow University dormitory room. It looked better than the tiny dark apartment in Moscow Elena shared with her aunt.

Flowers were everywhere—in cells, offices, the pharmacy, the twenty-four-bed hospital staffed by two full-time physicians. There was a baby ward in the prison hospital. The nearby conjugal visiting rooms reminded Elena of low-cost American motels she had been in when she had studied in the United States.

"The babies stay here for forty-five to ninety days after they are born," a young woman doctor in a white smock explained. "Then they go to relatives or the state center for orphans."

From the hospital Elena was taken to the heart of the prison, the textile factory. She was told that prisoners were paid to work an eight-hour-a-day schedule. There was also schooling in weaving, sewing, and knitting.

"The policy of Fidel, the Central Committee, and the Ministry of the Interior is reeducation before release," Lieutenant Colonel Lopez said. "We have psychologists, social workers, and lawyers on the staff. Some of our women choose to live in the nearby towns when they are released. They can continue to work in the prison factory and earn the same or better wages than they would in the city."

Elena had asked a few polite questions, accepted the offer of orange juice, and was led to the cafeteria, where she sat drinking alone and listening to the distant sounds of the prison, the chatter of women's voices, the churning of sewing machines.

Then a woman guard appeared with a full-lipped, angry young woman. The young woman's dark hair was long, straight, and tied back at the neck. She was short and lean with the body of a model. She wore denim slacks and a denim blouse with denim buttons.

Elena asked Victoria to sit and the guard to excuse them for a few minutes. The guard nodded and disappeared, but Victoria did not sit. She crossed her arms defiantly and stood across from the Russian detective. Elena took her notebook from her pocket and went over her notes once more before looking back up at Victoria.

"You are not Cuban," Victoria said.

"I am not Cuban."

"You are some kind of Russian."

"I am some kind of Russian."

"Your Spanish stinks."

"We can speak Russian."

"I don't speak Russian. Just Spanish."

"Then you will have to suffer my Spanish."

"Or not talk."

"We will talk," Elena said. "Sit."

"You like men?"

"As a gender or . . ."

"For sex," said Victoria, rubbing her finger along her lower lip.

"That is not relevant to our conversation," said Elena. "Now sit."

"It is relevant to our conversation," said Victoria. "Maria liked men and women. Have you ever made love to a woman?"

"No," said Elena. "Now you sit."

"What is so important about my sitting?"

"I don't like looking up, and I don't want you uncomfortable and hostile."

Victoria shrugged and sat across from Elena on the stone bench. She kept her arms folded and her eyes defiant.

"Thank you," said Elena. "I have only a few questions."

"I'm not in a hurry. I go back to the pressing machine when we're finished."

"Did you see Igor Shemenkov murder Maria Fernandez?"

Victoria laughed. "I see. You're going to try to get him off. He's a Russian and you're . . . I saw him."

"You actually saw him stab her?"

"No," Victoria said. "One minute she was fine. Then we were out in the hall and she was alone with your Russian. The next minute we came back in and he is on his knees over her body with a knife in his hand and a scratch on his face."

"Carlos and Angelica Carerra were with you in the hall the entire time?"

"Yes," said Victoria, rolling her eyes to the ceiling at the stupidity of the question. "Yes. Yes."

"To your knowledge, had Shemenkov ever acted violently toward Maria?"

"To my knowledge?"

"Yes."

"No, but so what. He tried to hit me."

"Did he or anyone else threaten Maria Fernandez, argue with her, express a desire to harm her?"

Elena's question was routine and she almost wrote the answer before it came. But the answer she got was quite unexpected.

"Yes," Victoria said. "Can I ask you a question?"

"Yes," said Elena.

"Do you think I am pretty?"

Elena looked at the young woman who now pouted in poor imitation of a model in an American fashion magazine.

"Yes."

"You are pretty too in a heavy kind of Russian way."

"I'm flattered," said Elena. "You say someone threatened Maria Fernandez?"

"The *Santería*," said Victoria. "I'm in the band here. You should come and hear us. We do shows for visitors. I sing 'Blue Moon.' In English."

Elena closed the notebook, sat back, and looked at Victoria Oliveras. Shemenkov had said something about *Santería*.

"What? What are you looking at?"

"Sudden changes of subject are neither interesting nor attractive."

"Is this attractive?" asked Victoria. She stood up and pulled down her denim pants and underpants.

"No," said Elena. "Who is the *Santería*?"

"It's not a who, it's what," said Victoria, pulling up her pants and sitting again. "The Negroes brought it from Africa. They're like your gangs. You have gangs?"

"We have gangs," admitted Elena.

"They worship dolls and do magic. They kill. They kill and eat the hearts of their victims for their religion. I know. It was the son of a *babalau* who works at the Cosacos. Maria made fun of him. She got drunk, made fun."

"A '*babalau*'?"

"Holy man, *Santería*," Victoria said. "Like a . . . a priest or something. He's a waiter at one of the tourist bars. Just a waiter, but he comes on to Maria like she should be impressed because he's the son of a *babalau*. Hell, his father's just a second-rate bass player."

Elena was tired, and the woman in front of her seemed either very clever or very stupid.

"Maria offended this . . ."

"Javier. I don't know his last name."

"And you think Javier . . . ?"

"I don't think nothing. You asked me a question. I answered your question. I answered your question 'cause maybe I don't answer your question and they transfer me to another prison. This one is better than where I was living in Havana. Food's better. Rooms are safe if you watch yourself. Work's a bore, but easy."

"This Javier, he threatened Maria?"

"Yes," Victoria said wearily, looking toward the barred windows.

"Who heard this threat?"

"We all did," Victoria said.

"We?"

"Me, the Carerras, Maria, your stupid Russian."

"And Javier said?"

"Maria would die for insulting the son of a *babalau*. He whispered like a bad guy in a movie. Maria laughed at him. He walked away and Carlos told her it wasn't a good idea to make the *Santería* angry. Maria said she didn't give a shit. Her Russian would protect her."

"When was this?"

"Week ago."

"And you think the *Santería* might have killed Maria for insulting this *babalau*?"

"I know they could," Victoria said smugly. "I know people they killed. Antonio Reyes, the pimp from the Dominican. Donna Ramerez, worked the tourists near the ballet on Paseo

San Martí on the Prado. They could have sent someone to the apartment over the roof, climbed down in the dark, or maybe they had wings and floated away. They could have killed her, but they didn't. Your Russian killed her."

"There is no doubt in your mind that he killed your friend."

"She was not my friend," Victoria said, her face inches from that of Elena Timofeyeva. "For all but the first two weeks I knew her, she abused me, ridiculed me, tormented me. We were lovers for two weeks and then we were . . . I couldn't stop. I loved her. I never loved anyone before Maria. Not my mother. Definitely not my father. Not my brothers, not even my grandmother."

There were tears in the eyes of Victoria Oliveras, but she did not blink or look away. She did not try to hide them.

"I'm not going to be stupid enough to love anyone else again."

"How old are you, Victoria?" asked Elena.

"Seventy, maybe eighty."

"You are twenty-one," said Elena. "I've looked at your record."

Victoria's eyes scanned the clear-skinned, healthy-looking Russian woman, searching for a sign of the trick she must be playing.

"So?"

"Nothing," said Elena with a sigh, standing up and putting her notebook away.

"You know something?" said Victoria, standing up as the guard who had brought her to the cafeteria returned and took up a position near the exit. It was evident from the perfectly timed appearance of the guard that the conversation had been listened to and someone had decided it had come to an end. Elena was annoyed because they hadn't had the courtesy or in-tellect to hide what they were doing.

"No," said Elena.

81

"I don't like Russians," Victoria hissed. "I don't like you. I think you would be a cold grouper fish in bed with a man or a woman. Russians are cold. That's why fools like Shemenkov lose everything for a Maria Fernandez who warms them."

Elena nodded to the guard, who moved forward. Elena caught the pain and anger in Victoria's eyes as she turned, tossed her braid of long hair back, and advanced to meet the guard.

The ride back to Havana was quiet except for the blowout, which required the two drivers to put on a spare that had no tread at all.

When she got back to the El Presidente Hotel just before ten, there was a note waiting for her from Inspector Rostnikov.

"Come to the pool whenever you return. Igor Shemenkov seems to have attempted suicide. The management has informed me that there will be no music tonight."

This did not promise to be a good morning for the Gray Wolf-hound, though he was sure no one in the conference of his senior staff was aware of his foreboding.

The colonel was wearing a perfectly pressed brown uniform with three ribbons of honor and one special medal of valor.

His hands were behind his back, his staunch chin held up, his blue-gray eyes scanning the men seated before him.

Only Rostnikov was missing, and, though he did not wish to admit it to himself, the colonel felt relief at the absence of his senior investigator. Rostnikov never seemed to be paying attention at the morning meetings and had a disconcerting habit of asking questions or coming up with answers that seemed to have little to do with the subject under discussion. On the other hand, Karpo, who was at this morning's meeting, had the equally disconcerting habit of paying close and critical attention to everything Colonel Snitkonoy said.

Facing the Wolfhound at the right end of the solid wooden table sat his assistant, Pankov, a near dwarf with thinning hair who was a perfect contrast to the colonel. Regardless of the season, Pankov's perspiration soiled and sagged his small collection of suits; the colonel's uniform never showed a stain or crease. Pankov's few strands of hair refused to rest in peace against his pink speckled skull; the colonel's full mane of perfectly groomed white hair was admired by all who met him, particularly women. When he stood, Pankov came up to the colonel's chest. When he spoke, Pankov's insecure high-pitched stammering played the flute to the Wolfhound's confident baritone. In appreciation of Pankov's inadequacies, Colonel Snitkonoy treated his assistant with the respect due a faithful dog.

Next to Pankov sat Major Grigorovich, a humorless block in his late forties who wore a neatly pressed brown uniform with no medals or ribbons. The major's lack of decorations reflected his remarkable ability to survive based on his uncanny ability to determine just how far to go without upstaging, embarrassing, or challenging whoever his immediate superior might be. Rostnikov, when he was in attendance at the colonel's morning meetings, always sketched in his notepad. One of Rostnikov's favorite subjects was the major. Grigorovich had once had the opportunity to glance at one of Rostnikov's sketches. The figure in the picture looked remarkably like the British actor Albert Finney.

Next to Grigorovich, sitting upright, his long-fingered pale hands palms down on the table, sat Emil Karpo, dressed in black slacks, sweater, and jacket.

From the window, Colonel Snitkonoy looked down into the courtyard of the central police building on Petrovka Street. The shrubs and bushes were green from recent rain, and the iron fence had recently been repainted black. The dogs that were kenneled on the opposite wing seemed particularly quiet today.

In fact, thought the colonel, they had been growing more and more quiet for some time. Was someone eating them?

The Wolfhound dismissed the idea and forced himself back to the task at hand.

The colonel savored his morning sessions and had recently begun to consider taping them. Then Pankov would transcribe them to be edited into a book that would provide startling models for criminal investigative procedure. Though the colonel was always confident that what he was saying was pointed, correct, and inspiring, two minutes after he had begun he was certain that this was one session he would not have included in his contemplated text.

"Ours is a nation of *pravo-voye gosudarstvo,* a state based on law," the Wolfhound said, taking two strides from the window toward his seated staff. "A true market economy, which is now required for Russia to prosper, must be grounded in law with a fully supportive judicial system."

He looked at each of the three faces before him and saw complete admiration in Pankov, respectful acceptance in Grigorovich, and nothing discernible in Karpo.

"Do you concur, Inspector Karpo?" the colonel couldn't resist asking.

"The law," said Karpo, "is simply a superstructure for the existing system of power, whatever that power may be."

"Lenin," said the Wolfhound, glancing at Pankov, who gave him a small smile of awe.

"Marx," Karpo corrected.

"We are in a new era, an era of landscaping, styling, pruning," said the colonel, seeking a quick recovery in an immediate attack. "Each tree, each bush and shrub in the new Russia is the people rooted in the soil of all our history from the day the first stone was laid in the Kremlin wall in 1367 . . ."

And here the colonel hesitated in anticipation of a correction by Emil Karpo. Not hearing any objection, the Wolfhound plunged on, ever deeper into an analogy which he sensed was decidedly weak.

". . . through the contributions of Marx and Lenin to the trials of a new, emerging Russia whose leaves and limbs must be carefully contoured to form a beautiful and mighty new forest of pride. Do you understand, Inspector Karpo?"

Karpo, palms still on the dark wooden table, replied, "I am not sufficiently well read in poetry or literature to fully appreciate the allusion, but historically, one might go back not to the stone walls of the Kremlin but to its first fortifications built from the wood of the virgin forest which became Moscow."

Grigorovich shook his head almost imperceptibly to make clear that he thought Karpo was making a grievous political error. The major was sure that Colonel Snitkonoy saw the sympathetic movement of his head.

Pankov had simply cringed.

"Major Grigorovich, your report on illegal arms in the city," the colonel said, and he resumed his pacing beside the conference table.

Grigorovich opened his notebook and looked down at the sheets before him. Each sheet was neatly typed with oversize letters. The major wore his glasses infrequently and never in public.

"Our best estimate is that about fifty thousand black market weapons—semiautomatic guns, pistols, canisters that spray nerve gas, handguns that shoot gas jets—are being brought into Moscow every month for distribution not just to criminals but to honest citizens who believe the police are no longer able to protect them from the beggars, the drunks, and the Gypsies. It appears that one of the most popular weapons is the AK-47. Russia manufactured and distributed them throughout the world and now they are being sold back to our people at double the price for which they were purchased from us."

Grigorovich looked up from his notes to see what effect his

report was having. The colonel was at the window looking out. Pankov was looking at the colonel. The only one looking at Grigorovich was Emil Karpo.

Colonel Snitkonoy, who had access to more accurate and disturbing reports than the one that Grigorovich had just given, was aware that violent crime involving weapons had increased by 50 percent in the past year.

"The safeguards of socialism departed with the Soviet Union," the colonel said, still looking out of the window. "Inflation and unemployment, though temporary, have driven many to poverty and crime. Too many people now feel that they must arm themselves. . . . Grigorovich."

"A gas canister can be purchased by anyone at an Arbat kiosk for eight hundred rubles, five American dollars. Firearms can be had in most bars for three hundred American dollars. The weapons come from Poland, Germany, on trains from Estonia, Lithuania, and Latvia, across the borders from Azerbaijan, Armenia, and Georgia. The borders are a sieve."

"Conclusion?" said the colonel.

"More men, women," said Grigorovich. "The borders must be controlled, the laws against possession of weapons renewed. The—"

"Major," the colonel interrupted, "it is too late. Freedom has brought us the blessing of destruction. We now have the right to commit suicide, and where a right exists there will be people who wish to exercise it. Source, Inspector Karpo?"

"I do not know."

"Tolstoy," said the Wolfhound triumphantly. "Major Grigorovich, the responsibilities of our small staff grow with each day. The successful accomplishment of our duty will best be accomplished if we choose our responsibilities with caution. There is no way, outside of a return to the Communist party, to control arms, drugs, or offensive public behavior. We will leave the matter of weapons in the hands of Deputy Police Chief Sedov and hope that he and his men can perform a miracle. As for the Mafia and the gangs, we leave that slough of despond to the Ministry of the Interior gang division."

The colonel looked up at the clock on the wall behind his desk. The clock, a gift of the Workers of the Volga Automobile Associated Works, told him it was nearly eight in the morning. The colonel stood erect, boots heel-to-heel, arms folded across his chest, and said, "Inspector Karpo, you have something to report on the murder of the young woman in the park."

Eighteen minutes later by the clock on the wall Emil Karpo completed his report on what he now believed was at least the thirty-fifth and probably the fortieth murder by the man who was known inside Petrovka as *Tahpor*, the Ax, in spite of the fact that not one of the murders had been done with an ax. Karpo, however, did not refer to the killer as the Ax. He left the assignment of code names to Colonel Snitkonoy, who enjoyed the idea of a battle with a formidable adversary, providing the adversary was quickly apprehended and the colonel and his department given full credit. Karpo preferred to give a killer no identity other than a file number. Those who abused the system deserved no special recognition. They deserved only punishment and anonymity.

"Continue your investigation," said the colonel. "If additional people are required . . ."

"Investigator Tkach and I will be enough for now," Karpo said.

"Very good," said the colonel, unfolding his arms and moving to his desk. "If that—"

"The foreign minister from Kazakhstan," said Karpo, opening the second file in front of him.

"Yes," said the colonel, sitting down in his large dark wooden desk chair and putting his fingertips together.

"Died of a heart attack Monday afternoon," said Pankov quickly.

"I have reason to believe," said Karpo, holding up the first sheet of Paulinin's report, "that the foreign minister was murdered."

Grigorovich shook his head again, this time in more open exasperation. Fifteen minutes later, when Emil Karpo had finished reading, Colonel Snitkonoy took the report, ordered the three men at the table to maintain absolute secrecy on this possible crime, and dismissed them.

When they were gone, Colonel Snitkonoy scratched his head. He had been suffering an overpowering itch of the scalp for more than half an hour and had resisted the pleas of his body to respond. Now he indulged and opened the file.

Rostnikov, he thought, would have handled this better. Rostnikov would have given him the information privately and said no more if he were not directed to pursue this bizarre possibility. Well, that was not quite so. Rostnikov would probably pursue it, but he would do so with some sense of discretion. Karpo was a dangerous man. All zealots were dangerous.

Karpo was a Communist. When others had taken the opportunity to renounce and abandon, Karpo had quietly insisted on retaining his Party identity and membership. At first this had seemed an act of near suicide, but recently, as food and jobs disappeared and Yeltsin began to appear in more and more devastating cartoons hung up for sale along the Arbat, Colonel Snitkonoy had begun to wonder if he should not keep his portrait of Lenin handy.

Now, in these explosive times, a bomb had been placed in the colonel's hands, a bomb that could well destroy him. The implications of this murder, if it was a murder, were inescapable. Even if no one in the government or bureaucracy had murdered the minister, someone had certainly acted to conceal the cause of his death.

The colonel laid the file neatly before him on the empty desk, smoothed his hair, and reached for the phone.

Though there were many who considered Colonel Snitkonoy a buffoon who had been propelled to significance by a combination of impressive bearing, very good luck, and a highly professional though eccentric staff, there were few who doubted his professional integrity. It was one thing to survive by avoiding missions that ran high risks to one's career. It was quite another thing to shirk responsibility when it was placed in one's lap. He would have to bring Karpo's report on the dead foreign minister to the attention of his superiors.

While the phone rang, the Wolfhound had only one major regret: that Rostnikov was not in Moscow so the whole thing could be dumped in his more ample lap.

SIX

Elena Timofeyeva found Rostnikov in a white plastic chair next to a white plastic table at the side of the pool of the El Presidente Hotel. The sun was low and a cool breeze wafted in from the Caribbean Sea a few hundred yards beyond the hotel. There were six similar tables around the pool in which no one swam. One table was empty. At the other tables sat small groups: a couple, a family that might have been Germans, a quartet of men between forty and sixty arguing in English and Spanish. And seated alone, a bottle of beer before him and a magazine in his hands, sat Povlevich, the thin KGB man whom Rostnikov had pointed out to Elena on the plane.

After Jaime and Abel had sheepishly dropped Elena at her hotel, she had rushed to her room, washed her face, combed her hair, and hurried down the stairs without waiting for the elevator, which she had already discovered suffered from chronic malaise.

When she arrived at the pool, Rostnikov was drinking something from a tall glass. Next to him sat a little man in thick glasses who was leaning forward and talking emotionally in barely passable English.

"I risk my job, maybe my life to talk to you," the little man was saying as Elena approached. "But I must, Rosenikow."

The man sensed Elena beside him, went silent, and turned his head to see her. His eyes were hilariously magnified behind the thick lenses. He was older than he had first appeared, maybe sixty, possibly even older.

"Señor Rodriguez," Rostnikov said in English. "This is my colleague, Investigator Timofeyeva."

The little man rose from his chair and took Elena's hand. She was five-foot-five. The man barely came to her shoulder. He wore a disheveled, slightly oversize Madras jacket over a faded blue shirt and dark baggy pants.

"Mucho gusto," she said.

"Servidor de usted," he replied. *"Habla Español?"*

"Sí," she said. *"Pero es mejor si habla un poco despacio."*

"She espeaks Spanish, Rosenikow," Rodriguez said to Rostnikov.

"I observed," said Rostnikov in English. "Please sit, Elena Timofeyeva. Señor Rodriguez is a journalist and a novelist. He is with that group at the other table, all writers here for a week of meetings. They have been drinking."

"We have been drinking too much," Rodriguez expanded.

"Too much," said Rostnikov.

"I see," said Elena. She placed her notebook on the table and sat down. The four men at the table across the pool reached a crescendo of Spanish-English argument.

"In the interest of international brotherhood," Rodriguez said, "we meet every year and fight about nothing with great passion."

A waiter appeared, a man in his thirties in black slacks and a white shirt.

"I suggest you have a rum drink and a hamburger," said Rostnikov.

"I . . ." Elena began.

"It is all right," Rostnikov said. "I have an adequate supply of Canadian dollars."

Rodriguez nodded in agreement. Elena ordered and the waiter moved on.

"Señor Rodriguez . . ." Rostnikov began.

"Antonio," said the little man. He placed his right hand on his chest as if he were about to make a sacred vow. "*Por favor,* Antonio."

"Antonio and I have made an exchange," said Rostnikov. "I have given him my four rolls of toilet paper, three bars of soap, my Bulgarian pen, and the promise of a shipment of paint from Moscow in exchange for four hundred Canadian dollars."

Antonio Rodriguez shrugged and whispered, "I cannot spend foreign currency. It is against the law for Cubans. So what good does this money do me? What good does it do my country? You want to know how I got Canadian dollars? No, better for me you don't know. Let me tell you somethin'."

From the bar behind them came the smell of grilling burger and the sound of a Mexican mariachi band on the radio. Antonio was forced to raise his voice.

"I love my country. I would never leave Cuba. If we were attacked by the Americans or the Cuban exiles in America, I would fight them. I say you this knowing what I risk. I say you this knowing I am a lot drunken. Fidel doesn't know what to do. He mus' step down, Rosenikow, you know?"

Rostnikov nodded and drank.

"But this you do not care," Antonio continued. "You want only to save one fool of a Russian. I want to save my country, my people. I don't hate Russians."

Antonio Rodriguez was looking at Elena, so she replied, "I am pleased."

"Pleased," Rodriguez said with disgust. "The Soviet Union looked at us like some kind of troublesome peon colony. They found Fidel an annoyance. But when they needed good medical care, your leaders, where did they go? Right here, to Cuba. Did you know that?"

"Yes," said Rostnikov.

"Good," said Rodriguez, looking at each of the Russians. "Good."

"What do you know about the *Santería*?" Elena asked.

"More than any man alive who is no a *Santería*," Antonio Rodriguez said with a satisfied smile. He adjusted his heavy glasses on his rather small nose. "I have written of them, gotten to know them. Most of what you hear is crap shit. *Despenseme*, but I hear so much garbage, it would make me to laugh if I wasn't so fretting about my country."

Elena looked at Rostnikov, who put down his drink and gave her a very small nod of understanding.

"Antonio," he said, "the *Santería* are a subject of great interest to Russians—a curious alien thing. It is something like the interest the English had in American Indians in the eighteenth century or . . ."

"I'm no a fool, Rosenikow. Hey, you want to be my friend, my *amigo*, my *tovarich*? See, I speak few words Russian."

Rodriguez laughed and removed his glasses to wipe his eyes with the backs of his hands. With his glasses off, he looked to Rostnikov like a small mole.

"This *Santería* question, it has something to do with your Russian in jail, *verdad*? I'm a journalist, remember?"

"Yes, perhaps," said Elena, wondering whether Rostnikov disapproved of her pursuing this before she discussed it with him.

Antonio Rodriguez put his glasses back on and clapped his hands. "Then," he said, "I speak."

The radio was now playing a loud Spanish version of a song

Elena had heard in the United States. It was something about virgins.

"The *Santería* are the biggest religion in Cuba, bigger than Catholics," Antonio said, holding his hands out to show how big they were. "But they got no pope, nothing like that, just branches, groups, dozens, maybe hundreds, big, small, each with its own *babalau* who leads his group like a family."

"Are they violent?" asked Elena.

"Violent," he repeated, shaking his head and looking at the sky. "Who isn't violent? Some of them they are. Most of them are no violent. There are stories yes of spells, sacrifices, all kinds of stupid stuff. Most of the *Santería* are Negroes. They brought their religion from Africa and had to hide it even before the revolution. They hid their gods, giving them the names of Catholic saints, celebrating them on the Catholic saints' days, but hiding their saints in jars, turning desks into altars. They are powerful, here, all through the islands, New York, Miami, but not organized. Now you tell me, Rosenikow, why you want to know these things?"

Rostnikov turned his eyes to Elena. She opened her notebook and slid it in front of Rostnikov, who shifted in his seat and read the notes by the quickly fading light of the setting sun.

Antonio Rodriguez looked at the notebook in Rostnikov's hands and then over at his fellow writers, who seemed to be getting along quite badly enough without him.

Rostnikov took his time going over all of Elena's notes. Her handwriting was firm and flowing, and the notes were a combination of data and personal impressions. Karpo's notes, which Porfiry Petrovich had grown accustomed to, were, in contrast, printed in small, efficient block letters, easy to read and with no personal impressions.

Satisfied, Rostnikov closed the notebook and returned it to Elena. It was only then that he realized that he had been sitting in nearly the same position for a long time. The drink, the sounds of the sea, and the lights around the pool had lulled him into forgetting his leg. Now, suddenly, this rebellious appendage had gnawed into him and brought him to consciousness. Porfiry Petrovich had no choice but to stand, holding the edge of the table, and begin to coax his leg into some level of reluctant cooperation.

"You wish I should leave?" asked Antonio, also rising. "I have give offense?"

"No," said Rostnikov. "Sit, sit. My leg fell asleep. It will pass. You have a wife, Antonio Rodriguez?"

"Wife, two sons. I have pictures in my wallet, but old, very old pictures, not my sons old, the pictures. My sons are grown but . . . my pictures are of children."

Rodriguez sat suddenly, looking quite glum.

"I have a wife and son, one son. His name is Iosef," said Rostnikov.

"One of my sons is José. Same name, is it not so?"

"El mismo, verdad," said Elena as the waiter returned with her drink and American hamburger. When the food was in front of her, Elena realized how hungry she was. Rostnikov paid the waiter in Canadian money, and she lifted the sandwich as the waiter departed.

"A witness told Investigator Timofeyeva," Rostnikov said, "that the son of a *Santería* priest—"

"*Babalau* or *Obba,* keeper of the secrets," Rodriguez corrected.

"This *babalau*'s son had threatened the victim, Maria Fernandez, threatened her with death."

Rodriguez shrugged.

"Is possible," he said. "People get angry, say things. Is possible. Which *Santería*?"

"Javier, the son of . . ." Elena began, and Rodriguez finished.

". . . a very important *babalau* named Manuel Fuentes." He

began to laugh so loud that even his journalist friends at the table across the pool paused to look at him.

"Forgive me, Rosenikow," he said. "We are lucky I do not choke. Manuel would hurt no one, would not permit his people to hurt anyone."

"You know this Manuel?" Rostnikov said.

"I know many people in Habana," Antonio whispered, his magnified eyes darting around the remaining patrons poolside. "*Sí,* I know him. Actually, I know one of his people, a Communist youth leader. Irony, no? A Communist youth leader is a secret *Santería.* But that's nothing. A cabinet minister was last year made a *santo,* how you call a saint by the *Santería.* See, I trust you. I tell you things that could get my friends in trouble. You should trust me."

"Perhaps," said Rostnikov, feeling painful life returning to his leg. "But experience in my country has taught me that trust must be earned slowly and relied upon almost never."

"You read Lorca," Rodriguez said with a smile.

"Gogol and Ed McBain," Rostnikov said. "Can you arrange a meeting for us with this *babalau*?"

"Maybe," said Rodriguez. He scratched his chin and looked at Elena as if she held some special answer to the puzzle before him. "But I will have to be with you."

"You would be most welcome," said Rostnikov, sitting down carefully to avoid angering his leg.

"Then," said the little man, "I shall get back to you very soon. If I do arrange this, however, is important you respect the *babalau*."

"Once," said Rostnikov, watching Elena take the final bite of her sandwich, "I saw an Inuit holy man do things that may have been miracles. One of those things may have saved the life of my wife. I always respect what I do not understand until it proves unworthy of my respect."

"You are a crazy Russian," Antonio said, "or maybe I no understand your English as good as I like to think."

"I think you understand," said Rostnikov.

"Ah well, so maybe I do. But as you can tell I am fond for you and more than fond for this lovely lady who has the appetite of a Cuban. I will talk to you soon."

"Soon, I hope," said Rostnikov.

"Tomorrow," said Antonio. *"Buenas noches, señorita."*

"Hasta mañana," answered Elena.

The little man turned and tottered toward the end of the pool.

"I hope he doesn't fall in the water," Elena said.

"He won't fall," said Rostnikov.

"A coincidence, his approaching you." She picked up a few overlooked crumbs on the end of a finger and guided them to her mouth.

Rostnikov shrugged.

"Povlevich sent him to you?"

"Perhaps, but probably our Major Sanchez," said Rostnikov. "Do you know that song?"

Elena didn't. It was a plaintive song, sung by a woman who was almost in tears.

"What is she saying?" Rostnikov asked, looking over his shoulder toward the radio in the bar.

"She says, When one loves too strongly, one is a slave, and a slave is doomed to misery until she dies. But since one has no choice when love comes . . . I don't know the word . . . then one must learn to accept, and get whatever pleasure one can for as long as it lasts."

"I'm a little drunk, Elena Timofeyeva," he said. "So that may account for my telling you this. Say nothing, just consider. Remember the first time you met my son, Iosef?"

"The birthday party for Sasha Tkach at your apartment," she answered.

"He told me in the bedroom that he loved you and that he intended to marry you. It is dark. I cannot tell if you are blushing or angry."

"I don't think you are drunk, Inspector Rostnikov."

"Perhaps not," he said. "Maybe it's the island breeze and . . . If Povlevich didn't look like such a boor, I would invite him over to our table for a drink. I have tried not to think about him. KGB people have no sense of humor, and once they get started they talk too much. This one . . . I can't tell if his being sent with us is an insult, or if the KGB now has only mediocrities because the best have fled."

The Americans and Antonio were getting up now, arms around each other, problems resolved in the temporary mist of alcohol. The family of Germans had already left and the sun was all but gone. A few pool lights came on and Rostnikov and Elena said nothing for a few moments as they watched the noisy writers walk across the open patio and enter the hotel.

"Shemenkov," she finally said, feeling very tired. She wondered what her reaction was to the declaration of love from the son of Porfiry Petrovich Rostnikov.

"I was informed that he tried to hang himself in his cell. Tied his socks and shirt together to make a noose, hung it from a water pipe, and jumped from his bed. The makeshift rope tore, but not before causing a burn around his neck and altering his voice. All this I got from our Major Sanchez. We will be permitted to talk to Shemenkov in the morning."

Elena tried to hold back a yawn.

"I'm sorry."

"Your day has been long," Rostnikov said. "It is still early. If there is water, I'll take a bath and read my novel, an Ed McBain, about women."

Elena hardly heard.

"Tomorrow then," she said.

"I'll call you when we must go," Rostnikov said. "Go ahead.

You've done well. I'll finish my drink. Leave the notebook with me."

Rostnikov watched the young woman move across the patio. A new song began, unfamiliar, upbeat, instrumental. Elena was built more solidly than his Sarah. Elena's skin was fine and her mind alert. There was an uncertainty in her that worried him, but all in all she would be a fine daughter-in-law. Deep within him he wished that it might happen soon so that the possibility of a grandchild . . . but that was for Sarah. He wanted very much to talk to his wife.

"Ridiculous," he said softly to his glass. "They haven't even gone to a movie together."

Rostnikov sensed the eyes of Povlevich of the KGB looking at him over the magazine. Should he call the man over, offer him a drink? The man looked lonely, but Rostnikov was tired. Perhaps tomorrow.

Rostnikov got up carefully, tucked Elena Timofeyeva's notebook under his arm, and slowly made his way across the patio, through the lobby, and up to his room, which had, according to Major Sanchez, been used frequently by Maria Fernandez. Rostnikov drew himself a tepid bath.

He closed his eyes and thought of Maria Fernandez, who had certainly bathed in this same tub. He imagined her looking down at him with a smile. But the figure above him was uncomfortably pale and vague. He reminded himself to ask Major Sanchez for a photograph of the dead woman. The warm water appeased his leg sufficiently for him to work his way out of the tub, dry himself, and put on the boxer shorts in which he slept.

He lay in bed for a while reading about Carella and Brown. Finally, with the ghost of Maria Fernandez lying next to him in the darkness, Rostnikov turned off the light and closed his eyes.

While Rostnikov was reading his book, Major Sanchez and Antonio Rodriguez met in the major's office, where they drank from glasses filled with Russian vodka.

"He knows," said Rodriguez, adjusting his thick glasses.

"That doesn't surprise me, Antonio."

"Nor me. Does it matter?"

Sanchez looked at his drink and pursed his lips.

"Who knows? Probably not."

"I like him, the Russian policeman."

"He is likable," said Sanchez. "But . . ."

"But?"

Major Sanchez put a finger to his lips and said quietly, "Antonio, my friend, there are things it is best that you not know, things I wish I did not have to know."

The major held up his glass.

"To the Russian."

Rodriguez blinked once, raised his glass, and repeated, "To the Russian."

"But if the devil springs forth suddenly from the earth . . ." Sanchez said.

". . . then may he spring forth not under us but under the Russian."

"*Salud.*"

"*Salud.*"

Emil Karpo sat upright in his straight-backed wooden chair staring at the wall of his room.

Earlier, as he did every morning before dawn, Karpo had wrapped himself in the thick, dark robe he had been given by his mother two decades ago. He had taken a clean blue towel, the blue plastic container that held his soap, and the black plastic container that held his straight razor, and had gone to the communal shower at the end of the hall. Under the stream of cold water, he had carefully soaped and washed his body and hair. He had then shaved without a mirror. When he was done he had carefully rinsed his razor.

Back in his room, Emil Karpo had dressed and brushed his hair back with the same bristle brush he had used since coming to Moscow years before. He had taken good care of his few belongings, and they had endured.

He had eaten his bread and tomato, drunk his glass of cold tea, and cleaned his already clean room.

Now he sat facing the wall, his dark shades and curtains drawn to keep out the sun, a bright lamp turned to face the map of Moscow on his wall. It was not as elaborate as the map in Yevgeny Odom's apartment, and the names of the streets had not yet been changed to eliminate the revolution, but otherwise it was the same.

Karpo had prepared four Lucite overlays for his map. He had purchased the thin Lucite sheets at a market not far from the Kremlin. Each sheet had been covered with advertising for some French cigarettes. Karpo had painstakingly removed the advertising with a sharp knife.

The four overlays, each marked in a different color, were arranged so that they could be read even if all were placed over the map at the same time. One overlay showed the location of each murder he felt reasonably certain had been committed by Case 341. A second overlay showed the date, time of day, and weapon used in the murder. A third overlay gave information on each victim by location. A fourth overlay indicated if any witnesses had been found and what, exactly, the witnesses had seen.

Karpo had looked at his map and overlays for hours. There should have been a pattern, but there appeared to be no pattern—no relationship between the days of the week of the murders, the intervals between, the times of day, the phases of the moon, the victims (though he seemed to prefer them young), the weapons used, the locations.

Yet perhaps there was a pattern. The killer was working hard to keep from falling into a pattern. He had even attacked twice in the same location, among the stand of birch trees behind the USSR Economic Achievements Exhibition. The pattern was the conscious avoidance of a pattern.

Karpo's task was to outguess the killer. To do this he had to figure out where and when he was least likely to attack next.

So Emil Karpo sat for a time, his eyes on the map. Occasionally he got up to switch the overlays, then sat down again to stare at the map, consider a new possibility, take more notes.

He was going over the relationship of night attacks to day attacks when he sensed the sound of footsteps long before he was fully aware of them. They came up the stairs toward his landing, moved down the uncarpeted floor of the corridor. The pace slowed a few dozen paces from his door, and he rose silently, crossed the room, and opened the door. It was Mathilde Verson.

"You don't ask who's knocking before you open your door at five in the morning?"

Karpo stood back to let her in.

"You didn't knock."

"You didn't give me a chance. But it doesn't matter. You knew it was me," she said, stepping inside. He closed the door.

Her red hair flashed fiery in the light of the lamp as she walked toward the window.

"May I let in the sun?" she asked, reaching for the shade.

Karpo said nothing.

"The sun is up," she said.

"Five forty-seven," he said.

She eased the shade up and let in the day. She wore an orange dress with yellow flowers.

"You have something to ask me, Emil Karpo?"

Her hands were on her hips. With the open window behind her he could not clearly see her face, but he was sure she was smiling.

"You are going away," he said. "An emergency. You will not be gone long."

"My detective," she said, looking about the room.

"If you were in trouble, you would have said so in the hall. It would have been evident from the tension in your muscles and your voice. However, if it were not an emergency, you would not have come here this early. If you were going to stay away long or were planning never to see me again, you would not be in a playful mood."

She sat on the edge of his bed and looked at the map on the wall.

"And where am I going on this brief trip?" she asked.

"Odessa," he said. "Your sister is getting married, an unexpected marriage."

He could see her face now. She smiled and cocked her head to one side.

"Absolutely wrong," she said.

Karpo stood rigid.

"No." She sighed. "Don't worry. You are not wrong."

"Your family is in Odessa. Births, marriages, and honors are nontragic emergencies. Your sister is unmarried and so—"

"And so," Mathilde interrupted. She got up from the bed. "How many years have we been together, Emil Karpo?"

"Four years, two months, and twelve days," he answered instantly.

"I know better than to assume romance, Karpo."

"It is both a failing and an asset that I am committed to precision," he said.

"But our relationship has changed greatly in that time," she said, taking a step toward him.

"Yes."

"You began as a client and became a friend," she said.

"That is accurate," he agreed.

"And," she said, stepping even closer to him, "I have learned that behind your dedication to duty is a human with needs beyond those of a cyborg or an animal."

Karpo said nothing.

"What is on the wall?" she asked.

He told her. She looked at the map and the Lucite coverings.

"There are so many," she said.

"And no pattern," Karpo said.

"Then something's missing," she said.

"No," said Karpo. "It is complete."

"No," she insisted, walking to the map. "Something looks . . . You have a Metro map?"

"Yes," he said.

"Same size?"

"Yes, and one for bus lines. But he has, as far as we know, never used the Metro in any—"

And Karpo stopped, the right corner of his mouth moving slightly in something only Mathilde Verson would recognize as a smile.

Moments later the Moscow Metro map was on the wall covered by the clear plastic sheets.

"Every murder has taken place within a five-minute walk from a Metro station," he said.

"No attacks in Metro stations?" asked Mathilde.

"No. Nor right outside of them."

"Maybe he wants to be near them," she said. She was sitting in the straight-backed chair in the middle of the small room and looking up at Karpo. "But why?"

Karpo looked at the map again.

"Every Metro line," he said. "Kirovsko-Frunzenskaya, Arbatsko-Pokrovskaya . . . Not just one or two lines."

"Perhaps," she said, "he is unaware that he is doing it. Or, perhaps, he cannot move far from the Metro yet wants to draw our attention away from it."

"Because," Karpo said, "he may work near the Metro."

Karpo moved to his desk, gathered his notes, and turned to face Mathilde.

"I should have seen this," he said. "What do I lack that prevented my seeing this?"

"Imagination," Mathilde said.

"There may be some other link, some other grid that also matches. It could be a coincidence."

"But you don't think so," she said.

"No. If this is right, we have narrowed our search down to perhaps eighty thousand people."

"I did not say I could solve your problem, Emil. I simply pointed out a pattern."

"How long will you be gone?"

"Two weeks," she said.

"Then I shall see you when you return. I wish you a good trip," he said, moving toward the door.

"Where are you rushing to?" she asked.

"I shall wake Sasha Tkach and proceed to consider the relationship between the killings and the Metro."

"He has a wife, two children, and a mother," Mathilde said. "Let him sleep a little longer."

Karpo considered the suggestion.

"Perhaps. He may be more useful if he is fully rested."

Mathilde stepped toward him again.

"Emil Karpo, I am in a good mood. I have just given you a useful suggestion for finding a murderer. I am going to see my sister married. Therefore, though it is not Thursday, I suggest that you and I get undressed, get on top of your little prison cot, and make love."

Karpo simply observed the woman who was now only inches from him.

"I am not proposing marriage," she said. "Just a major deviation from routine."

"When must you leave?" he asked.

"My train leaves at eleven. I'll have to be out of here in no more than an hour."

"That will give Sasha Tkach another hour and ten minutes of sleep. That should be sufficient," said Karpo.

Mathilde shook her head, took the notebook from Karpo's hand, and whispered, "How could any woman resist such a romantic offer?"

SEVEN

It was raining. No, to call it rain was an injustice to the madness that the skies had unleashed. The sheets of dark water that poured down were like nothing Porfiry Petrovich had ever seen. First there had been a gradual gathering of dark clouds as he drove toward the police station. Then came a distant cracking that might have been thunder or sounds from a construction site.

By the time Rostnikov arrived in the small cell in which Igor Shemenkov now sat at a small wooden table, the sky had gone insane. Rostnikov was fascinated. He stood at the window, his back to Shemenkov, whose neck was surrounded by a crude metal brace that made it impossible for him to turn his head.

"What are you looking at?" Shemenkov rasped.

"The rain," said Rostnikov. "I have never seen rain like this."

"It always rains like this," Shemenkov croaked.

A loud crack and a bolt of lightning tore through the sky.

Rostnikov turned to face Shemenkov. "Moscow," he said, "was built to make people feel small against the magnificence of the revolution. The streets are eight lanes wide, the statues are five stories high, the buildings are as big as mountains. But this—look at it, Shemenkov—this really makes one feel small. You feel we could be washed away in an instant."

"I have been impressed by the weather since I came to Havana," Shemenkov said. "And by the women. I wish I had never encountered either."

Rostnikov looked at the disheveled hulk before him. Shemenkov had his head in his hands. Wisps of whatever hair he had left crept through his fingers. His eyes were puffed and red.

"If you kill yourself, Igor Shemenkov, you will be assumed guilty and I will have come to Cuba for nothing."

Shemenkov pressed his head more tightly in the vise of his fingers.

"I did not attempt suicide to embarrass you," said Shemenkov. He coughed painfully.

"Don't do it again," said Rostnikov. He crossed the room and sat down in the chair opposite the prisoner. "I bring you something that might be hope."

Shemenkov's eyes scanned the face of the detective.

"Someone threatened Maria Fernandez three or four weeks ago, a *Santería* in a place called the Cosacos."

"Yes," said Shemenkov. "I told you. His name is Javier."

"Do you think this *Santería* might have killed Maria Fernandez knowing the crime would be attributed to you?"

"Of course," rasped Shemenkov so low that Rostnikov could barely hear him. "I didn't kill her. Those people . . . they can go through walls, cast spells. . . . Of course."

Another rumble of thunder and more lightning made them pause.

"I hate this country," said Shemenkov.

"I thought you wanted to stay here."

"That was before Maria was killed. Now I hate this country."

"What happened the night this person . . . ?"

"Manuel's son, Javier," Shemenkov said. "We got into a fight. He was bothering Maria. She made him look like a fool. He was going to go after her with a knife. I stopped him. He tried to bite my nose. I broke his nose with my head. I have a hard head."

"An admirable asset," said Rostnikov. "And he said he would kill Maria?"

"And me too."

"What else?" asked Rostnikov.

"What else? Nothing else. Maria's dead and they say I killed her. What else is there? I can't talk any more. My throat is burning. I can't eat, I can't sleep."

Rostnikov nodded.

Then Shemenkov said, "These people, who knows? It's possible."

Rostnikov got up, unsure of whether Shemenkov was talking about Cubans in general or the *Santería* in particular. Rostnikov's leg felt as if it had been filled with water and a weak charge of electricity was being sent through it. It was an unfamiliar feeling, and not terribly unpleasant, which led him to the conclusion that the Cuban weather might actually be soothing to his leg.

"Then," said Rostnikov, who began moving toward the door, "stay awake and stay alive."

"Look at me," said Shemenkov, rising. "I'm a shell, a worthless shell. They won't let me live. You don't know these Cubans. They won't let me live. Even if some crazy African killed Maria, they won't care. They are going to punish Russia for abandoning them. They are going to punish Russia by killing me and throwing my body into the sea for the sharks. They are going to spit on my body. They are going to laugh at us. And I," he said, pointing to his chest, "I am going to . . . I am a dead man. I am worthless."

As he spoke Shemenkov had turned around completely to

face the departing detective. He almost fell from the awkwardness of his stiff-necked movement.

"I did not kill Maria," he said. "I did not—" Another crack of lightning broke through the ocean that was falling upon Havana.

Rostnikov called the guard to let him out. As he stepped into the corridor he heard Shemenkov shuffle toward his cot in the corner of the room. Rostnikov made his way down the corridor to Major Sanchez's office, where he knocked. He heard *"Entra"* and stepped in.

Sanchez was seated behind his desk drinking from a steaming cup. He pointed to another cup across from him on the desk and said, "Coffee, Porfiry Petrovich?"

Rostnikov nodded and sat. He took the coffee in his hands and enjoyed the warmth of the cup against his palms. The room was pleasantly air-conditioned, and though it was morning and he had slept remarkably well, the drum of rain, the hum of the air conditioner, and the warmth of the coffee made Rostnikov drowsy.

"I like your coffee and your rain," said Rostnikov.

"*Gracias*. My father had a theory," said Sanchez, looking into his coffee cup. "If a Cuban is home when the rains come, he feels protected. It is like being in a castle with a great moat. No one will enter. It is a time for peace and security. All are equally trapped and protected by it. It is a time for coffee and love. Is it the same with snow and cold? Is that why Russians are willing to live in Siberia?"

"Your father was a philosopher," said Rostnikov, finishing his coffee.

"Stonemason," said Sanchez.

"You heard what I told Shemenkov, what he told me?"

Sanchez simply smiled.

"And?" Rostnikov went on.

"I think this pursuit of a vengeful *Santería* is a waste of time and energy," said Sanchez. "Everyone who commits a crime blames it on the Catholics or the *Santería*. More coffee?"

Rostnikov held out his cup, and Sanchez refilled it from the pot behind him on the table.

"But it is my time and energy," said Rostnikov.

"Your time and energy," Sanchez agreed. "You have the services of myself and my staff in your fruitless enterprise."

"I will call upon them if I need them," said Rostnikov.

"Let me try another way, Inspector," said Sanchez. "Havana is divided into ninety-three zones of the Provincial Court. Each zone has its own court division with professional judges. Each zone has its own prosecutors, attorneys, and others affiliated with the integral Vigilance and Protection System, the SUVP. Each zone has representatives of the National Revolutionary Police. Things are done quickly within this system. Do you understand?"

"If a person is arrested for a crime, it is almost a certainty that the system you have described will swiftly convict him," said Rostnikov.

"It was the same in your country before it was stricken with chaos," Sanchez went on. "Not only is it unpopular for anyone within the system to represent the accused, it is practically impossible. I have been at trials in which the attorney assigned to the defendant attacked his client with greater zeal than the prosecutor. In this way he let the court know that he was not being disloyal."

"I appreciate your telling me such things."

Sanchez shrugged and played with a pencil in front of him.

"I am trying to save you time and effort. I will speak even more frankly if you do not mind," said Sanchez.

"By all means."

Sanchez rose, put his hands behind his back, and strode to the window. There was something of the Gray Wolfhound in the move, a certain calculation for effect that alerted Rostnikov.

"There are dangers in Havana as there are in any city," said Sanchez. "If you remain within the protection of my office, we will see to it that such dangers are avoided. I can offer no such guarantees if you choose to . . . you understand?"

"Perfectly," said Rostnikov. "Consider yourself absolved."

"Unfortunately," sighed Sanchez, "absolution is not within your power. It is my own superiors to whom I would have to answer should something happen to you or your charming assistant."

Rostnikov nodded.

"I understand," said Rostnikov, rising with remarkably little protest from his leg. "The rain seems to be stopping."

"And its protection fading," said Sanchez. *Cuidado, amigo.*"

"I will be careful," said Rostnikov, moving toward the door. "A request."

"Yes."

"I would like Igor Shemenkov to survive at least until I have completed my investigation, however pointless that investigation might be."

"He has been moved to a cell with a video camera. He will be watched constantly. There will be no more suicide attempts."

"Gracias," said Rostnikov.

"Nyeh zah shto," replied Major Sanchez.

"Right there," Angelica Carerra said. She pointed to a wooden-legged tan lounge chair that Elena Timofeyeva thought would be better suited to the waiting room of a medical clinic than an apartment.

Sheets of rain slapped against the windows and roof of the Carerra apartment. The place smelled of must and mildew.

Elena examined the lounge chair. Its recently cleaned pillows still showed the stains of whatever had been used to remove the blood of Maria Fernandez.

"We didn't want to keep it," said Carlos Carerra, "but what could we do? Even if we could afford new furniture, where could we buy it?"

The large room was remarkably bare, as if someone were moving in or out. The floor was gray tile. In addition to the lounge chair, there were three white wicker chairs. All faced a low, dark wooden coffee table that matched none of the other furniture. Against a wall stood a heavy, black mock-Chinese serving table on which sat a Chinese-made LP record player. The only decoration on the wall was a crude oil painting of Castro as he might have looked two decades before.

The Carerras had been solicitous. They had welcomed Elena and offered her a towel to dry herself after her dash from the taxi to the apartment building. They had given her a tall glass of lemonade as she apologized for being late. The taxi driver had been unable to find the house. He had been unable, in fact, to find the housing complex or the street. He had lived in Havana his entire life, but he had needed to call his dispatcher for instructions and the dispatcher had not known for sure.

"Havana is a maze of high-rise houses and renamed streets," Angelica Carerras told Elena.

The rain came down so loudly they had to raise their voices. The wind rattled the windows.

"We are lucky to have this apartment," said Carlos. "When the rain stops, look around out there. There are only four floors in this building, only eight apartments. It was built before the revolution. The walls are thick. It stays cool. We are lucky."

The Carerras were standing side by side, concerned, grateful that Elena could speak Spanish, anxious to cooperate.

Carlos was in his late thirties, perhaps forty. He was thin and good-looking, with a broken nose and thinning black hair that he brushed back. He wore faded white slacks and a pale blue cotton shirt with the top button unfastened to reveal a stand of hair on his chest. His wife, Angelica, was of a similar age. She had blond curly hair, wore a lot of makeup, and was quite pretty. Her dress was a pale blue that almost matched her husband's shirt. Angelica's body, only slightly fuller than that of Victoria Oliveras, once again made Elena acutely aware of the body she had inherited from generations of Timofeyevas and Lipinovs.

Angelica glanced at the shaking windows.

"When the hurricane came through years ago," Carlos said, "it took out those windows. Even then it was difficult to get glass. Now, if the windows go, we'll probably have to board them up."

"But that is a sacrifice we will make gladly if it will help the revolution," Angelica added, looking at the painting of Fidel on the wall.

"Please sit," said Carlos with a sad smile.

Elena sat in approximately the same place where she was sure Maria Fernandez had died. Sitting made Elena acutely aware of how wet she had gotten in her dash from the cab. Angelica sat in one of the wicker chairs.

Carlos asked Elena if she wanted more lemonade. When she declined, he sat in another wicker chair, adjusted the crease in his trousers, and looked at Elena, who put her lemonade down on the coffee table and took out her notebook.

"What do you do for a living?" Elena asked.

"Tours," said Carlos quickly. "We arrange tours of entertainers throughout Cuba and, when we are lucky, we arrange for Cuban entertainers to travel to other countries. We sent a folk band to the Soviet Union three years ago. Great success."

"Until a few years ago," Angelica said, "Carlos and I performed. Dancers. My parents were ballroom dancers before the revolution. They appeared all over the world—Miami, New York, Rio, Madrid. Santos and Anita."

"I was a great admirer of Angelica's parents," said Carlos as lightning cracked outside again. "I wanted to be a dancer. I became a soldier."

Carlos laughed. Angelica joined him. Elena did not laugh, but she did manage a small smile.

"How long did you know Maria Fernandez?"

"Well," said Carlos. "Not very long. A year, perhaps."

"Yes, a year," Angelica agreed. "She wanted to be a singer. There are too many singers. Some of them very good, but too many, even too many pretty ones."

Carlos nodded in agreement.

"But we liked her," he said. "We hired her to help us. And she was very good."

"Very good," Angelica agreed, folding her hands in her lap.

"And Victoria Oliveras?" Elena asked, trying not to think of a quick return to her room at the El Presidente and a change into dry clothes.

"Well," said Carlos, looking at Angelica and sighing. "To tell the truth, Victoria was a friend of Maria's. I don't know how they met. I think Victoria attached herself to Maria. We warned her about Victoria."

"We had heard some . . . things about her," Angelica said, almost too softly for Elena to hear.

"Things?" Elena asked.

The rain suddenly subsided. Within seconds it turned into a light drizzle.

"None of our business," said Carlos, "but we heard she was into things, perhaps illegal things. And some of the people she knew . . . Well, sexual preferences can sometimes . . ."

"Not that we condemn," added Angelica.

"What about Shemenkov?" said Elena.

"Ah, the Russian," said Carlos. "Maria met him at the Russian club. She was there with a show, managing, setting up, you know."

Elena nodded and wrote in her notebook.

"He approached her," said Angelica. "That's what she said. And to give him his due, she encouraged him. She thought he was funny. She called him her Russian bear, said she would train him to do tricks."

"Were you at the Cosacos bar when the man called Javier threatened to kill Maria and Igor Shemenkov?"

"Who told you that?" asked Carlos.

"Victoria Oliveras."

"It wasn't such a great thing," Carlos said. "Yes, he got into an argument with Igor. Javier had said some things to Maria. Maria had tried to ignore him. Javier was a little drunk and so . . ."

"Did Shemenkov strike him?"

"No," said Carlos. "Push a little, maybe. But strike? No." He looked at Angelica, who nodded her head in firm agreement.

"Javier is a *Santería*," said Elena.

"Perhaps," said Carlos. "Many blacks are."

"Whites too," added Angelica. "More now that Fidel is enlisting the *Santería* in the revolution. Even Gramma carries articles now on the 'colorful' high priests and their support of the revolution."

Carlos closed his eyes and nodded in assent.

"The *Santería* can be violent," Elena went on.

"Yes," said Carlos.

"The night Maria Fernandez was murdered, did you see anyone nearby?"

"You mean like a witness?" asked Angelica.

Elena nodded.

"I don't know," Angelica said. "Who remembers?"

"I don't remember," said Carlos, playing with a large silver ring on his finger. "Just Martin, the building maintenance man. He was sweeping the stairs when we came in, I think."

"Yes," Angelica confirmed.

"Where does he live?"

"In the basement," said Carlos. "A room. But he is . . ." Carlos touched the side of his head with a finger.

"What happened the night Maria Fernandez was murdered?" Elena asked.

"You know we have told this three, four times to the police?" asked Angelica.

"I have seen their report. Please, once more."

Carlos sighed and said, "We came here for drinks, to talk, and to be sociable. Victoria showed up. There were words, stupid words. Angelica and I wanted them to go. Maria and Igor started to argue. We got Victoria into the hall and tried to get her to leave."

"No one on the stairs?"

"No," said Carlos. "No one came up. Our neighbors across the hall, the Hernandezes, are away, on business I think. We were trying to get Victoria to leave, had her halfway down the stairs, when we heard the scream and the noise. We all ran back up. The Russian was standing over Maria. She was covered in blood. I think my wife screamed."

"I did. And Victoria attacked Igor even though he had a knife in his hand. She kicked him in the face."

"He didn't hurt her?" said Elena.

"No, he didn't," said Carlos. "He just looked . . . I don't know. Stunned."

"Did he speak?"

"Yes," said Angelica. "He said, 'Someone has killed Maria.' I think that's what he must have been saying in Russian. It took a while to get him to say it in Spanish."

The rain had definitely stopped now and a hint of sunlight came through the window. Distant thunder whispered in retreat.

"Was that window open the night of the murder?" asked Elena.

"Yes," said Carlos. "It is always open at night unless it is raining."

Elena got up as gracefully as she could and moved to the window, notepad still in hand. She opened the window and felt a rush of warm moist air. She looked four stories down at the empty street and then, holding the side of the window ledge, leaned out to look upward. The roof was two or three feet over her head.

"Can I look at the roof?" she asked, easing back into the room.

Angelica did not join them on the trip to the roof, though the ascent was not particularly difficult. On the interior landing outside the apartment, Carlos stepped back into the shadows and reached up for a metal chain. The chain, sleepy with rust, came down reluctantly. When pulled it released an equally rusty ladder. A sudden clang echoed across the landing as the ladder came down.

"Careful," Carlos called out as he headed up the ladder.

Elena followed him up and through the trapdoor to the roof, which was covered with pebbles. Water from the rain could be heard trickling down a metal drain. There were five bent television antennas lashed to the stone balustrade that fenced in the roof at hip level.

"Did the police come up here?" Elena asked.

"Up here? I think so, but maybe not. Why?"

Carlos had somehow managed to make the climb without creasing or soiling his white trousers. He carefully removed a handkerchief from his pocket and cleaned his hands.

Elena looked outward at the expanse of high-rise white-block apartments, trees, and departing clouds. Then she moved to the edge of the roof. The next apartment building, about eight feet away, seemed to be a duplicate of the one on which she stood, except that it had only three antennas. On the opposite side there was only an empty lot.

"Your window?" she asked, and Carlos led the way to the edge of the roof facing the street.

"Just below, here I think," he said.

Elena moved past him, leaned over to be sure he was right, and felt along the stone wall above the window. The cement was chipped away, but most of the chipped cement was dark with dirt. There was one small chip that looked more recent. At the base of the wall, she searched and pushed away small stones.

"What are you looking for?" Carlos asked.

Elena said nothing. Almost instantly she found two holes. She pressed the tip of her finger into one of the holes and brought it back out with the dust of clean moist cement.

"What did you find?" Carlos asked as Elena rose.

"I would like two things, Señor Carerras," she said.

"Of course."

"First, I would like to have the use of your handkerchief so that I may clean my palms as you have. Second, I would like to get on the roof of the apartment building next door."

Carlos nodded, fished out his handkerchief, and handed it to her.

"Some people are joining us for dinner tonight," Rostnikov said when Elena reported to him at the table near the pool of the El Presidente Hotel. The table was fast becoming Porfiry Petrovich's unofficial office.

He was dressed in dark slacks and a yellow guayabera shirt. His forehead was slightly sunburned and he sipped on a tall drink.

Elena sat down and placed her notebook in front of her. Rostnikov was looking at a pair of children, a boy and a girl, splashing in the pool and arguing in what might have been Portuguese over an inflated toy that looked like a cross-eyed pink pony.

"Would you like to know who is joining us?"

"Yes," said Elena.

"Major Sanchez and Povlevich of the KGB. At breakfast this morning he looked so lonely I took pity on him. We will meet at eight, have some drinks, perhaps see some of the town. When we return I will excuse myself for a well-earned night of sleep while you entertain Major Sanchez, who has a decided interest in you, and Povlevich, who is decidedly glum and in need of as much of the Russian language as he can get."

The waiter reached over Elena's shoulder and placed a duplicate of Rostnikov's drink before her.

"And the reason for this merriment and revelry, Inspector?" she asked.

"Ah," he said, shifting in his chair to look at the group of American and Cuban writers, who were making an early start at drinking and arguing. "I will slip away with our nearsighted journalist Antonio Rodriguez in search of our *Santería.*"

"But have we not concluded that Rodriguez is probably in the employ of Major Sanchez?"

"We have so concluded," said Rostnikov. "Our conclusion is tentative, but . . . given our options and the fact that our Major Sanchez has suggested that the Cuban judicial system is likely to move swiftly in this case . . ."

"Perhaps I have some information that will make your search more promising." Elena opened her notebook.

"It was my impression that you were filled with revelations."

"Am I so obvious?"

"You are very wet, very tired, and glowing with life. Speak."

"The Carerras pretend to be what they are not," she said. "Their furnishings are spare but there are marks on the floor which indicate that other furniture has been moved. There was one painting on the wall, but clear outlines from the sun indicate that the walls had been covered with pictures or photographs. Carlos Carerra suggested that they had little money for food and drink and gave me only lemonade, but there was a distinct smell of meat recently cooked. I was not shown the kitchen. The table in the living room was filled with bottles. I heard them when I touched the surface."

"Good," said Rostnikov. "But that is not the news with which you are bursting."

"There are signs that something, perhaps a rope or metal ladder, was recently lowered from the roof to the window of the Carerras' apartment. On the adjacent roof, perhaps eight feet away, I found a wooden painters' platform leaning against the wall where it could not be seen from the roof of the Carerra apartment building. It was too heavy to move but it is sturdy and about ten feet long."

"Major Sanchez's report indicates that the police found no sign of possible entry to the Carerra apartment from the roof," said Rostnikov.

"Perhaps they did not look carefully enough," said Elena Timofeyeva. She put her hand to her hair and realized with horror that it was a wild mop. It had probably been just so from the moment she entered the Carerra apartment.

"Or perhaps they did not wish to look carefully enough," said Rostnikov. "You've done well. Go to your room. Take a bath if there is any hot water. Take a nap, prepare to have a good time."

Elena rose, closed her notebook, and nodded.

"In a little while I am going to the stadium across the avenue where I have been told there exists a passable collection of weights. I order you to enjoy yourself, Elena Timofeyeva."

"I'm not sure that enjoyment is something that one can be ordered to engage in."

"Perhaps not, but my doing so gives you leave to make me responsible for allowing you to abandon your post."

"May I say that I find your reasoning convoluted," she said.

"It is a skill which I have nurtured and in which I take some pride."

Elena was about to speak again when the children in the pool shrieked and Rostnikov turned his head to look at them.

Five minutes later Elena was in the bath with the water running. Twenty minutes later she was asleep in her bed. Five floors below children were still squealing in the swimming pool.

Had he arrived five minutes earlier or later, Emil Karpo would have missed the boy with the red Mohawk and the slender blue-haired girl in black leather. The sky was dark with the threat of rain or early snow, and people were hurrying in and out of Petrovka to beat the weather.

They were at the sentry gate, arguing with the uniformed guard, who was repeating that they could not see Inspector Rostnikov, that he was unavailable, that they could leave a message, that they were holding up the line. The line consisted of a short, fat, shivering man carrying a briefcase and looking at his watch with impatience.

"Capones?" Karpo said, stepping around to the sentry station.

The red-haired boy looked up at him, and the girl, whose eyes were made up with dark circles so she looked like an owl, smiled.

"Yes," the boy said. "We need to see the Washtub."

"Come," Karpo said, motioning them to follow him into the street. The uniformed young officer motioned for the short businessman to step forward.

Karpo crossed Petrovka Street with the two Capones at his side. A low fence and some trees faced the Petrovka station. Karpo stopped beneath the trees near the bus stop and turned to the Capones.

"We want to see the Washtub," the boy said defiantly.

"What is your name?" Karpo asked.

"I'm called Matches."

"Why do you want to see Inspector Rostnikov?" asked Karpo. He was aware of the owl girl looking at him with something that appeared to be fascination.

"We want Yellow Angel's body," said the boy.

"Her name was Iliana Ivanova," said Karpo.

"She hated her name," said the girl. "She didn't want to be buried with that name over her. She wanted a headstone with a yellow angel."

"We are trying to find her family," said Karpo. He felt the first drops of slushy rain begin to fall.

"You found it," said Matches. "The Capones are her family."

"When the examiners are finished with the body, I'll see what can be done," Karpo said, looking at the girl.

"You're the Vampire," she said. "The one they call the Vampire."

Karpo pulled the leather notebook from his pocket.

"When?" asked Matches, nervously pulling up the collar of his jacket to keep the sleet from his neck. "When can we get her?"

"Have Xeromen call me at this number in an hour, at nine-thirty," Karpo said, handing the boy the sheet of paper.

Matches looked at the sheet and then at the girl, who was still admiring Karpo.

"Take it," she said.

Matches put the paper in his jacket pocket.

In the red treetops of Matches's hair, beads of gray sleet clung, slipped, and melted.

The girl smiled at Karpo again and shifted her weight from foot to foot. Her dress was short and her legs covered with thin tights. Karpo was sure she was no more than fifteen or sixteen. The cheeks and thighs of childhood gave her away, even though her eyes revealed experience that added five years to her heavily made-up face.

"Well?" said Matches, reaching up to brush the sleet from his hair.

"Nine-thirty," said Karpo. He now looked directly into the girl's eyes.

Her grin disappeared. She blinked and turned away.

"Let's go," said Matches, touching her arm. "Ginka, let's go."

The sleet was falling harder now. Matches pulled at the girl's arm, and finally, reluctantly, she followed him. As they hurried down the street she looked back at the motionless pale policeman in black, whose eyes followed them as they reached the waiting black Volga and got in.

EIGHT

The Moscow Metropolitan Railway, with more than 100 stations, 160 miles of track, 8,000 trains, and over 2 million passengers a day, is—in terms of layout, efficiency, extent, and even beauty—the best subway system in the world. It is probably the highest lasting achievement of the Soviet Union in Moscow.

Stations are scrubbed and polished constantly. Air is changed four to eight times an hour depending on the traffic. Smoking is forbidden in stations and on all trains, which run until one in the morning and arrive every ninety seconds at all stations during the rush hour.

There are seven lines, each color coded, with convenient transfer stops in the center of the city and along the Koltsevaya Line, which runs in an almost perfect circle around the central city. A map of the system looks like the wheel of a cart with its spokes extended well beyond the rim.

The cost of travel on the Moscow Metro is one ruble, the equivalent of an American penny.

The system is semiautomatic, operated by computer, monitored by uniformed drivers who check the control settings.

When plans for an underground railway were considered before the revolution, in 1902, the newspaper *Russkoye Slovo* called the proposal "a staggeringly impudent encroachment on everything Russian people hold dear in the city of Moscow. As the tunnel of the metropolitan railway will pass in places only a few feet beneath churches, the peace and quiet of these sacred places will be disturbed." The Moscow City Council, the Duma, rejected the proposal.

The first shaft of the Moscow Metro was finally sunk in 1931. When the first train ran on May 15, 1935, there were thirteen stations. Even when the war with Hitler began, construction continued.

Stone and wood from all over the Soviet Union were used to construct each station. Architects, sculptors, painters, and designers considered it a great honor to be assigned to a Metro station. Many of the stations in the center of the city look more like cavernous museum galleries than train stations.

Each stop on the Metro line is different from all the others. The Mayakovskaya Station is known for its massive red marble columns and its mosaics created from the cartoons of Alexander Deineka. The lighting system in the Kropotkinskaya Station was designed to give the impression that the station is on the surface and that sunshine is beaming in on a bright summer morning. Supported by seventy-two pillars, the Komsomolskaya Station, with its eight massive mosaics depicting the struggle for independence, is more than two hundred yards long.

In the winter, Gypsies and the wandering homeless ride the trains for warmth and the opportunity to beg from captive travelers.

The Metro police division, a branch of the Moscow police with almost one thousand uniformed and plainclothed men and women, patrols the vast system, dealing with a range of crimes that includes purse-snatching, pocket-picking, and the recent outbreak of American-style muggings by youth gangs.

"And so," said Sasha Tkach, sipping tepid tea, "what does this tell us about *Tahpor*? Is he a Metro employee? A frequent rider? A lunatic who loves or hates the Metro? This could also be a coincidence."

Karpo stood next to him in the office of Inspector Rostnikov looking at the Metro map he had brought from his room and carefully laid out on the desk.

"I have considered this," said Karpo. "The odds are approximately two hundred to one against the selection of forty murder sites in close proximity to Metro stations being random."

Sasha poured himself some more tea from the thermos Maya had prepared for him. Some time during the night, Sasha had begun to develop a slight cough and when he got up in the morning he thought he might have a temperature.

"Why didn't anyone notice this connection to Metro stations before?" asked Sasha.

"Perhaps," said Karpo, "because there is no overt connection, only a proximity that becomes remarkable when the sample becomes large enough. Coincidence would have had at least one of the murders taking place farther than five minutes from a station, or one or more of the murders even closer to a Metro station. It would appear, therefore, that 341 does not want to act too near a station and is afraid of getting too far from one."

"I'm catching a cold again and I distrust such statistics," said Tkach.

"I have noticed that you are remarkably prone to viral attack. I suggest large doses of citrus and aspirin and I share your skepticism, but I think the possibility that I may be correct is worth pursuit unless you have a potentially more promising conjecture."

"I have a cold."

"I'm sorry, but you have colds with increasing frequency."

"Pulcharia asked about you," said Tkach, stifling a sneeze. "She likes you."

Karpo allowed himself a smile, though no one, with the possible exception of Rostnikov, would have recognized it as such. He looked up at the clock on the wall of Rostnikov's office. It was a few minutes before four.

"I read," said Tkach, returning to his skepticism, "that a researcher for the American Encyclopedia Britannica determined the square footage of forest in the Soviet Union by calling a forest ranger and asking how many trees grew on an average square acre of forest. The researcher then looked at a map, added up all the area marked in green in the Soviet Union, divided it by acres, and multiplied it by the number the forest ranger had given her. That figure then appeared in the encyclopedia and has subsequently been picked up by almanacs and even used by *Izvestia*."

"And you find a relationship between this anecdote and my conclusions about 341?" asked Karpo.

"You see spots on a map and draw a conclusion." Tkach sniffled. "You see a pattern. You connect the dots to make the picture you want to see."

The tinkling fluorescent light from the single fixture above Rostnikov's desk sent long shadows down Karpo's pale face.

"I see no other reasonable conclusion," said Karpo. "I think 341 will realize this too," he said.

"Realize what?" asked Sasha, holding back a sneeze that confounded him by emerging as a cough.

"Perhaps soon, or perhaps after more killing, he will become aware of his pattern."

"And perhaps never," said Tkach. "But, assuming you are right, what will he do?"

"Force himself to kill a great distance from a Metro station, if he is capable of doing so. Or commit a murder in a Metro station, if he is capable of doing so."

"Or," said Sasha, "simply go right on the way he has been. We can search far from a Metro station, inside a station, or near a station. The circle is closing around our killer, Karpo. We have him trapped within the confines of greater Moscow."

"I assume that was sarcasm. I do not find sarcasm productive," said Karpo.

Someone tapped at the door and Sasha called for whoever it was to enter. A female clerk with very short hair stuck her head in and announced that Sasha had a call.

Karpo responded by looking down at the map.

"Deputy Inspector Tkach," Sasha said into the phone.

"You sound worse," said Maya. "Did you drink the tea?"

"I'm drinking," he said. "I'll get an orange or some pills."

"Pulcharia has a cough too."

"I'm sorry."

"If it gets worse, I'm calling that doctor, Sarah Rostnikov's cousin, the one we met at the party. The clinic lines are getting longer and the nurses always take your temperature and give you the same bottle of red syrup."

"Good idea," said Tkach. Karpo, standing pale and still, reminded Sasha of the statue of Lenin in October Square. Then Sasha remembered that the statue of Lenin was no longer in October Square.

"Try to come home and get some rest," Maya said.

"I'll try," Sasha said, aware that home and rest were antagonistic concepts. His greatest chance at recuperation would probably be to remain right here in Rostnikov's overly warm office pondering the Metro theory of Emil Karpo.

When Sasha hung up the phone, Karpo spoke.

"We have a profile of victims. Central Computer indicates that they are sixty-four percent males and thirty-six percent females. The median age of victims is twenty-one, with the range from fifteen to thirty. An examination of the victims suggests that the younger ones looked a bit older and the older ones looked younger than their age. All of the victims were approached while traveling alone."

"So," said Tkach, leaning back dreamily, "the odds are approximately three to one that *Tahpor* will next attack a male traveling alone who is in his early twenties or seems to be. The odds are perhaps eighty to one that this attack will take place near a Metro station."

"So it would seem."

"Ah," said Tkach, fighting a strong urge to close his eyes and lean far back in Rostnikov's desk chair. "And when?"

"Soon perhaps," said Karpo, still staring at the map. "He killed two days ago. He has killed on consecutive days. He has waited months to kill. What he has not done is strike three days after a murder."

"But he might go back to an old pattern," said Tkach, resisting the urge to touch his own forehead to check his temperature.

"All things are possible," said Karpo. "We are dealing with a madman. Like all mad people, he has a set of needs, a pattern that compels him."

"Like killing always five minutes from the Metro. So, what is your plan?"

"My plan," said Karpo, "is to find as many young people as we can who fit 341's victim profile, and place them where they can be watched if they are approached by anyone."

"And how many decoys and watchers would that take to have any statistical chance of finding 341?" asked Tkach.

"Several hundred," said Karpo.

"We'll need the Wolfhound to get the Metro police to cooperate," said Tkach. "You are talking about one hundred police."

"Then we shall ask him for that. We shall convince him that it is imperative."

"And the decoys? Even if we get enough police, which is not likely, where are we going to get a hundred decoys who fit the victim profile?"

Karpo simply looked at Sasha and said nothing.

"You have at least one in mind," said Sasha.

"Yes," replied Emil Karpo.

"So, you have me. All you need are about fifty more."

"I think I may know where to get them," said Karpo.

The phone on Rostnikov's desk rang. It was precisely nine-thirty.

Yevgeny Odom was a hardworking man. Not only did he carefully plan murders and protect Kola, he also worked two jobs.

Since his full-time job did not start till early in the afternoon, he put in two or three hours each day in the blood bank at the hospital. His army service as a medical assistant had taught him how to draw blood, and his pleasant disposition had earned him his civilian position. Donors frequently reported to doctors and nurses that the tall man with the small smile drew their blood with almost no pain and great good humor, both characteristics that were traditionally in short supply in Russia.

When he went to the hospital in the mornings, he always carried his flat, compact, blue carry-on bag, an imitation Delsey he had purchased at a street market. It contained, among other things, hundreds of rubles. It had become a necessity with insane inflation to carry a bag of money to buy even the most mundane of things. Street vendors sold cans of Pepsi, jars of pickles, postcards, and political sketches at one stand, pathetic onions, fur hats, religious icons, and cans of olives at the next. Food was suddenly plentiful and the lines were short in stores.

The problem was that very few Russians had enough money to buy anything.

Yevgeny's needs were limited, but one had to be prepared.

This day should be no different from all the rest. He placed the bag behind the table at which he drew the blood and entered into the morning routine with enthusiasm, offering support and sympathy to each person who dutifully made a fist while he prepared the needle.

During the previous night he had made his decision. It had come partly from logic and cunning, partly from this faint sense of separation he had begun to feel. He would double-check before locking the plan into place, but he could see no great problem with it.

"Fist please," he said to the heavy, dark man in the chair. The man was frightened and trying not to show it. There was the look of a drinker in the man's skin and eyes; his blood would probably be rejected, but that was not Yevgeny Odom's concern.

The man cringed as Yevgeny tightened the yellow elastic band around his bicep. The man tried to look away as the needle approached skin but he could not resist and turned at the last instant. Into his arm went the needle, smoothly, easily. The man let out the breath of air he had been holding.

"Hurt?" asked Yevgeny.

"No," said the man with a smile.

"Good, it's over."

The man moved away quickly, and Yevgeny smiled in amusement. He hoped that there was a policeman or a team of policemen assigned to him. It was reasonable that there would be. He preferred to imagine real human beings rather than a computer and a set of standard Ministry of the Interior guidelines for identifying and apprehending serial killers.

Yevgeny had considered his options carefully. He contemplated a faceless, androgynous victim along a riverbank in Klin, but rejected the distant riverbank as somehow unsatisfying even though it would make sense to strike next far from the city. He chose not to explore the reasons for this decision, but something inside told him that the decision to remain in the city was correct.

A thin, thirtyish woman with an aggressive look on her face was the next donor. Her washed-out blond hair was tied back with a band, making her face even more taut and tense than the situation merited.

"Sit, please," Yevgeny said, holding his large hands open to show they were empty and harmless.

The thin woman sat cautiously.

"This will not hurt. I promise you."

She watched him aggressively and he smiled at her. He preferred the aggressive ones like this to the ones who chatted, seeking contact and kinship in an effort to obtain more gentle treatment. They always walked away thinking that their transparent efforts had been the cause of his care. He preferred ones like this, who had no choice but to credit him for the ease of these few moments.

"Please pull up the sleeve of your dress," he said. Reluctantly the woman did so.

Perhaps she was one of those who believed that her anger would generate a fear in him that would result in his taking extra care. Then she, too, would walk away crediting not him but her own actions. In fact, it mattered not to Yevgeny whether they pleaded, tried to make friends, cast warning looks, or resigned themselves to their fate. He treated them all the same. He wanted donors, victims, and the police to treat him with the respect he deserved as a professional.

The woman turned out to be another satisfied donor. Her anger turned to relief, and she managed to mumble a thank-you as she rolled down her sleeve and hurried away.

At precisely 11:00 A.M., Yevgeny was relieved by Karin. He

did not know her last name, nor did he want to know. She was his age perhaps, a bit plump, with dark hair and good skin. She was not terribly bright and tried to mask it with a weary Moscow cynicism. Yevgeny knew that if he wanted her she would be more than willing to come to his apartment, but he did not want her. He exchanged pleasant greetings, wished her a hearty good day, and hurried off with his carry-on bag. He had just enough time to change into his uniform and make it to his shift on the Kaluzhsko-Rizhskaya Metro Line.

Two of the three young men who waited for Rostnikov outside the sports center were getting impatient and distinctly nervous.

Their names were Juan and Martin. They were twin brothers, but not identical. Juan looked very much like their mother—thin and dark—while Martin was the image of their father, who was also named Martin. Martin was very big and looked quite as stupid as he was. People who met the brothers often mistakenly believed that the crafty-looking one, Juan, provided whatever thinking the pair could generate. In fact, Juan was every bit as stupid as his brother. Martin's pride, what there was of it, came from his strength, which he had been born with. Juan's pride was derived from his knife.

Both Juan and Martin relied on the third young man who stood with them. His name was Lupe and he was younger than they. He was a brooding, good-looking young man with thick dark hair and full lips. Lupe had led the twins from failed career to failed career. They had failed in the black market trying to sell imitation American clothes. They had failed at petty extortion, almost getting caught when a shopkeeper on Calle Composteta called for the police. They had even failed at reasonably honest work, first because they had no heart for long hours and later because there was no work to be had.

Supposedly the trio were now farmworkers on a citrus farm

somewhere in the northern provinces. In fact, they were muggers with a reasonably successful two months behind them.

Lupe chose their victims well, foreigners who would be carrying hard currency or jewelry that could be sold for hard currency. The foreigners were usually women or men who did not look as if they could defend themselves.

The one he had chosen today seemed perfect, a washtub of a man comically dressed in a sweat suit, a towel draped around his neck, and a light jacket over his shoulders. The man walked with a decided limp. There was no way he could chase them. They would simply wait till he emerged from whatever workout he had planned, pull him behind the tin-roofed hut beyond the sports complex, grab his jacket and wallet and the wedding band on his left hand, and run while he shouted for help and limped after them.

The only question was, how long would the lame foreigner be inside the sports complex?

The answer was forty-five minutes.

Inside the complex, in a vast room the size of a small airplane hangar, the sound of grunts and the echo of weights clanging on gray mats was music to the ears of Porfiry Petrovich. There were perhaps fifteen people using the old, worn weights, of which there were plenty. Rostnikov preferred to work out alone in his own apartment, on his own pull-out bench, with his own weights that he stored in the cabinet in the living room–kitchen. At home he savored his routine, but he was not at home.

He found a relatively private corner, removed his sweatshirt, and pulled down the T-shirt that bore the fading words "Moscow Senior Championship 1983" across the back.

The bench nearby was not as low as his own bench, but it was not bad. He arranged the weights, preparing them so that he could alter the weight on the bar. Even though there were enough weights and bars to allow him to use different ones, his familiar routine was more important than convenience.

As he set to work, humming "Mean to Me," he tried to recall the almost childlike trill in the voice of Dinah Washington as she sang "It must be great fun to be mean to me."

Soon he was almost lost in the memory of his tape and the painful comfort of the weights. He closed his eyes as he sat on the bench doing his set of forty curls with a fifty-pound weight in each hand.

When he opened his eyes, he found himself looking at a quartet of boys all around ten years old who were leaning against a pipe railing about fifteen yards away.

Rostnikov smiled at the boys. They smiled back and it was clear that they were not going to depart. So Rostnikov moved away from the bench to pick up the bar on which he had placed two hundred pounds. He bent over and knelt toward the bar. It would have been better if he could squat, but his damaged leg had never permitted him the proper form.

He chalked his hands, closed his eyes, gripped the bar, and tried to think of the circle of the moon as he merged with the weight. When he was ready he stood erect, swept the mass of clanking balanced metal first to his chest and then, taking a step with his weak leg, skyward. When it was firmly overhead and in control, Rostnikov opened his eyes to the applause of the smiling boys.

As he brought the bar down and pressed it back up, the boys counted joyfully,

"*Uno . . . dos . . . tres . . . quatro . . . cinco . . . seis.*"

When he brought the weight back down to his chest and eased it to the mat with a satisfying clank, the boys again broke into applause. Rostnikov stepped over the bar and bowed formally to the quartet. This had been as much fun as when he had won the senior weight-lifting championship and met the great Alexiev.

When he finished the entire routine, the boys approached

him as he gathered his things. They jabbered quickly in Spanish he could not understand.

"American, Canada?" asked a thin boy.

"Russian," answered Rostnikov.

"Ruskie, Ruskie," the boys chanted.

"Va a volver mañana?" asked another boy, pulling at the sleeve of his jacket.

"Mañana, sí," said Rostnikov.

They left him at the door of the building and ran back inside. He wiped himself with his drenched towel and headed down the concrete path toward the Avenida del Presidente.

Normally, Rostnikov would have sensed the attack, but conditions were not normal. The sun was hot; he was exhausted and in a country whose sounds were unfamiliar.

In front of him stood a good-looking young man with a smile on his face. The man's legs were slightly apart and he clasped his hands in front of him like a soldier at ease. Suddenly an arm circled Rostnikov's neck and a thin young man at his side held the point of a knife to his stomach.

"Shhh," said the good-looking young man in front of him as the young man with the knife reached for Rostnikov's jacket pocket. The good-looking young man had stepped forward. Now he lifted Rostnikov's left hand and put his fingers on the wedding band.

Rostnikov took two shallow breaths. Then he threw his left hand up at the thin man's wrist. It snapped, sending the knife flying into the air. With his left hand Rostnikov grasped the wrist of the man in front of him and pulled the man's nose into his forehead. The nose collapsed in a crunch of bone. Then, as the grip around his neck tightened, Rostnikov tensed his neck muscles, grabbed the fingers of the man behind him, and bent the fingers back, quickly breaking three of them. Rostnikov turned and faced the startled man, who looked first at the other two, one who was howling in pain as he staggered away, and the other, whose face was a sheet of gushing blood. The man with the broken fingers turned and ran.

Rostnikov picked up the knife and turned to the confused man with the shattered nose.

"Don't touch it," Rostnikov said in English. "You understand?"

The man nodded dumbly.

"Good. If you know a doctor, you should go see him. Might be bone chips. But remember, don't touch it."

The man seemed uncertain of which way to go for an instant. Then he hurried after the other two, leaving a trail of dripping blood behind him. Rostnikov adjusted his wedding band, mopped his face with the towel, and continued his walk back to the hotel.

In Moscow, he thought, they would have had guns. In Moscow, they probably would have belonged to some extended Mafia like the Capones. They would have had backup.

It was a relief, Rostnikov decided, crossing the avenue behind an ancient Volkswagen, to be in Cuba, where some crime was still, at least for a while, in controllable infancy.

NINE

Colonel Snitkonoy was dressed in mufti. This was, as his staff knew, very unusual. His perfectly fitted dark suit had been painstakingly ironed by his housekeeper only an hour before, as had his white English shirt and serious blue-and-red-striped tie. His black shoes were military shined, and his hair had been perfectly trimmed by the same housekeeper, who had been his aide-de-camp when both were spreading Soviet dominance in the days not so long gone.

The Gray Wolfhound pulled out his antique gold pocket watch. "I have," he said, "exactly five minutes before I must leave for my presentation on the alleged murder of the Kazakhstani foreign minister."

"We understand," said Karpo, who, along with Sasha Tkach, stood in front of the colonel's desk.

"I am to meet with the Council of Deputies for Internal Security in the Kremlin," the colonel went on.

There was a long pause while the Wolfhound sat erect in his chair facing the two detectives.

"I have your report, Emil Karpo," he said, holding up an envelope. "I have contradictory laboratory findings. I am walking into a room of important people who want irrefutable evidence."

And, he thought, a room in which, if this report is correct, several of the people around the table may well be parties to the murder of Foreign Minister Kumad Kustan. Some facts were quite clear. The foreign minister had been in Moscow two days before his death. An overweight, surly man with a mop of white hair that matched Yeltsin's, he had conducted his search for Russian support in a rumpled suit. Things seemed to have gone well, so well that an announcement had been made by both the Russian foreign minister and Kustan that a new era was about to begin. Kustan died in a lounge at the Hotel Russia following a small reception, which only a dozen members of the government, both pro- and anti-Yeltsin, had attended. Security had been tight. Kustan had died. Now it seemed he might have been murdered. The murderer was likely to have been at the highest level of government. But why kill the foreign minister? To stop the agreement and embarrass Yeltsin? Or to protect Yeltsin? But why? Had the talks fallen through? It was not impossible that the murderer of the Kazakhstani foreign minister would be sitting in the room where Colonel Snitkonoy was going to make his report.

"We cannot be wrong, Emil Karpo," said the Wolfhound, putting the report down in front of him and folding his hands on his shiny dark desk. "Have you noticed that there are few dogs in the police kennel? Food is scarce. Luxuries are few. Those who produce survive. Those who do not are eaten."

"We are not wrong," said Karpo.

Colonel Snitkonoy nodded. He knew he had no choice but to go to the meeting and present the evidence. He had rehearsed his presentation for forty minutes before the mirror in his bedroom. He hoped it would go well.

It would be a difficult morning. He glanced out the window.

At least the sleet had stopped and the sky held a gray hope of light.

"Speak, Inspector Karpo," the colonel said. The Vampire was one of the few people he knew who made him truly uncomfortable.

"We have developed a plan," said Karpo, "which we believe can result in the resolution of Case 341."

"Tahpor," said the Wolfhound.

"It will require the services of the Metro Railway security forces," said Karpo.

The Wolfhound nodded and looked at Tkach, who was doing his best to hold back a sneeze.

"It will also require one week of round-the-clock shifts by perhaps one hundred armed officers and as many as fifty decoys who will have to look as if they are approximately twenty-two years old."

Employing self-control developed through four decades of service, Colonel Snitkonoy simply nodded for Karpo to begin.

Karpo outlined his plan and the Wolfhound listened.

Three minutes later, the colonel stood up, put the report on the Kazakhstani minister in his black Samsonite briefcase, and said, "I can ask for a day or two, perhaps three, but a week is out of the question. Can you narrow this down to a day or two with reasonable certainty that we will get 341?"

"No," said Karpo, "but . . ."

"I'll see what I can do," said the colonel. "As for the decoys . . ."

"That will be our responsibility," Karpo said.

The Wolfhound's eyes met and held Karpo's, which revealed nothing.

"Very well. Go. I will let you know."

Karpo nodded, and he and Tkach turned to leave.

"Attend to that cold, Deputy Inspector," the Wolfhound said.

"I will," answered Tkach, anxious to escape so he could let out the cough that he had choked down.

When the two detectives had gone, the Wolfhound considered whether he should indicate to the council that a plan had been suggested to catch the man who had murdered at least forty people in the past three years. He would then be placing not one but two distasteful decisions before them. If the council agreed to assign officers and Karpo's plan failed, the council would know it quickly, for he would be expected to follow up with a report. If he did not report and word of it got back to any of the men in that room, he would have to explain why he had not done so. There was no help for it, he concluded, but to face the possibility of failure on two fronts of his besieged operation.

Though he usually enjoyed being the focus of attention, Colonel Snitkonoy did not walk into his outer office with the enormous confidence he usually projected.

When the colonel's door opened, the startled Pankov rose quickly from behind his desk. He bumped his knee as he made a useless effort to pat down his hair.

"I'll be gone two hours," said the Wolfhound. "I want Major Grigorovich in my office at three-fifteen this afternoon. Also, put in a call to Inspector Rostnikov in Cuba. I want a full report from him in writing before the end of the day. He can dictate it to you."

"Yes," said Pankov, his hopes dashed for an easy day of paperwork.

"Havana is a city of misleading surfaces, you know?" said Antonio Rodriguez, taking off his thick glasses to wipe them on his shirt.

Rostnikov looked at the little man at his side. They were

stopped at a red light on the Prado, a street whose broad median strip had benches, ornate iron railings, and stone lions at the corners. But the buildings that had once clearly been spectacular were all falling to ruin. Atlantis, thought Rostnikov. It is like Atlantis risen from the sea.

Rodriguez squinted into the afternoon sun, put on his glasses, and looked startled, as if the world had magically changed in the time it had taken to clean his glasses.

Rodriguez had been waiting at the hotel when Rostnikov returned from his workout, had greeted him saying, "Change your clothes quickly. I have something to show you."

Rostnikov had gone to his room, showered and dressed, and returned to the excited little man, who urged him out into the street and into an automobile pitted with acne.

Rodriguez looked at the light, which was now green, and carefully changed gears on his 1954 Chevrolet. The car moved forward with a shake of metal. In a few places, the floor below Porfiry Petrovich's feet was worn through with age and rust. It was disconcerting and fascinating to watch the brick street pass beneath him. Rodriguez talked excitedly.

"There," he said. "That white house was Batista's capitol. Now it is the headquarters of the Cuban Academy of Science. See there, right there, across from the ballet? That statue? Saint Martí. I was here the night in the 1950s—it was summer—when some U. S. Marines climbed on the statue. The people tried to kill them."

"Have the Russians climbed any statues?" asked Rostnikov.

"Worse," said Rodriguez. "They piss on the statues."

A familiar red bus, the same kind of bus that traveled the Moscow streets, passed them quickly going in the opposite direction. Rostnikov looked up at the street signs carved into the building at the next corner. They were at the corner of Colón and Agramonte.

"There," said Rodriguez. "You must look. Big white build-ing. It was the Presidential Palace. Now it is the Museum of History. And here . . ."

He pulled the car over to let traffic pass and pointed to a small park surrounded by a dark iron fence. The park was clut-tered with an odd assortment of gray-green trucks, jeeps, two airplanes, and a small boat.

"This too is a museum of the revolution," said Rodriguez. "The boat is the *Gramma,* the ship Fidel used to come to Cuba to begin the revolution. Nobody knew what *Gramma* meant. They thought it was Latin or something. It means *abuela,* "grandmother," in English. We have a newspaper named *Gramma*, lots of things named *Gramma*. Those vehicles were used to storm the palace, and the airplanes fought the Americans at the Bay of Pigs."

"Fascinating," said Rostnikov. "But, Antonio Rodriguez, you did not snatch me from a few hours of rest to show me the sights of Havana."

"We are a bit early," the little man answered, putting his finger to his nose. "I wanted to be dramatic, you know. But, let's go."

He pulled the car back onto the Prado, made two left turns, and found a parking spot.

"We are lucky," he said, backing into the space with a grinding of worn-out gears. "Tourists—Germans, Canadians—usually take all the spaces."

When they got out, Rodriguez said, "This way." Rostnikov followed him to a corner where they stood in front of a bar.

"La Floridita," said Rodriguez proudly. "Hemingway's favor-ite bar, where the daiquiri was invented. They have kept it up for the tourists. Don't get anything to eat. Just a drink. Over-priced. Next door is a good Cuban restaurant if you want to eat. That's overpriced too, but not like La Floridita."

Rodriguez led the way inside and they were met by the sound of an accordion playing "Fascination."

To the left was a bar with a line of white-seated stools before it. The array of amber, white, and green bottles in front of the bar mirror was the most extensive Rostnikov had ever seen. On the wall was a large photograph of Ernest Hemingway. The small round tables in front of the bar were red with metal chairs around them. The metal chairs had white plastic seats and Rostnikov saw that the back supports for each chair were up-right metal arrows.

The floor beneath their feet was black with small white squares embedded in it. To their right, the windows were closed, and each had a box in front of it filled with plants.

"As it was when Hemingway himself he sit on that very stool," said Rodriguez. "I saw him myself in here one time. Or I think I did. Who remembers when history, memory, and wishes come together. You know?"

"I know," said Rostnikov.

The accordion was joined by a violin and a bass. Rostnikov could see the musicians on a small platform in the next room, the room he assumed was the dining room of La Floridita. There were a few other people in the bar. Rodriguez moved as far from them as he could and indicated one of the small tables to Rostnikov. The moment they were seated a waiter dressed in white with a red tie appeared before them.

"Daiquiris," said Rodriguez. *"El mismo que bebió Papá."*

When the waiter had gone, Rodriguez adjusted his seat and said, "So?"

"So, indeed."

"Tomorrow I take you to the Miramar," said Rodriguez, looking around the room. "Used to be very exclusive in the 1930s, even the 1950s. Then the Russians took over. Russians and Bulgarians."

Rostnikov sat stoically looking at the little man, who grinned back at him.

"I'm joking," said Rodriguez. "Teasing. Forgive me. Our Cuban sense of humor it grows strange in isolation."

"As ours has grown strange with the opening of borders," said Rostnikov. "Why are we here?"

"The band," Rodriguez said, leaning forward to whisper.

"They are adequate, but hardly memorable."

"Wrong," whispered Rodriguez. "Look at them."

The trio were blacks with more than a trace of both Spanish and Indian blood. The violinist was a man of about forty with a round smiling face and a full mustache. The accordion player was a woman about the same age with very long, dark hair pulled back in a knot. The bass player was tall, perhaps fifty, with a flat African nose. Both men wore gray slacks and white short-sleeved shirts with black ties. The woman's dress was colorful, a splash of orange, yellow, and red.

"I have looked," said Rostnikov, turning to Rodriguez.

The trio launched into a spirited version of the Beatles' "Norwegian Wood."

"That, the bass player, is Manuel, the *babalau,* the father of Javier who threatened to kill Maria Fernandez."

Rostnikov looked again at the man playing the bass fiddle. The man turned his gaze to the detective, and when their eyes met Rostnikov was sure that Manuel knew who he was and why he was there.

The waiter returned, placed the daiquiris in front of Rostnikov and Rodriguez, left a check, and disappeared without a word.

"And," said Rodriguez with great satisfaction, "you have just met Javier."

Rostnikov looked at the pale drink before him and said, "The waiter?"

"The waiter," Rodriguez confirmed. "How you like that?

Javier works here. He gets his father to fill in with his group once in a while."

Rostnikov looked at Javier, who was waiting on a quartet of tourists—two blond couples who looked Scandinavian.

Javier was tall and light-skinned. His hair was cropped short. He had a clear, handsome face with a sculpted nose quite unlike the nose of his father. Rostnikov was sure that beneath the uniform was a strong, sinewy body. Nothing in the man's face or dark eyes betrayed anything he might be feeling or thinking.

"You want to meet them?" Rodriguez asked.

"Very much," said Rostnikov.

Rodriguez began to rise, but Javier, who had returned, leaned past Rostnikov and collected the Canadian bills Rostnikov had put out. He did not look at Rostnikov as he picked up the money and departed.

"You won't get change," said Rodriguez. "How you like the drink?"

Rostnikov hated the frigid, sour-sweet liquid.

"It is interesting."

"You hate it," said Rodriguez. "Russians always hate it. Americans pretend to love it. They even order a second. Americans. They think they're going to return and turn us into a Disneyville."

"Do you like daiquiris, Antonio Rodriguez?"

"They taste like frozen goat piss."

"You've tasted frozen goat piss?"

"When pushed to the wall and thirsty," said Rodriguez with a straight face.

"But you just drank one."

"It is the thing to do in La Floridita. Wait here. I'll talk to Javier."

"No," said Rostnikov.

"I thought you wanted . . ."

"I changed my mind," said Rostnikov. The band moved to something Latin but without heart. Rostnikov stood up.

Rodriguez shrugged.

"Russians make no sense," he said, following Rostnikov to the door.

At the door, Rostnikov turned to look at Manuel the bass player. There was no expression on the face of either man but their eyes met once again.

Rodriguez drove back along the Malecon, past the monument to the victims of the *Maine*. He also pointed out the American Embassy Building and the statue of Antonio Maceo on horseback in front of the Hermana.

"There, that building used to be the National Bank. Still has vaults, still has Cuban money in it, but now is a hospital, best hospital in Central America, even your big shots come here."

Rostnikov looked but he was not really listening. He kept his hands folded in his lap and wondered why his leg was causing him so little trouble. He resisted the urge to reach into his pocket and read the note that Javier had slipped into it.

The twenty-story-high Soviet embassy in Havana stands behind a seven-foot-high iron fence. The embassy itself is a modern brick monolith surrounded by lower buildings and ample lush grounds. It culminates in a tower that looks like a squat letter *T.* At one corner to the right as one faces the embassy a faded red flag hangs waiting for the wind.

Next to the embassy is a Catholic church, its spire matching the height of the embassy tower in an uneasy contest for dominance of the street.

Major Sanchez, in full blue uniform complete with blue baseball hat, parked his white Lada on the nearly empty street in front of the embassy gate and looked out of the curbside window past Elena Timofeyeva.

"Impressive, eh?" he said in Russian. "Just a year ago it would have been impossible to park on this street. Cars, trucks, people in and out. Now, empty. Fidel has a house near here. It is said he can see the tower of the embassy from his bedroom window when he wakes up."

Sanchez's face was inches from Elena's. When Sanchez had picked her up that morning, they had breakfasted on toast, oranges, and bananas in the rooftop cafeteria reserved for guests of the hotel. Their conversation moved from Russian to Spanish and back to Russian again for no reason that Elena could perceive.

As they ate, Sanchez had asked Elena how she became a police officer. Elena told him about her aunt Anna, who had been a Moscow procurator, and about her father, who had been in military intelligence. Throughout the conversation, Elena had been acutely aware of the major's eyes scanning her, watching her, saying something without speaking.

Now, as she felt his breath on her cheek, she had no doubt about his eyes and his body language. Elena suspected that the major behaved in the same way toward all women. She had no illusions about her looks. Her face was oval, clear-skinned, and healthy-looking. Her hair was short, brown, and straight. Her body was not yet heavy, but it was certainly ample, and her condition, from a strenuous routine of running and exercise, was excellent.

Sanchez and Elena got out of the car and moved to the iron gate.

"Who knows how many millions it cost to build it?" Sanchez said, pressing a bell in the gate. "You have anything like it in Moscow?"

"Nothing this new," she said. "Many things this large."

The gate clicked open.

"You people are impressed by size," he said, holding the gate open so Elena could step inside. "Russians think the bigger something is—a statue or a building—the more it will impress.

149

They are right, but their mistake is in equating beauty with size alone."

Elena counted the twenty-eight serpentine marble steps as they moved upward toward the embassy entrance.

"And Cubans, what do they find impressive and beautiful?" she asked as they approached two massive wooden doors at the top of the steps. Each door was studded with vertical rows of wooden spheres.

"Intricacy, music that makes one weep, the remembered shape and touch of a woman's body, paintings that burst with color and life," he said, looking at her with a smile.

Elena had worn her suit—gray skirt and matching jacket—with an off-white blouse. The suit had belonged to her aunt, with whom she lived in Moscow. A neighbor had miraculously altered the suit to fit Elena, for Anna Timofeyeva was significantly larger than her niece.

The door opened and a tall, thin man with unkempt white hair stood before them. The man needed a shave and looked pained by the brightness of the morning sun. He wore a blue shirt only partially tucked into his matching blue trousers. He wore black socks and no shoes.

"*Qué hora es?*" he said in heavily accented Spanish.

"Seven-ten," Sanchez answered in Russian after checking his watch.

The white-haired man brushed his hair back with his long fingers and stepped back to allow them to enter.

"You are Major Sanchez?" the man asked in Russian. He closed the door behind them. "And you are Assistant Inspector Timofeyeva from Moscow?"

"Yes," Elena said.

Their voices echoed through the empty corridors and the three-story entryway as the man shook his head.

"*Prahsteetye,* forgive me," he said. "We used to have so many people answering phones and doors, making appointments."

He looked around the room in search of the departed and then turned to shake hands with both Elena and Sanchez.

"Gleb Tarasov, deputy attaché," he said. "One of the ghosts who still walks the corridors of what was once the heart of Soviet benevolence in the Americas. Sometimes I think we have been forgotten by Moscow. Sometimes that is fine with me. *Prahsteetye,* forgive me again, I'm rambling."

"No need to apologize," said Elena.

Tarasov nodded again, considered apologizing for his apologies, caught himself in time, and turned his back on his visitors to lead them down a darkened corridor. As he walked he tucked in his shirt.

"I must confess," Tarasov said as they passed empty desks and silent offices, "I had a bit to drink last night. Till a few hours ago. My wife is Cuban. She is partial to vodka. Second wife. First wife was partial to young men."

He put his hand to his mouth. After padding a little farther down the corridor he removed his hand and said, "Can't stop babbling. Can't stop begging your pardon. I'm afraid I will be a sad source of information for you. Here we are."

He stopped at an office door, pushed it open, and stepped inside. Sanchez and Elena followed.

Though the office was bathed in morning light through two large windows, Tarasov hit a light switch. Elena watched the deputy attaché move behind a steel desk on which a computer rested.

"Please, please," he said, "have a seat. I can find someone for coffee if you . . ."

"No, thank you," said Elena. "We won't take much of your time."

The two chairs in front of the desk were chrome with black leather seats and backs. Elena and Sanchez sat.

"I have not been to Moscow in five years," Tarasov said. He had seated himself behind the desk and was looking out the window in the general direction of Moscow. "It is hell here. I hear it is worse there."

"We have been through a great deal in a single year," said Elena. "And there is more we must endure."

"There is always more, young woman," Tarasov said, rubbing his gray-stubbled chin. "There is always more to endure, more to sacrifice. More . . . You came about an embassy employee, the one who was arrested."

"Igor Shemenkov," she said, taking her notebook from the bag she had placed on the floor.

"Igor Shemenkov," Tarasov repeated softly as he scratched the back of his right hand. "Losing his hair, shaped like an egg. Dresses badly, but at the moment who am I to talk?"

"Yes," said Elena. She looked at Sanchez, who seemed amused.

"Let's see," said Tarasov, rubbing his eyes. He blinked and reached over to turn on the computer. The machine emitted a tone, chugged softly, and let out a low *ping* to announce that it was ready.

Tarasov's long fingers began to dance over the keyboard as he looked at the screen in front of him. The computer clacked steadily and Tarasov was transformed—a borderline alcoholic with a hangover had become a wizard of the electronic landscape.

"Coming," he said, eyes still on the screen. "Ask questions if you have them."

"Whatever you have," said Elena. "Friends, relatives, activities."

Tarasov nodded. He reached over to hit a button on a white box without breaking his rhythm on the computer.

"Printing in the next office," he said. "It is a long document. Seventeen pages."

"Is that unusual?" asked Elena.

"No, many are much longer. Ask."

"Friends," said Sanchez.

"Acquaintances," answered Tarasov. "None in the embassy or in his apartment in the Sierra Maestra. He does not make friends easily."

"His job?"

"Documents processor. Coded dispatches from the embassy to Moscow and from Moscow to Cuba. Important, but routine. Takes no intellect."

Tarasov's fingers were no longer dancing. A single finger hit a button to scroll the open file before him.

"Work record is very good. No problems, at least not since he came to Cuba. No—"

"And before he came to Cuba?" Elena asked.

Tarasov looked up as if seeing Elena for the first time.

"Before," he said, and turned his eyes back to the computer screen. "Twice arrested for assault following fights in Odessa. Suspected of black market activities. But that is common. Considered to be loyal, without great intellectual resources, a natural gift with computers, drinks a bit much on occasion. So did his father. So did my father and so do I for that matter."

"What else?" asked Elena.

Tarasov looked at Sanchez and then back at Elena, who said, "Go on."

"Shemenkov has a wife and two children in Odessa. He also has an inclination toward Cuban prostitutes. He has been warned about this many times and has been treated on four occasions for sexually transmitted diseases. Because of this inclination, Igor Shemenkov has been considered a security risk."

Tarasov looked at Major Sanchez and so did Elena.

"He means," said Sanchez, "that your embassy believes that Cuban prostitutes have been used to get information from embassy employees and pass it on to security forces in the Cuban government."

"Believes?" asked Elena.

"Believes," said Sanchez. "But I would say there is far more reason to believe such a tale than there is to pray to the saints or expect the Communists to rise again and reunite the Soviet Union."

"Anything else?" asked Tarasov. "I have plenty of time."

"No," said Elena. She stood up. "Just a copy of the report."

"Other room," said Tarasov, standing up also.

After they had obtained the report from the printer and Tarasov had put on his shoes and accompanied them to the gate, Elena got back into the Lada with Sanchez.

"And now?" the major said.

"Back to the hotel. I'll read the report and take it to Inspector Rostnikov."

Sanchez did not start the car.

"A suggestion," he said with a small smile. "We go to your room and make love."

"No."

"I am an accomplished lover," he said. "And you are very inspiring."

"No," she said again. "You have a job to do, Major. It is not to make me uncomfortable and distract me from the investigation."

"How do you know?" he asked, putting his right hand on the back of her seat very close to her face.

"Know?"

"That my job isn't to make you uncomfortable and distract you from the investigation," he said.

"I do not know and I do not care," she said. "I wish to go to the hotel."

"*Servidor de usted,*" he said, moving his hand, sitting back, and starting the car. "But it is a waste of two perfectly healthy bodies."

Major Fernando Sanchez drove into the empty street.

TEN

Yevgeny Odom was certain that the next one would be the most satisfying yet for Kola. It would take place within the bowels of the earth, in the tunnels of life and dreams. It would take place in Yevgeny's world, the one place they would never imagine it could happen.

As he pulled into the Academicheskaya Station, he realized that after he had lured the victim into one of the storerooms or tunnel alcoves, he would have to move the body to someplace more public, someplace the police wouldn't connect with someone who knew the system well.

Although he was well aware that people would not notice a uniformed man who minded his business, he did not want to be seen simply wandering the outlying stations. Someone, perhaps even a Metro police officer, might remember his odd behavior after the body was found.

Inside of Yevgeny Odom the animal pulled and demanded release. Yevgeny resisted, but the effort was greater than had ever been required before. Kola had desires, appetites that Yevgeny did not understand, but he knew they were part of him. He knew that Kola had to be cared for.

Yevgeny Odom closed his eyes, took a deep breath to soothe the animal, and opened his eyes again as the train slowed and stopped at the Profsoyusnaya Station. On the almost empty platform stood a figure in black, a gaunt, pale figure with unblinking eyes. The figure turned his eyes to the arriving train and looked directly at Yevgeny Odom. In that moment as the train stopped and the doors opened, it seemed to Yevgeny Odom that the ghost on the platform looked into him, saw the snarling animal within him, and understood. The creature on the platform had such an animal within him too. It was like looking into a mirror and seeing one's own darkness.

Then the doors closed and the train pulled away slowly, smoothly building up speed. Yevgeny commanded his body and face to show nothing, his mind to feel nothing. Yet he had the feeling that someone else was looking at him.

Through the small window behind him, Yevgeny saw him, a jowly man in a cap. The man nodded dreamily as he looked across the rows of seats at Yevgeny Odom, who responded with a sincere grin.

The man in the cap did not grin back. He had been awakened from a dream of demons by the lurching of the train car leaving the station. He was going to Belyayevo, the end of the line, so he had no worries about falling asleep. But then his eyes had opened and he found himself looking at a devil dressed as a Metro trainman, a devil grinning at him ready to leap forward through the door and over the seats to rip out his eyes. The man sat upright, careful not to look at the devil again, and resolved not to fall back asleep. He adjusted his cap, checked his watch, and pulled a battered paperback novel from his pocket. He pretended to read for four stops and then, unable to help himself, he glanced up to find that the devil had turned his back.

Emil Karpo had spent the night riding the Metro, getting off at
outlying stations, determining which ones were least used late
at night. A Metro police officer, a woman named Katrina Vross,
had been assigned to show him the stations, point out the likely
areas of attack, tell him about security, the nature of crimes encountered, the recent history of bizarre underground behavior
and outbreaks of madness.

Karpo had listened to her without response for over an hour
and then indicated that he wished to proceed on his own. This
was fine with Katrina Vross, a weary, short, baggy-eyed chain-
smoker with the put-upon air of many Russian bureaucrats
whose attitude suggested that any question you might ask was
a major imposition on their time, a reflection of your own stupidity, and a confirmation that life was an endless series of de-
bilitating repetitions.

Karpo had considered bringing Sasha Tkach on his rounds
but there were many good reasons why this was a bad idea.
One reason was that Tkach's cold had gotten much worse and
he needed rest and a quick and at least partial recovery to put
Karpo's plan into action. Another reason was that Tkach should
not be seen with Karpo or any other members of the police. A
third reason was that Sasha Tkach had no faith in Emil Karpo's
plan.

"Your evidence is weak," Sasha had said as they drank tea at
the kiosk near the small park across from Petrovka.

The tea had been Karpo's idea and as soon as the morning
rain had stopped, they had walked across Petrovka Street between the cars and headed toward the kiosk.

"It is not a matter of evidence. I have a conviction now that
I understand something about 341's processes," Karpo had
answered.

After he had sneezed and wiped his nose, Sasha had said,

"Karpo, have you abandoned logic for mysticism? Even if you are right, even if he will strike next time or the time after that in the Metro, we can't possibly have any idea of when it will be."

Karpo looked down the street at the cars sloshing through the puddles of rainwater and shook his head.

"Intuition is a form of logical empathy, not mysticism," he said.

"Karl Marx?" Tkach guessed.

"Pavlov."

"And so"—Tkach sniffled with some disdain—"we are to haunt the tunnels and stations because you have a bond with 341. I would prefer some evidence. You are the one who always demands evidence."

Karpo did not answer. Sasha shook his head and blew his nose.

The rain began again. Not hard but dank, cold, and oppressive from the gray sky. They took refuge under a broad tree, Sasha clutching his tea in two hands and looking quite miserable.

"Alternatives, as you well know, are being pursued. Park patrols with plainclothes officers are doubled. Sites of previous attacks are being patrolled by cars on their rounds."

"And so," said Tkach with some sarcasm, "you do not fully trust your intuition."

"It would be a mistake to do so. Here."

He handed Sasha Tkach a small amber bottle. Sasha took it.

"Paulinin said that you should take one every three hours with food," said Karpo.

Tkach looked at the unmarked bottle.

"What is it? Where did he . . . ?"

"He got it from the pocket of a dead prostitute," explained Karpo. "He analyzed it and found that it was English, a new antibiotic. It should help you."

"Your concern for my health is touching," said Tkach, pock-
eting the pills.

"I need you healthy and quickly," answered Karpo. "The rain
is stopping. We must get back."

Sasha nodded and returned his plastic teacup to the kiosk
manager, a short, fat man with an enormous nose.

And so Emil Karpo, after meeting with the deputy director of
the Metro police and setting up a special-force low-profile pa-
trol plan, had wandered the trains and stations listening to the
subterranean rush of the cool air, watching faces, considering
contingencies, and taking notes when he was alone.

It was on the platform of the Profsoyusnaya Station that he
was observing an incoming train, scanning it to determine the
number of passengers at this hour, when he saw the uniformed
operator on the train.

The man wore a trainman's cap that cast a shadow over his
eyes, but Karpo knew the man was meeting his gaze. It was not
unusual for people to stare at the vampire image of Emil Karpo
if they felt it was safe to do so, as the girl Ginka in the owl
makeup had done this morning. Occasionally, a person, usually
a child, would look at him transfixed, wondering who this creature might be, their curiosity overcoming their fear.

But the man in the train, the man in the uniform, had looked
at Karpo as if he recognized him, as if he had a question to ask,
an important question. As the train had pulled away, his own
reflection in the window was superimposed over that of the
man within and Karpo had the fleeting impression that he was
looking into himself at something he preferred not to see. Then
the reflection, the man, and the train were gone.

Emil Karpo was not a man of great imagination. In fact,
though he could see the occasional value of imagination in the
methods of Porfiry Petrovich, his own strength had come
through determination and a dogged loyalty to the law.

But Rostnikov was in Cuba. Mathilde, who had both imagination and a sense of humor he did not understand, was in Odessa. Paulinin had no interest in the living, and Tkach was too emotional and unfocused.

Karpo, therefore, was forced to rely on his own rudimentary imagination and was not sure whether his attempts were helpful or an impediment.

He stood on the platform, late-night commuters, Gypsy beggars, and occasional tourists giving him a great deal of room, as he tried to imagine the act of murder itself, tried to imagine himself in the park three days ago standing over the kneeling, perhaps pleading victim, Iliana Ivanova. He focused on a brick in the wall across the tracks, but the image that came was of Sasha Tkach's daughter, Pulcharia.

Weeks ago, at a party for Tkach's thirtieth birthday at Rostnikov's apartment, Pulcharia Tkach had suddenly rushed across the room and leaped into Emil Karpo's arms. Without thinking he had scooped her up and the child had nestled her head against his shoulder. He had smelled her hair, seen her pink bow mouth and the thin blue veins of her closed eyelids. And something had happened, a deeply buried feeling had pulsed, a feeling of an almost forgotten childhood, of a child he had not seen or thought about for more than two decades.

Now he stood, alone, on the platform of a Metro station trying in vain to remember a quote that would sustain him. Communism had been his only god and foundation for most of his life. A return to the company of mankind was an alien concept that he was reluctant to embrace, though the altered world offered him little choice. He could not cling to a system that had failed, yet he was reluctant to betray it. So, in an era when it was no longer profitable to be a Communist, he retained his membership.

He had seen the old Czarists and White Russians in the park, heard them talk furtively and futilely of the return of the Father. He had been moved by his conversation with an old nun before she was murdered, but the fire of religion did not burn hot enough within him to replace the solid, now toppled, figure of Lenin. One could not believe simply because one sought meaning in chaos.

Emotion was not a familiar companion. He had felt it more and more in the last year as the Union tottered and collapsed, and he was wary of these feelings. They seemed to accomplish so little and to promise only the anguish he witnessed in the faces of others. He had worked honestly and hard, had devoted himself to a lifetime of duty, party, and the law. The warmth of Mathilde and the trusting leap of Pulcharia gave him not hope but fear. Emil Karpo did not know what he would be if he ever set free the animal he had kept caged within him for more than thirty years.

Out of the dark tunnel another train approached. Emil Karpo had lost track of time. The air on the track and in the station was alive. He checked his watch. Four minutes. He had been told that it was four minutes between trains at this hour but he had to be sure, had to see it, hear it, confirm it, and record it in his notebook. Four minutes. That was the approximate time 341 would have in which to kill if he chose the platform of a Metro station.

When the train pulled in, Emil Karpo got on. He found a seat in front, looked through the window at the hole of darkness before him, and waited to plunge into it.

Then a quote did come to him, not from Lenin or Marx, but from Mao:

"Taught by mistakes and setbacks, we have become wiser and handle our affairs better. It is hard for any political party or person to avoid mistakes, but we should make as few as possible. Once a mistake is made, we should correct it, and the more quickly and thoroughly the better."

ELEVEN

Sasha Tkach had a cold. There was no denying it, no avoiding it, and no hiding it from Maya, who, Sasha was sure, was growing weary of his recurring bouts with viruses. He stood in the small cubbyhole that was the toilet and shower room of the apartment and looked at his face in the mirror. His nose was slightly red. His eyes looked moist. He wasn't sure if he wanted to cough. He was certain, however, that he had a cold.

The prospect for the rest of the evening and the next morning was bleak. Neither Maya, his mother, nor the baby had any symptoms, but Pulcharia had a slight fever. He was the carrier. And that meant that certain things were inevitable. First, he had passed his cold on to his daughter, and the two of them would pass it on to the rest of the family if they had not already done so. Second, he would have to accept and swallow at least two of the vile little balls of Chinese medicine that his mother kept in a jar in her drawer.

He would have liked a shower but the water was, as always, tepid. Since there was no heat in the apartment and the weather was cold, he was afraid of risking a chill in spite of his mother's repeated assurances that one did not make a cold worse by being cold. On the contrary, keeping cold kept one's temperature down.

Yes, no doubt. Sasha now had the first sign of chills. He checked his shaved face, looked at his reasonably clean teeth, put on his robe, brushed his unruly hair back, and stepped out to face Maya, who was waiting her turn for the washroom.

"*Yah plokhah syeebyah choostvooyoo.* I'm not feeling well," he announced.

In the next room, the only other room in the apartment, he could hear his mother urging Pulcharia to eat something.

Maya, who was sitting on the edge of the bed in her purple Chinese robe, stood and moved toward him.

"You are warm," she said, touching his face.

"Because I am ill," he said. "I just—"

"*Yah nye galohdnah.* I'm not hungry," came Pulcharia's small voice from the next room.

"Shh," Maya said, touching her husband's lips with her finger and then speaking softly. "I am not going to make you take care of the baby. I'm not going to ask you to make love. I am not going to give you a reason to fight with me because you don't feel well."

He had to admit that he had armed himself with anger, but that didn't stop him from saying, "I'm not looking for a fight. Why would I look for a fight? I'm just . . ."

Maya's soft round face moved to his and kissed him softly.

"Thank you," he said. "But now you are certain to catch my cold."

"It was inevitable," she said.

Maya leaned against him.

"Why are you in such a good mood?" he asked.

"I don't know," she answered. "I have as many reasons to be as discontent as you and as many reasons to be in a good mood.

We have too little money and no privacy and no likelihood that it will change. But we have the children, a place to live, and each other."

"I must work tonight," he said. "And maybe for many nights."

Maya stepped back and looked at him, her cool palms against his cheeks.

"I doubt if you will be much use to anyone as you are."

"And . . . ?"

"And nothing." She moved past him to turn on the shower. "I have learned not to argue with you about such things. You will do them anyway."

"The water is cold," Sasha said.

"Invigorating," she said.

Sasha smiled.

"It's just potato soup," Lydia's voice crackled from the other room over the beat of the shower water. "It will make you well."

Maya took off her robe, moved behind her husband, and put her arms around his waist.

"I just told you, I'm sick," Sasha said, sniffling.

"Then there is no way to avoid it. It is better to get it quickly and get it over than try to hide from the inevitable."

"Now you are a philosopher," he said, putting his warm cheek against her cool one as she moved in front of him.

"I've always been a philosopher," she said. "What I lack is recognition."

"Perhaps I should pay closer attention."

"There is no 'perhaps' about it."

"A little. I eat a little," said Pulcharia from the next room.

Maya smiled, her face inches from Sasha's nose.

"You know you are depriving me of my righteous self-pity and anger," he said.

She nodded.

"I could sulk and be angry about that."

"Not once you have recognized it," she said.

"Philosophy and psychology," he said with a sigh. Then he stepped back from her. "I think I am going to sneeze."

And, indeed, he did sneeze, a serious, moist, loud sneeze that brought his mother running into the room, Ilya in her arms clinging to her neck.

"Sasha, you are ill," she announced in the loud monotone that confirmed her growing deafness.

"I sneezed one time," he said, holding up a finger for her to see. "One time. One sneeze. One—"

And he sneezed again.

Triumph and disapproval clouded Lydia Tkach's face as she looked at her naked daughter-in-law.

"Here, take," Lydia said, handing the baby to Maya.

Pulcharia came padding barefoot into the bedroom. She wore a small T-shirt that advertised a French movie called *La Triste*.

Lydia was scurrying toward the dresser in the corner.

"*Shto,* what?" asked Pulcharia.

"Your father is sick," bellowed Lydia. "Sick like you. Probably gave it to you."

Sasha looked at Maya, who stroked the confused baby and shrugged helplessly at her husband. Pulcharia began to cry.

"Found it, here," said Lydia, stepping back from the open drawer and holding up the milky bottle. For all Sasha knew, the marble-sized gray-white pellets that rattled around in it contained powdered excrement of eel.

"I am not ill," Sasha insisted as his mother advanced on him, opening the bottle and paying no attention to his protest.

Considering the fact that he would spend all of the next day and who knew how many days beyond wandering through crowded, drafty Metro stations in the hope of attracting a serial murderer, Sasha looked at his wife and baby and then at the face of his red-nosed daughter and had the sudden urge to laugh. It made no sense. Only moments before he had been filled with anger and self-pity, but now it all seemed so absurd.

"Here," Lydia said. In her outstretched palm rested two round pellets.

Sasha took them and winked at Pulcharia. The little girl appeared amazed at the size of the objects in her father's hand and at the fact that he was putting them in his mouth.

"Water," Lydia said. "Wait."

She ran toward the outer room as Pulcharia ran after her.

"Why am I going to laugh?" he asked Maya.

"Because you are a Russian," she said.

"And why am I taking these things?" he said.

"Because you love your mother, who drives you mad," she said, rocking the baby on her shoulder.

Lydia returned holding up the half-full glass of water. He put the pills in his mouth, washed them down without gagging, grimaced at the strange bitter aftertaste, and handed his mother the empty glass. Maya laughed and Lydia looked at her.

"What is she laughing about?" asked Lydia. "And why doesn't she have any clothes on?"

"She's a Ukrainian," said Sasha. "They laugh about things that are the pain of others and they have strange and ancient urges to run naked in the woods."

"I hope my grandchildren do not inherit this," Lydia said, turning her back and walking toward the door.

Sasha shook his head and looked at Maya.

"I hope they do," he said quietly.

Then he sneezed again.

The woman on the low stage was very fat and very black. She wore a dress the color of *pyehrseekee,* peaches, a fruit of which Porfiry Petrovich was particularly fond.

The woman threw her head back and sang in this huge room filled with the smoke of cigars and the sweat of many bodies pressed around too few tables. She sang loud and deep with a trill in her voice of *"Mariquita Linda, La Paloma."* She sang *"Yo Te Quiero Mucho,"* and though he could understand almost none of the words, Rostnikov was sure the songs were sad and plaintive; they could be nothing else.

There were several hundred people in the room, most of them Cubans who joined the wailing black woman in choruses and sometimes for an entire song. The men smoked, looked sad, smiled knowingly, and sang with emotion, their arms thrown around each other as they grew more drunk from the bottles of rum, wine, and vodka that were brought to the tables by sweating, mirthless waiters with rolled-up sleeves.

"What do you think, Porfiry Petrovich?" asked Major Fernando Sanchez, who was dressed for the evening in a pale green button-down shirt with an open collar. Since Rostnikov was seated across from Sanchez, the major had to raise his voice.

"She sounds Russian," said Rostnikov.

Sanchez grinned, puffed on his cigar, and looked at Elena Timofeyeva, who sat to his right. She had attempted to sit next to Rostnikov but Sanchez had insisted that she would have a far better view of the singer from his side of the table. With a nod to the dour blond man at the door Sanchez had managed to get a table very close to the low stage.

Elena wore her flower-print dress, a green background with small red-and-orange multipetaled flowers. She also wore the imitation pearls she had tucked into the bottom of her travel case. The decision to put them on had taken her five trips to the mirror and moments of near agony. When it had been time to join Rostnikov in the lobby, she walked to the door of her room, hesitated, removed the pearls, placed them on a chair, and left the room. When she got to the elevator, she changed her mind again and went back for the pearls. A young couple, probably Canadians, had held the elevator for her.

Now she sat next to Sanchez, who looked at her approvingly, evidently pleased that they were color-coordinated. On Sanchez's left was Antonio Rodriguez, the little journalist with the thick glasses. Rodriguez seemed to be deeply moved by the music and, from time to time, he redirected Rostnikov's attention from the stage to a new singer or group of singers waiting to come on.

It was awkward for Rostnikov to face the performers since his back was to the stage. The chairs and tables were packed so tightly together that he could turn his chair only about one quarter of the way to glimpse the stage over his shoulder.

Povlevich, the thin KGB man with spaniel eyes, sat between Rodriguez and Rostnikov. Povlevich's eyes seldom left the black singer as he drank steadily and deeply. Though he was attentive, his face betrayed no emotion.

A tap of wood against metal and the pointing of Rodriguez turned Rostnikov awkwardly once again to the stage, where a drummer, a guitar player, and the fat black woman prepared to sing again. The drummer and guitar player were dressed in identical white shirts and pants stained with perspiration even before they began. Both men, who looked like brothers, were dark and narrow of face and body.

The low level of chatter in the room stopped almost completely and the drum began a slow beat picked up by a languid tune on the guitar. Most of the patrons already knew the song and sighed in anticipation. Then the woman began to sing "Bésame Mucho."

"That's American," Povlevich said softly under the music. "I heard the Beatles sing it."

"The Beatles aren't American," said Rodriguez. "And what does it matter? American, Brazilian, Chinese."

Povlevich shook his head and drank. Though he was turned

partly toward the stage, Rostnikov was aware of Major Sanchez's arm as it moved to the back of Elena Timofeyeva's chair. She shifted uncomfortably as the audience joined in the chorus of the song and brought it through to an emotional conclusion.

The applause was wild, sincere. The trio onstage bowed and wiped their brows. Rostnikov turned, caught Elena's eye, and then began to get up.

"What?" asked Major Sanchez, his arm coming down from Elena Timofeyeva's chair.

"The rest room," said Rostnikov.

"You just went to the rest room," said Rodriguez.

"Perhaps an hour ago," said Rostnikov, plotting a path through the chairs and tables. "I can only apologize for my inherited insufficiently small bladder."

Rodriguez's thick lenses turned toward Sanchez. The major looked at the little man with no movement of his head and no change of expression.

"I think I go with you," said Rodriguez. "My bladder is also a small one."

Povlevich hardly looked up as the two men made their way through the maze of people and furniture. The trio on the platform launched into *"Todos Vuelven."*

The rest rooms were near the front of the club in an alcove of three doors, one marked with a dark cutout of a man, one with the cutout of a woman, and the third unmarked. A bored-looking man with broad shoulders and dark hair combed straight back leaned against the wall watching people enter and leave. He wore a black long-sleeved shirt with a turtleneck and black pants and shoes.

Rostnikov pushed ahead of the little journalist and went into the one-seat toilet. He put the flimsy hook into the eye screwed into the molding and moved to the commode.

Earlier he had examined the rest room and for the instant that he had been alone in the alcove, he had opened the door that was not marked. It had been dark, and he saw only that it led to a room beyond, in which he could see a faint light.

Rostnikov used the toilet, rinsed his hands in water at the small sink, and then shook them rapidly to partly dry them. There was neither soap nor towel in the rest room and the toilet paper was narrow strips of old newspaper.

He opened the door and let Rodriguez, who would have to at least make a pretense of using the toilet, enter.

"I will be just a moment," said the little man over the wail of the black woman and a loud riff on the drum.

Rostnikov nodded.

The instant the washroom door was closed, Rostnikov went through the unmarked door, closed it, and groped into the dark for a lock or latch. There was none. His hand found a low table or cabinet. He pulled at it and full bottles rattled inside it. He got a grip with both hands and pulled hard. The cabinet reluctantly moved across the floor and Rostnikov dragged it in front of the door through which he had come.

The music beyond the door stopped. Applause. Then the flushing of a toilet.

Rostnikov looked around in search of the distant light he had seen earlier. For an instant he did not see it and then something moved and the light was there.

"This way," a voice said in English.

Rostnikov took a step forward. His knee hit something solid.

"Wait," came the voice, and Rostnikov could hear chain rattling against glass before the light came on, a single dangling bulb under which stood a lean, erect, young black man in jeans and a red T-shirt. The young man was eating a sandwich and seemed to be in no hurry.

"Take a bottle," the young man said, nodding to his right.

Rostnikov looked at the boxes full of bottles that lined the room and moved to one of the boxes.

"Next one," said the young man. "Better rum."

Rostnikov obeyed. Out of the next box he pulled a dark brown bottle.

Someone tried the handle of the door through which Rostnikov had come. The door did not move.

"Strong," said the young man softly, looking at the cabinet Rostnikov had moved. "Come."

The man finished his sandwich, reached up, and turned off the light.

Colonel Snitkonoy slept in pajamas. He owned five pairs, all two-piece cotton with drawstring pants, all in muted solid colors, all made in Nigeria. The Wolfhound shaved each night before going to bed and again in the morning when he awakened. He brushed his teeth both morning and night.

He would have preferred to shave in the morning and sleep in the nude. He would have preferred to have a woman in the bed next to him. But the Wolfhound had decided long ago that he would share his life with no one lest he be vulnerable. He had also decided that he would go to bed each night fully prepared to be awakened in the core of darkness by a group of men in uniform accusing him of treachery.

Colonel Snitkonoy was a man who went through life immaculately prepared for disaster and reasonably confident that he was skillful enough to keep that disaster from taking place.

Today had been a supreme test of his skill.

As he sat in the chair of his small bedroom drinking the nightly cup of herbal tea his aide had prepared for him, the colonel went over the fifteen minutes he had spent in the Kremlin boardroom that had once been Stalin's private sitting room.

He had entered, folder in hand, to face a dark wooden table at which sat ten weary-looking people, three of whom were women. Though the Wolfhound knew that four of the men were in the military, no one wore a uniform.

In front of each of the ten was a pile of papers, an ashtray, a coffee cup, a glass, and a carafe of water. The papers were disheveled, the ashtrays full, the coffee cups empty, and the water that remained in the carafes dusty.

There was an empty chair at the end of the table. General Karsnikov, once a bureau head in the KGB and now a military adviser, nodded to the empty seat. Colonel Snitkonoy took the chair, placed his files before him, and met the eyes of each of the ten with a sad, very small smile that he had practiced before his mirror. The smile was meant to convey the sense that he had bad news that it pained him greatly to present to these already sorely tried patriots, but that he felt was his duty to pass on for them to deal with in their greater knowledge and wisdom. Further, he wanted the smile to say that he was but their servant in this difficult situation. It was a lot to ask of a smile, but the Wolfhound was confident that he had succeeded.

General Karsnikov, a white-haired bull of a man with a too-tight collar and small round glasses, cleared his throat and looked at the colonel.

"We have read your report, Colonel Snitkonoy," he said. "You and the Special Investigation Office are commended for your zealous efforts."

This, the Wolfhound knew, was a bad start. Praise, especially from the man whom the Wolfhound knew would dearly love to take over the Special Investigations operation with one of his own people, meant only that condemnation was coming. It would have been better had they come at him with questions.

"I will convey the commendation of the committee to my staff," he said.

There was a pause during which those around the table looked at the colonel, searched for something in the stacks before them, made notes, or did something of no consequence to keep from having to look at each other. These were people, as Colonel Snitkonoy well knew, with power but no consensus.

The new Russia had not yet been defined. Those who ran it came mainly from the ranks of those who had run the Soviet Union before. There was little choice. To avoid complete chaos, Yeltsin had been forced to accept the hasty democratic conversion of thousands of former Party members. Among them, even in this room, were a smattering of true believers in the hope of a new Russia, believers without experience who had never participated in the apparatus. Though they were learning, the wisest of them were insecure. There were also those around the table whose uniforms and Party memberships lay neatly folded and ready in closets.

"The report presents several problems," came a woman's voice from the far end of the table. It was Olga Dimitkova, the youngest person in the room, an economist who along with her husband, a journalist, had stood with Yeltsin during the siege of the White House, the Parliament Building. She was thin, had short hair, and was rather pretty.

The Wolfhound dutifully opened his copy of the report.

"If what the report implies is true," she said carefully, "it could have very severe consequences for Russia at a time when we are dependent on a sincere though fragile alliance of neighbors."

She had prepared well and, the colonel was certain, had memorized what she was now saying. It would not be a good idea to interrupt or even imply by a nod that he had something to say. Snitkonoy folded his hands on the table and gave Olga Dimitkova his full attention.

"Our interests generally coincide with those who surround us," she went on. "But there are tensions. There are also many Russians residing within the borders of sister states. One of those harboring a significant number of Russians is Kazakhstan. As you know, there have been ethnic conflicts throughout the former republics. Many thousands have been killed. This is perhaps inevitable as ethnic identities resurface. Were it to be thought that the foreign minister of Kazakhstan had been murdered while on a mission to Moscow the safety of several million Russians within Kazakhstan would be uncertain."

"And," came the voice of a tall, erect man in his late sixties, "if a minister from one of the former republics had been murdered while under our protection and it became known that we had not immediately disclosed the fact, other republics would view us with suspicion. The entire fragile network of the continuing alliance would be in jeopardy."

The speaker, Maxim Popolov, had been carefully chosen to speak at this point. Popolov was the closest thing to an old friend the Wolfhound had around the table. Popolov had at one time been information director in the Ministry of the Interior. He and Colonel Snitkonoy had eaten together, exchanged information, and even, on occasions when it was mutually beneficial, supported each other's careers. Now, Maxim Popolov's eyes met those of the colonel and urged him to make no mistake.

"We are inextricably tied together in the collective minds of the Western nations," Popolov went on, "and we are desperately in need of the financial support and goodwill of these nations if the new Russia is to survive."

Popolov paused and reached for his cigarettes. Someone coughed.

"Therefore," Popolov went on, "if a force within Russia, perhaps even within a government in transition, wished to cause upheaval by murdering the Kazakhstan foreign minister, it would not be in the best interest of the State to play into the hands of such a force by announcing to the world that the murder had taken place."

Now General Karsnikov spoke. "The original report on the death of Kumad Kustan states that he died of a heart attack," said the general. "The contradicting report comes from a single laboratory technician whose results in the past have ranged

from the extraordinary to the eccentric. A panel of distin-
guished physicians has reaffirmed that the original finding of
death by heart failure is accurate. The body of the deceased and
all of its organs, with the agreement of the Kazakhstani parliament, have been cremated according to the wishes of the foreign minister's family. You may now make your presentation
of evidence and speculation to this panel for review and
disposition."

The Wolfhound looked around the room at each of the
ten who had put him in this awkward position. No, that was
not fair. He had put himself in this position, but he had
had no choice. If someone had found that Karpo had presented him with a report concerning the possible murder of a
foreign minister and he had chosen to suppress the report, it
would surely have been held against him in the future. In years
past it could have led to his imprisonment or execution. Now,
who knew?

Some around the table looked at him with a challenge, almost willing him to put his neck in the noose. A few, including
Popolov and Dimitkova, urged him with their looks to retreat
with dignity. Others did not meet his eyes at all.

"I am here," said the Wolfhound, in the deep, confident baritone he had perfected, "solely to inform this committee that
such speculation exists and should be taken into account, dealt
with as you see fit. I will support and execute any decisions you
make."

There was a rustling of papers and a sense of relief around
the table before Popolov spoke again.

"We would like all copies of your report, all computer disks,
and all information relating to it."

"My assistant will have it in your hands by four o'clock," said
the Wolfhound.

"If you do not mind," said General Karsnikov, "a member of
my staff and an associate of member Olga Dimitkova will ac-

company you to your office immediately following this meeting to expedite this relay of information."

The Wolfhound knew this meant that those around the table distrusted not only him but each other. He said, "I welcome and appreciate the committee's willingness to act so quickly in resolving this issue so that I can get back to the mission of my office."

"Your vigilance is appreciated," said the general. "Please continue to bring to our attention any problem that might have serious consequences inside or outside our borders."

In his mind, the Wolfhound translated this as, "If you put us in an awkward position like this again, you shall suffer for it."

"Unless there is additional business," said the general, turning to those at the table, "we shall now adjourn."

"One question," said Popolov, examining the burning end of his cigarette. "Colonel Snitkonoy, what progress has there been in identifying and apprehending the multiple murderer or murderers known as *Tahpor*?"

"Our office, in coordination with all other security services, is working to bring Case 341 successfully to a close," said the Wolfhound. "We have a new initiative which we have reason to believe will soon lead us to the murderer."

"Our security apparatus has suffered in prestige," said Popolov, glancing at General Karsnikov and then back to Colonel Snitkonoy. "Failure to resolve such a loathsome string of killings could also have political and international consequences."

"I understand," said the Wolfhound. "And with that foremost in mind I request additional manpower from the MVD and other services for a one-week surveillance."

"How many people will you need?" asked the general.

"At least one hundred armed officers."

"And this is your idea, Colonel?" It was a new voice, the voice of General Lugharev of Military Investigation.

"No," said the Wolfhound, "it is the idea of one of my men who has been on the case for several months."

"Karpo," said General Lugharev.

"Yes."

"The same one who prepared the report on the alleged murder of Minister Kumad Kustan?"

"That is correct," said the colonel.

"And you agree with his suggestion?"

"I believe it has merit," said the colonel, "and that is why I presented it to you."

"Given the current crisis in Moscow," said Lugharev, "the gangs, the possibility of riots, I do not see how we can commit a small army of men and women without a stronger case for taking them from present important tasks."

"I am afraid," said General Karsnikov, "that you will have to tell your staff to engage in this speculative venture with whatever help the Metro division can give."

"We will make do," said Colonel Snitkonoy. It was what he had expected, no more, no less.

"We are adjourned," General Karsnikov said abruptly.

Colonel Snitkonoy had waited for the members to begin rising before he got up, gathered his files, and allowed himself a moment of relief for having escaped with only a rap on the knuckles.

Following the meeting, Olga Dimitkova and a nonuniformed captain from General Karsnikov's staff accompanied Colonel Snitkonoy back to Petrovka. They refused his offer of tea and waited in his office for Pankov to gather the records and both the original disk of Karpo's report and his own backup, plus original and file copies of the autopsy report on the foreign minister and the conflicting report on vital organs.

Conversation had been brief and Pankov had scrambled as quickly as he could to furnish the information.

Now, in the familiarity of his bedroom five hours later, Colonel Snitkonoy assessed the events of the day and concluded that he had done well. Everyone on the committee would assume that he had another copy of the evidence. But he had gone on record as having turned everything over to the committee. He had assured the committee that he understood the stakes and was prepared to cooperate.

The Wolfhound was confident that General Karsnikov had been a party to the death of the Kazakhstani minister, and he knew the general would appreciate his not forcing an issue that, at best, would lead to the general's embarrassment.

The colonel finished his tea and looked at his lamp, an ancient stained-glass and lead monstrosity that had belonged to a member of the Czar's private guard before the revolution. The problem was no longer the committee. The problem was Emil Karpo. The Wolfhound did not relish the prospect of conveying the committee's decision to Karpo.

As the colonel turned off the light and climbed into bed, he considered the ways in which he might turn the events of the day into the promotion that would mark the successful culmination of a lifetime of service, success, and, above all, survival.

He was not quite asleep when he heard the rap on his door. The rap was followed by a louder rap, and Colonel Snitkonoy sat up and turned on the light. He automatically smoothed his hair back with his hands and straightened his pajamas.

"Come in," he called out.

"Telephone," came the voice of the colonel's man. "General Lugharev. He says it is urgent."

The Wolfhound got out of bed and picked up the phone from the bedside table. Outside the door he heard his aide padding away.

"Colonel Snitkonoy," he said.

"Lugharev," came the general's tired voice. "I have good news. My men have found the killer of the Kazakhstani foreign minister. A Moslem separatist, from Kazakhstan, who was working as a waiter at the Hotel Russia the night of the reception. We have a full confession. He was given the drugs and the syringe by a radical group. We have the name of the Moslem doctor who prepared the injection and instructed the waiter."

"I am pleased to hear it," said the Wolfhound.

"Your information was invaluable," said Lugharev with perhaps a hint of sarcasm. "The confession and the name of the Moslem doctor have been turned over to the Kazakhstani government with our assurances of cooperation should the man still be in Russia."

"The waiter," said the Wolfhound.

"Unfortunately," said General Lugharev with a sigh, "he is dead. Threw himself through a window after he signed the confession. But do not worry. We have four witnesses to the confession."

"I had no fear, General. I am certain that you and your staff know what you are doing."

"Your office will receive an official commendation from the committee," said Lugharev. "Possibly another medal if we can ever agree about what our medals will look like from now on."

"My staff and I need no medals," said Colonel Snitkonoy. "It is sufficient that we have contributed to the apprehension of a criminal whose crime could have embarrassed many people."

"You have always been adept at understanding political reality, Colonel," said the general.

"Thank you, General. About those additional men . . ."

"I'm sorry," said the general. "As much as I would like to contribute to your office having two major successes in a short period, I cannot release any officers. There are needs . . . I hope you understand."

"Completely," said the Wolfhound.

"Sleep well, Colonel."

"And you too, General."

When he hung up the phone, Colonel Snitkonoy got back

into bed, allowed himself a small smile in the dark, and went instantly to sleep.

Yevgeny Odom stood at the window of his apartment looking at the apartment building across the way. He held a pair of binoculars in his right hand as he scanned the windows, secure in the knowledge that with his lights out he would not be seen.

Since he had arrived at the perfectly logical decision to make his next attack in a Metro station, he had been uneasy. He knew he should wait at least a week, but Kola pounded in the cage of Yevgeny's chest, urging him to go out now, find a victim, and let the beast free to attack, to feed, to gorge on a young body.

Planning was essential. The charts were essential. But it was impossible to keep track of his records with Kola in a near-constant frenzy now. Yevgeny even had difficulty remembering whether the last one had been the young man with the backpack behind the opera or the blond girl in the park.

In the past, Kola had been content between killings to be thrown chunks of imagined horror. Eva at the clinic had once asked Yevgeny what he was smiling about after he had drawn blood from a pretty young woman. He had been smiling because he had imagined plunging the needle deeply into the woman's arm and breaking it off for Kola, letting him watch her face as the horror came to her. He would never have actually done such a thing to someone at the clinic. He would always be gentle and give the least possible pain, so that returnees would ask for the nice man who didn't hurt them and always had something cheerful to say.

But that impulse throbbed in him so powerfully now that Yevgeny Odom considered selecting one of the people he could now see across the street. He would charm his way in, let Kola kill them, and leave a note or a clue. It would put the beast to sleep for a while and give Yevgeny at least a night of rest. In the next apartment building, a woman and baby were alone because her husband worked nights. There was the young man who came home early from work before his sister, mother, and father. There were so many. . . .

After Kola had killed one of them he would come back here and watch from the darkness as they discovered the body. There would be no danger in an attack so near his home. After the first four or five attacks he was sure the police had wasted no more effort on the assumption that the killer might be someone who lived or worked nearby. They simply didn't have the resources. It would have been a waste.

Yevgeny tried to focus on the chart on the wall, but it was no use. Before he could change his mind, he went to the door of his apartment, stepped out, locked the door, and hurried down the stairs whistling something from Prokofiev to drown out the cries of Kola throbbing through him.

The rain had stopped and the sky was clear, but it was growing cold and the streets were slick and icy.

Near the Metro station he found an outdoor phone that worked. They might try to trace the call, and Yevgeny knew enough from technical journals to be sure that they could do it in seconds with the proper equipment. He would make no mistake.

He put in his kopecks, dialed 02, and waited for the three rings and the voice of a woman who said, "Police."

"I wish to speak to someone in charge of the *Tahpor* investigation," he said, raising his voice to near falsetto.

"One moment," the woman answered.

Yevgeny had decided that he would wait no more than ten seconds for someone to answer. Then he would hang up. Perhaps Kola would be quiet and let Yevgeny rest. The urge would leave him by morning, and he would not feel the need to call, but . . .

"Special Security," came a hollow voice.

"You are in charge of the *Tahpor* murders?" Yevgeny asked.

"I am an investigator," the man said slowly, much too slowly for Yevgeny.

"My name is Igor Polynetsin," said Yevgeny. "And you are . . . ?"

"Deputy Inspector Karpo."

Yevgeny hung up. It was enough. He had the name of an investigator. There could not be many Karpos in Moscow. It might take an hour or two to locate the right one, but when he did, he could call him at home in the middle of the night.

He stood shivering in the night wind, feeling the return of some control. The sense of exhilaration continued as he bounded away from the telephone, nodded to passersby in an un-Russian show of street goodwill, and considered what he might now eat since he was suddenly very hungry.

He also considered, and not for the very first time, that he might be mad.

TWELVE

There were two men in the front seat of the 1957 Chevrolet in which Porfiry Petrovich Rostnikov rode. One was the man who had been waiting for him in the storeroom of the bar. The other man was Javier the waiter, the son of Manuel the bass player at La Floridita.

Javier looked over his shoulder at Rostnikov as they bounced over pits in the dark street and around mounds where once someone had considered repairs. Javier wore faded pants and a yellowish-white buttoned shirt with an oversize collar.

"I did not do it," said Javier in English.

Rostnikov said nothing.

"Maria Fernandez," Javier went on. "I did not kill her."

Rostnikov said nothing.

"I don't kill women because they reject me. There are many women who do not reject me, many who do not put needles in their arms and sleep with foreigners."

Rostnikov grunted and said, "Do you kill women for other reasons?"

"I kill no one, not women, not men, no one," said Javier over his shoulder.

"Would you not say the same even if you were the killer of Maria Fernandez?" asked Rostnikov.

"If I were the killer of Maria Fernandez, you would not be in this car. I would not be stupid enough to talk to you."

"You might be smart enough to talk to me because I could not imagine the killer doing so," said Rostnikov.

"You think like a Russian," Javier said in exasperation, and then said something in Spanish to the driver, who answered, *"Sí."*

"May I ask you a question?"

"Yes."

"How old are the houses on this street?"

"The houses on . . . I don't know. Maybe two hundred years. What has that to do with the murder of Maria Fernandez?"

"Nothing," said Rostnikov. "I was curious. Your city has a sad decay. Noble houses that look as if they have been crying for a hundred years. The houses of my city are heavy shoulders against the wind, most of them without distinction or nobility. What the Nazis did not destroy of the past we tore down, with notable exceptions, and built concrete tombs. I like your city. It eases the pain in my leg."

Javier looked at the Russian silently for a few moments and then said, "Are you making a joke?"

"No," answered Rostnikov. "Another question?"

Javier nodded.

"Are you married? Do you have children?"

"No, but I will be married in a month if the police don't put me in jail for killing Maria Fernandez."

"Last question," said Rostnikov as they hit a particularly solid bump in the street. "What is the uniform of our driver?"

"He is a Communist Youth leader," said Javier.

"And he is a *Santería?*"

"Yes," said Javier. "We are everywhere. The Catholics are everywhere, but there are far more of us. Same like in Europe, your country. No religion for thirty, fifty, seventy years and suddenly it comes back. We come back. We hide our gods behind Catholic gods and when the Catholic gods are no longer tolerated we hide our gods in flowerpots. Our religion goes back long in Africa before the thought of Christ. When Castro goes, we will be here. Those who denounce us now will embrace us, African and European alike."

"I have a son about your age," said Rostnikov.

"I think we should be talking about the dead rather than the living," replied Javier.

The car stopped.

"This is the house where Hector Consequo lives," said Javier. "Hector is the handyman in the apartment where Maria Fernandez died."

Rostnikov looked out on a dark, narrow street with five- or six-story buildings on either side. The buildings looked neither new nor ancient.

"We are in the Central City," said Javier, "the part of the city that tourists are driven around. Here there is hell. Come."

Rostnikov got out of the car and stood in the street. Theirs was the only car in sight.

"George will stay with the car," said Javier. "If he did not, it would be picked clean the minute we were out of sight."

As it would be in Moscow, thought Rostnikov.

"Come," said Javier, moving slowly toward a faded yellow wooden door on the far side of the narrow street.

He pushed the door open and stepped through with Rostnikov behind him. A yellow glow provided the hint of light. The smell of something heavy and sweet was in the air.

In a narrow passageway they stepped over empty jars and bottles. On both sides in little alcoves people sat huddled under light bulbs or behind burlap sheets. A hand reached out, touched Rostnikov's arm. A man, or what was once a man and was now a wasted cord of bone, said something in Spanish.

"Drugs," said Javier, removing the man's hand from Rostnikov's arm. "He wants money or drugs. They all do. Let's go.

"There are hundreds of passages like this, thousands," said Javier. "The government says they do not exist, that there are no drugs. Do you do the same in Russia?"

"Yes," said Rostnikov. "I must ask you to move more slowly."

"I'm sorry," said Javier, "but it is not good to remain here too long. Word is already out that we are here. They probably think we are the police."

At the end of the passageway, Javier pushed open a door that led to total darkness.

"We must go up," he said. "The stairs are in need of repair and there is no light, but there is a railing. We go up three flights. At the top will be light."

Rostnikov groped for the railing, found it, and began to pull himself up. The sick sweet smell was still there, but more and more faint as they rose.

The stairs creaked as Porfiry Petrovich's foot touched a broken step and felt around it. The sound of Javier's footsteps came from ahead of him and the pain of climbing was much to bear. After a floor, Rostnikov relied only minimally on his screaming leg. He would have hopped up had the railing he clung to given him a sense that it would support him.

His eyes did not adjust to the stairwell for there was no hint of light, at least not until he neared what must have been the third flight. He found himself on a narrow walkway with windows along one side and a rotting wooden railing on the other facing into the open night.

Javier stood waiting. Another man, a short man with a very black face and hair cropped short, stood at his side.

Rostnikov gritted his teeth from the pain of the climb and steadied himself on the railing. The short man said something quickly in Spanish and leaped forward to remove the Russian's hand from the wooden railing.

"He says," said Javier, "that you are too heavy to lean all of your weight. It will break and you will fall and die."

The short man said something else in Spanish and Javier nodded.

"He says a child died that way last month. The other side of the building. This railing is very old wood and no one repairs it."

"*Gracias,*" said Rostnikov, moving to lean against the wall next to a yellow glowing window.

"*De nada,*" said the short man, whom Javier introduced now as Hector Consequo.

"Señor Consequo does some work at the building where the Carerras live, the building in which Maria Fernandez was murdered. He was there on the night of the murder."

A young man stepped out of the shadows and stood in front of Rostnikov.

"This is Señor Consequo's oldest son, José. He will stay out here and let us know if there is trouble. His father is a very respected man in this block and there should be no problems, but times have been very hard."

They moved past the young man through a door and into a room in which a black woman of no clear age sat in an unsteady wicker chair cradling a girl of about three. In front of them on a rickety table sat a television set on which a movie with the American actor Tony Perkins was playing. The top and bottom of the screen were black and the image was faint and distorted. There was a small bench against one wall, a wooden chair, and a table whose top had been bolted down to a broad wooden base. A refrigerator, pre-Batista, stood against one wall. There was no other furniture.

What struck Rostnikov was not only the emptiness of the room but the lowness of the ceiling. Anyone more than six feet tall, like the young man who stood guard outside the door, would have to stoop.

"There is a room above this one," said Javier, seeing Rostnikov's eyes. "Hector and his son built it. They all sleep up there. They have to crawl into their beds."

Hector introduced his wife, who took Rostnikov's hand with limp resignation. The child looked at him and without knowing why, Rostnikov reached for her. She came willingly and put her head against his shoulder.

Hector motioned to the wooden chair and Rostnikov sat awkwardly.

"Señor Consequo is not a *Santería*," said Javier. "They, the police, the Carerras, they say he is but he is not one of us. We are there for him should he change his mind."

Hector looked at his wife, who handed him a lit cigarette, which he took and put to his lips. He inhaled deeply before speaking again.

"He says Castro gave him an education, a knowledge of the world, and hope he cannot fulfill. Castro also took his faith. He says he cannot believe."

Hector raised his hand again as if he were a schoolboy who needed permission.

On the television, at which Hector's wife continued to look, Tony Perkins was growing hysterical. Hector Consequo spoke again, quickly, passionately, his eyes moist.

"He says he wants to tell you something, that he must tell you something that you should tell others. Then he will tell you what you want to know."

Rostnikov nodded and felt the breath of the child against his neck. He could tell she was either sleeping or in the stage just before sleep.

Hector spoke again and Javier nodded his head.

"He says there is no opportunity here for Negro people. They cannot fish in the sea. They do not hold public office. They do not have enough to eat and they are not allowed to make a living."

Still speaking rapidly, Hector rose and opened his refrigerator. It was empty and he urged Javier to translate.

"We are allowed only a bit of chicken and barely enough milk for the children. And it was no better before you Russians abandoned us. Before Castro we were oppressed and knew nothing better existed. After Castro we were educated and given a dream which we know can never be achieved."

Hector interrupted and pointed around the room as he spoke even more rapidly.

"He says, can you believe that we are considered the most successful family in the neighborhood?"

"No zapatos," said Hector, holding up a finger of his right hand.

"No shoes," Javier translated.

"No vestidos."

"No clothes."

Hector rattled on, holding up finger after finger, his cigarette dangling from the corner of his mouth, his voice rising.

"He says that he is given nothing and allowed to earn nothing. He can fix anything, but if they catch him charging for repairs, he will be in trouble. The police come through here whenever they wish to be sure he does not have more food than his quota and that he is not doing work to which he has not been assigned."

"Basta," said Hector with a sigh.

"Enough," Javier translated.

With Javier continuing to translate, Tony Perkins growing more calm on the thin screen, the child sleeping in his arms, and his leg throbbing painfully, Rostnikov listened to Hector Consequo's statement about the night Maria Fernandez was murdered.

The possibility existed, though Rostnikov doubted Hector's dramatic skills, that the man was lying. The possibility also existed that Javier was not translating accurately, but that was highly unlikely since Javier could not have been sure how much of the Spanish Rostnikov understood.

According to Hector Consequo, on the night of the murder he was in the basement trying to repair a wire when he heard screams above and people on the stairs. He stepped into the stairwell. There were voices above him but he couldn't hear what they were saying. No one came down the stairs and went out. Then the police arrived and Hector went out through a door in the rear of the building. He returned the next morning when he was sure the police were gone. Among the things he did was go to the roof to reattach a wire. He had no idea there had been a murder. He thought it had been a family argument. To reattach the wire, he had strung it across to the next apartment building. Hector swore that there had been no painter's plank, no ladder, nothing on the roof of either building.

"*Yo estoy seguro,*" Hector said emphatically.

"He is sure," Javier translated. "You have any other questions?"

"No," said Rostnikov. "Tell him that I know he has risked a great deal to talk to me and I am very grateful."

Javier translated and Hector nodded and rose.

Rostnikov handed the father his limp, sleeping child. The little girl had left a warm, damp impression on Rostnikov's shoulder. He watched the child being handed to the mother, who rose to take her, and he forced himself up out of the chair. Hector shook hands solemnly with both men.

"Is it proper for me to give him some money for his help?" asked Rostnikov.

"He is a proud man," said Javier. "To offer him money would demean the chance he has taken in talking to you. You can give me money later and I'll send him two packages of American cigarettes. It is enough."

Javier led the way to the door and into the night where Hector's son José waited.

"And now?" asked Rostnikov.

"And now," said Javier, "we go to see the *babalau*."

"Your father?"

"My father."

Emil Karpo was fully awake and reaching for the lamp next to his bed before the phone actually rang. The initial surge of electricity had set off an almost silent click that had him awake and half seated as the first ring started. The phone was in his hand before the ring had ended.

"Yes," said Karpo, looking at the clock and confirming his intuition that it was nearly three in the morning.

"Do you know who I am?" came the voice.

"You identified yourself earlier as Igor Polynctsin," said Karpo.

"And?"

"And you are not Igor Polynetsin. There are three Igor Polynetsins in Moscow, or likely variations. You are none of them."

"It is a cold night." Yevgeny Odom shivered as he looked both ways down Sherikpskaya Street from the public phone. Half the streetlights were out and no one was in sight.

"This was anticipated by the meteorological service," said Karpo.

He was seated on his narrow cot with his bare feet touching the cold concrete floor. Karpo slept two ways, in a clean black pullover cotton shirt, short-sleeved or long-sleeved depending on the weather, and a pair of washable black slacks; or he slept nude. Until the last two years, Emil Karpo had always slept clothed and under a blanket even in the musky heat of Moscow summer. Since meeting Mathilde Verson, he had become intolerant of any covering at night.

"Karpo."

"Yes," said Emil Karpo.

"Don't you want to know how I got your home phone number?"

"No," answered Karpo. "There are many ways. It is not difficult."

Sudden panic filled Yevgeny Odom. The man was too calm. Was his phone monitored? Had he said something in his earlier call that made the detective suspicious? No, there was nothing, but he should hang up. He knew he should hang up. And yet . . .

"I know the one you call *Tahpor*," said Yevgeny. He pulled the collar of his coat around his neck as a gust of chill wind came off the river and whistled down the street like a searching ghost.

"Case 341," said Karpo.

Yevgeny Odom laughed, but as the laugh echoed down the street, chasing the ghost of the chill wind, he stopped suddenly.

"Do you believe me?" asked Odom.

"I neither believe nor disbelieve. If you wish me to believe, you may give me details of some of the crimes in Case File 341."

"I don't like being a number," said Yevgeny seriously.

"The decision to assign this crime a number is a matter of investigatory policy. It was not done to please or displease you."

"Details," said Odom, turning around and leaning against

the kiosk next to the phone stand. "So many. The girl on the embankment, July 2, 1990. She was bitten on the back of her neck. I selected her because she looked so ripe, so clean. But she was evil. I did it for him."

"For him?"

"For Kola," Yevgeny explained.

"For Kola?"

"I think Kola might be growing fur."

"Fur?"

"On his back. I may throw up."

"You said he was evil," said Karpo quickly.

"No. You misunderstood," said Yevgeny with a sigh. Perhaps he had made a mistake. Perhaps he had made contact with a dull-witted policeman with whom he could not talk. "I said *she* was evil."

"You said *she* was evil," Karpo corrected himself. "She was a clerk in a government butcher shop. What had she done that was evil?"

"She was not a clerk in a butcher shop," Odom said with a smile. "She was a prostitute posing as a student in need of money to help her finish her education. Her name was Anya Profft. All this is on my board."

"Your board?"

"Never mind," said Odom impatiently. "Do you believe me?"

"Yes," said Karpo. "So you and Kola killed the girl."

In the long pause Karpo could hear the ambient sounds of a street.

"Yes, I am guilty. But only of finding them. Kola . . . This is lonely business, Karpo. I have to be strong. I have no choice. No one asked me if I wanted to do this. He was there, waiting, growing, demanding. Do you have any idea what that is like, what it took from me to keep him contained for all these years?"

"Yes," said Karpo, and Odom believed that the man with the flat voice on the other end of the line really did understand. "You will have to go underground soon."

The pause was long.

"What do you mean?" asked Odom.

"Hide."

"Perhaps."

"If you do not, you will be caught."

"Why are you giving me advice?"

"I am not," said Karpo. "I'm pointing out that you are a man scheduled for a long dark ride. I think you have no choice but to take that ride even if it leads you to your death."

"Everyone dies, Karpo. Do you have a first name?"

"Yes."

Pause.

"What is it?"

"I would prefer not to have you use it," said Karpo.

"Are you mad, policeman? You are supposed to be friendly to me. Exchange first names, life stories. I've read the manuals. Septnekvikov's biography."

"Do you wish to turn yourself in?" asked Karpo.

"Turn myself . . . No. I wish . . . I wish to be understood. Not forgiven. I've done nothing to be forgiven for. Kola has killed forty-one people. See, I'm not afraid of the word, *killed*. I don't use cowardly euphemisms. I don't say 'eliminated' or 'removed' or 'did away with.' He meant to kill them. And I helped. Yes, I helped. And I helped well. You've never been close to finding us."

"We have been very close," Karpo said. "And we are very close now."

The chill of hell ran through Yevgeny Odom and within him Kola whimpered.

"You lie to me, policeman."

"I do not believe in lies," said Karpo. "You have lied."

"No."

"Where is Kola now?"

"Screaming for a victim."

"Where is he?" Emil repeated quite calmly.

"I quiet him by rocking from foot to foot," said Yevgeny. "I keep him caged inside me, but it is hard. If he is growing fur . . ." Yevgeny sobbed.

"You have killed forty, not forty-one," said Karpo.

"You didn't find one of them or you didn't give me credit. Perhaps you didn't recognize Kola's work."

"There is no Kola," Karpo said.

"Listen, Karpo. Before Kola returned to me, I was considering suicide. Russia is a nightmare now. It was a nightmare before. Only those who are awake and strong, who live by their wits and dine on the bones of the weak, can survive. I needed Kola and he needed me, but now he grows fur. Don't laugh at me or I'll hang up."

"I never laugh," said Karpo.

Yevgeny Odom knew from Karpo's voice that this was true.

"Why have you called me?" Karpo asked.

"Because, I told you, I'm having trouble controlling Kola."

The sound of his own voice made him look down the street to see if he had awakened anyone or drawn the attention of a roving police car. Moscow was accustomed to drunks and noise, he told himself, and then returned to the phone.

"Then come to us. I will meet you. We can take you to doctors who can remove Kola."

"You don't understand. I can't betray him. I am nothing without him. I know if you take him I will die."

"Why did you call?"

"So someone would understand," cried Yevgeny in near panic. "Oh God. Shh. Shh. He's awake again."

"Kola?"

"I will try to make him wait till tomorrow."

"We will be waiting."

"No," sobbed Yevgeny. "We will strike where we have never struck before, away from the moon and the sun. I think I may be going mad."

His voice was almost imperceptible.

Another pause.

"Well," said Odom. "Aren't you going to comfort me, put an invisible arm around my shoulder, urge me again to give my-self up to be treated, understood, cared for?"

"No."

"What kind of policeman are you?"

"You called me to confess. I am listening to your confession."

"What? I accidentally called a priest?" Odom asked derisively.

"I believe in no god or gods," said Karpo.

"What do you believe in?"

"Obeying the law and seeing to it that others obey the law. Without the law, there is no meaning. Without the law, there is you."

"He will kill again," Odom said. "And again."

"Until we catch you," said Karpo. "I can talk to you no more. I have work to do, work that is more important than you. I need rest."

"More impor— What is more important than what *Tahpor* has done?" Odom said in disbelief.

"You do not merit an answer. You are Case 341."

Yevgeny Odom hung up the phone and fell back against the kiosk. His hands were trembling. His cheeks were cold and he was truly afraid.

THIRTEEN

"**D**id you believe Hector?" asked Javier, looking back at Porfiry Petrovich as George drove them through the dark night.

"I believe," said Rostnikov.

"And?" asked Javier.

"I believe that he is telling the truth as he experienced it," said Rostnikov, looking out of the window. He was still clutching the bottle of rum George had given him. "I believe that the truth may have been altered so that he could experience it according to someone's plans."

"Yes, I see," said Javier, biting his lower lip. "You think maybe I killed Maria Fernandez or had someone do it for me and then got rid of the ladder when Hector came and then put it back after he left and . . ."

"It is unlikely," Rostnikov admitted.

There was silence for a minute or two before Rostnikov said, "At night your apartment buildings look like those of Moscow. For a moment, I had the sense that I was dreaming."

"The same people who built your apartments for Stalin came

over here and built ours," said Javier, glancing out the window at the massive gray high rises set back from the street down which they were bouncing over mounds of gravel and forgotten potholes.

"I did not kill her," Javier said.

The car clattered dreamily into a neighborhood of narrow streets and old two-story houses. The houses were dark, though here and there groups of men and women could be seen watching as the car passed. The people here were almost all black.

Rostnikov felt himself dozing as they drove into a neighborhood of one-story homes. By the light of the moon he could see that all of the houses were badly in need of repair and paint.

The car suddenly pulled over a low curb with a jolt that shot Rostnikov forward. His leg hit the seat in front of him, and his dreams went flying. The car stopped and Javier stepped out.

"Here," said George over his shoulder as he too stepped out of the car.

Rostnikov joined them and found himself in front of a one-story once-white house. The lawn was a stretch of gray dirt, and a light shone through the first window they approached. There were voices within the building, perhaps the hushed sound of music.

Holding the bottle of rum, Rostnikov followed Javier and George down a narrow stone path around the side of the house. In spite of the hour, two old women sat on tree stumps in the yard as the three men passed. They neither paused nor looked up from their conversation. To his right, through the open window of the first room, a young black man lay on a bed. He wore a pair of faded pants and no shirt. His body was lean and muscular and on his knees was a very small child in a dress trying to keep from laughing by pushing her tiny fist in her mouth.

The path curved around a thick-based, gnarled tree whose

roots had long ago lifted the stones on which Rostnikov walked.

"Here," said Javier. He opened a door and stood back so Rostnikov could enter.

The room he found himself in was not large, about the size of the living room–kitchen of his two-room apartment in Moscow. The floors were ancient red terrazzo and the walls faded white stucco. Low, unmatched wood benches ringed the room against the walls. A handsome, light-skinned woman, perhaps in her fifties, sat in a small wicker chair in a corner. She held a bowl on her lap in which she was mashing a mustard-colored paste with her fingers. She wore a colorful dress that reminded Rostnikov of Africa. She looked up at Rostnikov, smiled, and returned to her work. In the center of the room was a white, peeling wicker chair; on it sat the man Porfiry Petrovich recognized as the bass player at La Floridita.

The man had clearly not dressed to impress his visitor. He was wearing a pair of frayed blue denim pants and a sleeveless undershirt. From the corner of his mouth a seemingly lifeless cigarette drooped. The man, whose hair was cut short and was steely white, looked older than he had on the platform of the restaurant. He was barefoot.

Rostnikov stepped forward toward the seated man and handed him the bottle of rum, as he had been told to do by George. The *babalau* nodded almost imperceptibly as he watched Rostnikov's eyes. Javier stepped forward and took the bottle. A young woman, a beautiful light-skinned woman in an African-style dress of yellow and brown, her head turbaned, entered through a maroon drape in the far corner of the room. The rum bottle was passed to her and she exited quickly and gracefully.

The *babalau* said, *"Sientese, por favor."* He held out his right hand, palm up, toward the bench nearest the door through which Rostnikov had entered. Rostnikov sat, his left leg extended, and George sat next to him.

Javier went through the maroon drapes and the *babalau* began to speak in Spanish.

"He says," George translated, "you should consider moving to Cuba before the earth shakes and the men who have ruled for the blink of Chango's left eye are gone. After they are gone, it will be difficult for a Russian to move here."

"Why should I move to Cuba?" Rostnikov asked, and Manuel began to speak before George translated.

"He says your leg, your wife, and your children," George translated.

"I have only one child," Rostnikov said.

Manuel spoke again and George translated.

"You have two girls in your house."

"Yes," said Rostnikov.

Manuel spoke again.

"The *babalau* has many children. His wife has been fruitful."

The beautiful girl in the yellow-and-brown dress came back through the maroon curtain carrying a metal tray with two glasses and the bottle of rum Rostnikov had brought. The glasses were common kitchen glasses much like the ones in his hotel room in the El Presidente Hotel. They were filled with rum. The girl with the tray bowed before the *babalau*, who took one glass; then she moved to Rostnikov, who took the other. Both men drank deeply. Although Rostnikov was not particularly fond of rum, this was good rum and the setting felt appropriate for its thick amber strength.

The curtain parted and people filed in. Rostnikov was aware of girls in African dresses and turbans, and shirtless young men with lean powerful bodies, including the young man Rostnikov had seen through the window playing with the baby. Two of the young women were carrying babies. A boy and a girl of five or six came in holding hands and sat together near the curtain. Javier entered and stood behind his father's chair, his arms folded. He had changed his clothes and wore a loose-fitting red shirt. Finally, an ancient woman came through the curtain, her dress a mad rainbow of colors. The young people parted and the woman moved to a bench in the corner. The woman with the bowl had stopped mashing her mixture and was wiping her hands on a towel a girl had handed her.

The *babalau* spoke again, and George said, "These are his children and the wives and husbands of his married children and these are some of his grandchildren. Behind his wife is his mother, who has powers of the eye and mind."

Rostnikov watched as the ancient woman scooped up a child who had waddled across the floor into her arms.

"They are beautiful," said Rostnikov, holding up his glass of rum.

The *babalau* smiled and also held up his glass as George translated. Both men drank and Rostnikov understood this part of the ritual. If either man drank, the other was obliged to do the same. The bottle was still nearly full and there was no knowing how much longer the night would be.

The *babalau* spoke. George and most of the people in the room nodded.

"You have missed a god's day by one day," George said. "Yesterday was the feast of Santa Barbara, who is the shadow face of Chango, our god of war. You would have been welcome. Our religion has been secret for two hundred years because of the intolerance of the Catholic Spanish and the atheist Marxists. Only now can we begin to show our ways."

The *babalau* spoke and the congregation nodded.

"*Santería* is open to all who embrace its truth," George translated as Manuel held up his glass, and he and Rostnikov finished what was left. "White and black. A Catholic can be a *Santería;* even a Hindu or a Jew can be a *Santería*."

"Entonces casi la sua esposa," said the *babalau,* holding out his glass to be refilled.

Rostnikov too held out his glass for the young girl. He hoped they would offer him something to eat.

Manuel leaned toward Porfiry Petrovich and spoke again.

"Then even your wife could be a *Santería,"* George translated.

The two men drank yet again.

"Preguntele," said the *babalau.*

"You have questions," said George. "Ask."

"I have been told that *Santería* kill their enemies," said Rostnikov. He was aware that he had begun to perspire.

George translated without hesitation both Porfiry Petrovich's question and Manuel's answer.

"There are many *Santería,* many *babalau.* There are those who take the path of the shadow and those who take the path of the light. The *Abakua* secret societies are sometimes confused with the *Santería.* The *Abakua* have been known to practice violence. We do not tell the others how to live their tradition. There is no right or wrong in your sense but there are more than one hundred secrets a *babalau* passes on to the one who will succeed him. Our *babalau* will be succeeded by his oldest son, Javier, and he is being taught the secrets."

"And," said Rostnikov, trying not to look around at the crowd of smooth sculptured faces and firm bodies that surrounded him in the warm room, "what do you do when you are attacked? How do you protect your people? You have men watching the front of your house. They watch for something. When someone comes, what will they do? What will you do?"

"Find a way within the paths given to us by our gods through tree, shell, and dream," George translated the *babalau's* answer. "You have more questions."

"Did Javier or any of the *babalau's* family or congregation kill or participate in the killing of Maria Fernandez?" Rostnikov drank deeply from his second glass of rum and wondered if he could possibly stand.

"No," said the *babalau*, the cigarette bouncing in the corner of his mouth. Then he spoke very slowly, very softly, to the hum of his family.

"He says, you now know who killed this woman, but you must have the courage to face the truth. The *babalau* believes you have this courage."

"And if I do not?" asked Rostnikov.

The *babalau* shrugged and spoke, and George said, "We will survive and prosper. Now listen."

Manuel spoke again, slowly and clearly, and everyone around the room nodded as he spoke and as George translated.

"He says that the *Orishas,* the gods of our people, spoke clearly to all the *babalaus* and told of the fall of Fidel. When the white dove landed on Fidel's shoulder more than thirty years ago, the *Orishas* blessed him. Now there are new signs, and Fidel has severed the twins."

Manuel nodded his head and spoke quickly.

"The twins are sacred, *Jimaguas*. Fidel ordered one of the LaGuardia twins executed, one of his closest advisers. He ordered the death of the general with the sacred name, *Ochoa,* Eight-A. Now, when the gods have spoken, Fidel wants to make peace with the *Santería*. He fears betrayal and seeks the blessing of those who first give him power—the poor, the Black, the ones who had been slaves."

Before Rostnikov could ask another question the *babalau* nodded his head slightly. Three of the sinewy young men produced drums of various sizes, each drum draped with beads and shells on strings.

"These drums have been among us for thousands of years," George whispered. "It takes a lifetime to learn to play them so others can hear them. Listen."

The three men began to beat the drums gently, humming,

chanting. The *babalau* motioned to one of the young women. She was very young, very beautiful, and very shy. Manuel gestured to her again and smiled. Those around her urged her forward.

The *babalau* reached back and took the drum from the youngest of the three men. He put the drum in his lap, began tapping its head gently, and shook the drum once. The rattle of the beads and shells shivered through Rostnikov like the sound of half-remembered rain. He smelled his wife's hair, Sarah's hair, clearly, unmistakably.

The *babalau* handed the drum back to the young man, who nodded in understanding, and the music rose as the young girl who had been summoned danced and the policeman and the priest drank their rum.

All three drums were rattling, and the steady rumble of hide surged through Porfiry Petrovich. The girl turned, smiled, and glided to the music. For an instant, Rostnikov had the feeling that he was leaving his body. He was leaving his body and it was not frightening. The feeling passed and then the music stopped.

Rostnikov's eyes met those of Javier, whose look seemed to say, "Now, do you see, do you understand?"

"That was beautiful," said Rostnikov. The *babalau* raised his glass and they drank once more.

"What do you enjoy doing, Russian policeman?" a voice asked, and Rostnikov was sure the question had come in precise English from the *babalau* himself.

"I like to lift weights, fix plumbing, read books, be near my wife and son and the girls who live with us, do my job, feel that I can rely on those with whom I work, and strive to be there so they can rely on me."

"Look," said the *babalau*. Rostnikov, whose eyes were half shut, forced them open as a necklace of shells left the *babalau's* hand and clattered to the red floor.

The necklace was twisted like a dead snake, the shells facing both up and down.

Manuel leaned forward to look at the necklace and examine the shells.

"Your wife has suffered but the suffering ends. You should go home to Russia as soon as you can."

This time Rostnikov was sure Manuel was speaking to him in English. Rostnikov did not speak.

"Do you understand all that I say?"

"Enough," said Rostnikov. The roomful of people hummed with approval.

"One more thing the shells say. When you face a bearded man, be careful to hide your gods as we have hidden ours."

"That," said Rostnikov, "I do not understand."

"You will," said the *babalau*.

Rostnikov was not sure how he got to his feet, whether he had stood or been lifted. The next thing he knew he was standing outside next to the big gray tree that cracked the stone walkway to the *babalau*'s room.

"We are here because this tree is here," said Javier in English. "The mother of the *babalau* brought us to the giver of life. It is not buildings or monuments we worship, but the symbols of life we respect and draw strength from. We do not kill women for their bodies, for spite, for revenge. We do not kill. The son of a *babalau* who will himself be a *babalau* knows better than to let the animal that lives within us all out of the cage of our ribs. We do not ask you to believe as we do. We ask you to respect who we are. Our tradition will not fall when a government dies. Do you understand?"

Rostnikov reached out and touched the tree, partly to steady himself and partly to reassure himself that he was awake. The tree felt cool and reassuring in the heat of the night.

Then Rostnikov was in the back seat of the car.

"The sun will be up soon," said Javier.

Rostnikov tried to shake off the taste of rum and the sound of imagined rain. He had something to say, but before he could say it he was on an elevator, one arm around George, the other around someone he vaguely remembered as a desk clerk at the hotel.

Then he was in his bed. He was alone. As he looked at the stains on the ceiling, he sensed that the sun was coming gently through the closed blinds and that the ghost of Maria Fernandez, which haunted this room, was whispering something he could not quite understand.

Something the *babalau* had said made him feel that he should take some action, but he also felt that it was too late and would be far too difficult.

Porfiry Petrovich closed his eyes. There was an image of snow, the Moscow winter snow of his childhood, and the sound of his friends, Mikhail, Ilya, Feodor, calling across the park in a language he did not know.

Later he would rise. Later he would face the killer of Maria Fernandez. Later when the snow of his dreams melted in the hot morning sun of the island.

Two floors below the room in which Rostnikov was falling asleep, Elena Timofeyeva opened her eyes and turned to look at Sanchez, who was wide awake and staring at her.

"Good morning," he said in Russian.

"Good morning," Elena responded in Russian.

"I must go," he said, getting out of bed. "I didn't want to wake you."

Elena nodded and pulled the sheet up to cover her large breasts.

Sanchez, as her fingers had confirmed the night before, was covered with scars. His back was scarred, he had said, from beatings by a street gang. Other scars, on his legs, stomach,

neck, came from encounters with drunks, petty criminals, and a
pair of women who didn't like the fact that Sanchez had
stepped into their quarrel. He had told her all these things in
the night. He had observed after touching her that she was very
young, that the smoothness of her skin attested to her inexpe-
rience as a police officer.

Elena had accepted Sanchez's offer to drive her back to the
hotel so that she could cover for Rostnikov. At least that was
what she had told herself, and Sanchez, she was now sure, had
let her get away with the illusion that he was being taken in.

"He is probably in his room," she had said. "But I would
rather not wake him. He gets little sleep and when he does he
sleeps soundly."

"Perhaps the desk clerk can confirm that he returned," Sanchez had suggested.

"I doubt it," Elena had said. "He doesn't check the key."

"Still," Sanchez had said, as they parked in front of the hotel
and he stepped out.

"Does it really matter?" she asked.

"I am concerned for the safety of Chief Inspector Rostnikov.
He is under my protection. You are both under my protection. When I leave you at your door, I will have to make inqui-
ries, perhaps knock at his door. I have no choice."

It was then that Elena had decided. When they arrived at her
hotel room door she had stood for an instant, long enough to
encourage him to lean over and kiss her. His kiss was soft and
lingering, and his arms pulled her close to him. She had felt her
breasts against his chest, his excitement between her legs.

She had invited him in.

He had been prepared, an American condom in his pocket,
and he had been gentle and loving. Elena had told herself that
she was doing it to protect Rostnikov, but she knew that it was
also from her own desire, perhaps her own need.

There had been none of the self-absorbed frenzy of the two

Russians she had gone to bed with, and none of the false concern of the American she had slept with when she was a student in Boston. Sanchez was older than any of these and he made love slowly, enjoying her growing arousal and matching it to his own.

In the middle of the night, he had awakened her for more with a hand between her legs. Or perhaps, if she wished to be honest, she had aroused him by rubbing against him as he faced away from her in sleep.

Now, with the morning, he stood by the window, his body dark and strong, his face lined and handsome.

She watched him as he dressed.

"You have the best breasts I have ever seen or tasted," he said, smiling at her as he buttoned his shirt.

"Thank you," she said. "What will you tell your wife?"

"I had to work all night. I have to work many nights."

"I see," she said.

"We have hurt no one," he said. "And we have given pleasure to both of us. We have also satisfied a curiosity which would have caused us an agonizing sense of lost opportunity."

He finished tying his shoes and stood to look down at her.

"Elena Timofeyeva," he said, "I know where your chief inspector went last night."

She said nothing. She wondered if he saw her as she saw herself—a puffy-faced creature with dull straight hair and a flat look on her face.

"I doubt if we will be able to do this again without someone finding out," said Sanchez. "I would like to, but it would probably be best for both of us if it did not happen. We will see. If you choose, the pleasure of this night will be forever sealed within my memory."

"Very poetic for a revolutionary," she said, knowing her voice was a morning rasp and her accent in Spanish almost out of control.

"I am a well-read revolutionary," he said with a sigh, moving to the bed and leaning over to kiss her.

Elena wanted to reach for him, pull him back to her, feel him beside her and then inside her. She wanted to lose herself in this man she did not know and who was almost certainly lying to her, but she did not.

She returned his kiss and let the sheet slip from her breasts. He moved his mouth to one exposed breast, tasted her nipple with his lips, and quickly left the room.

Alone, Elena felt neither guilt nor love. The moment of lust had passed and she wanted to get up and stand in the shower as long as the hot water was willing to trickle out of the corroded, ancient nozzle.

She wondered if she would tell her aunt about this when she got back to Moscow and decided that she would not if she could possibly keep herself from doing it.

As she got up she understood the feeling she did not want to face. She did not want Rostnikov to know what had happened. She did not want him to know because Rostnikov's son, Iosef, was clearly in love with her and she felt that she might want to accept that love. If Rostnikov knew, even if he never spoke, it would be too much to bear. Her hope now was that Sanchez would be true to his vow of silence. It was a hope in which, as she stepped out of bed to the bright reality of this Havana morning, she had little faith.

The fifteen men the Gray Wolfhound had managed to pull from the Criminal Investigation Division and the Traffic Division were far fewer than Emil Karpo and Sasha Tkach needed. If Karpo was right, *Tahpor* would attack tonight in or near a Metro station.

Following his conversation with Yevgeny Odom, Karpo had dressed and walked the two miles to Petrovka. He had written

his report and turned it in to Colonel Snitkonoy with a copy to
Sasha Tkach.

The Wolfhound read the report while Karpo and Tkach
waited. Sasha sneezed twice during the wait. He apologized
both times, and blew his nose as discreetly as possible.

"Remarkable," the Wolfhound said finally. "I have managed
to free some people from other branches to help you for a few
nights, but . . . but you are confident?" Snitkonoy looked re-
splendent. He wore a neatly pressed uniform with almost all his
ribbons and several of the most impressive-looking medals.

"There is no certainty with a madman," said Karpo.

Sasha sneezed.

"You should be in bed," said the colonel.

"Tomorrow, sir," said Tkach, trying to stifle another sneeze.

"Well," said the Wolfhound with a sigh. "Proceed."

Sasha turned and took a step toward the door, but Karpo
stood his ground.

"The murder of the Kazakhstani foreign minister," said
Karpo.

The Wolfhound turned his back and strode to the window.

"It has been taken care of," he said. "The murderer was a
Kazakhstani Moslem, an extremist. He confessed and then
committed suicide."

"I see," said Karpo.

"I believe you do," said the Wolfhound. "I would appreciate
your passing on our thanks to the forensics laboratory."

"Paulinin," said Karpo.

Tkach stood by the door, his hand on the knob.

"Emil," he said as the Wolfhound turned. Karpo had not
moved. "Let's go."

"You are dismissed, Deputy Inspector," the Wolfhound said
evenly.

"Emil," Tkach whispered again, and this time Karpo turned

without another word and followed Sasha Tkach into the outer office, closing the door gently behind him.

"We won't get more men," Tkach said as they sat in a canteen eating greasy vegetable pies and drinking tepid tea. "The Wolfhound is not going to get us any more help."

Karpo took a bite of his pie, and nodded. People at the other plastic tables did their best to pretend that the man who looked like a vampire was in no way worthy of their attention. They tried, but they failed or left quickly.

"All the more reason we must keep our appointment in Izmailovo Park," said Karpo.

FOURTEEN

Rostnikov blinked his eyes at the sunlit window, checked his watch, rolled toward the battered table next to the bed, and picked up the telephone.

"*Quarenta y cinco,*" he said.

"*Qué quiere?*" the hotel operator answered.

"*Quarenta y cinco,*" he repeated slowly.

"*No entiendo,*" said the operator.

Rostnikov repeated the number in Russian and English and then a voice came on, a man's voice, which said, "*Quarenta y cinco.*"

"*Ah, bueno,*" said the operator.

"Thank you," Rostnikov said to the man who must have been monitoring his phone.

The man didn't answer, but Elena did on the third ring.

"Elena Timofeyeva, are you dressed?"

"I am dressed," she said.

"We meet in the lobby in twenty minutes."

"Twenty minutes," she said.

There was something in her voice that he had never heard before, at least never heard in her. It puzzled him.

"Are you well, Elena Timofeyeva?"

"Yes," she said.

"Are you not going to ask where we are going?"

"Where are we going?"

"To see Major Sanchez about what happened last night," he explained.

"Last night?" she asked, clearly straining to sound normal.

"Twenty minutes, Elena. You have time for a cold shower."

He hung up the phone and went into the bathroom. He reached over to turn the hot water on and straightened to examine himself in the mirror.

The face was in need of a shave. The face was in need of sleep. The face was in need of the slap of cold Moscow winter. Cuba was fine for his leg but it was a narcotic against which he had to constantly struggle. The *babalau* had told him to leave as soon as he could and that was what he pledged to the flat-faced Russian face in the mirror. For an instant, as the steam began to cloud the mirror, Porfiry Petrovich had the impression that his image was grinning.

He moved away from the mirror and considered calling Elena back and telling her to meet him in an hour. He wanted to sink into the heat of the bath and read about some men who had killed Carella's father. But a call would require him to deal with the operator. He shook his head no and climbed carefully into the bath.

"The Washtub is in Cuba?" asked Anatoli Xeromen. He sat on a park bench looking up at two policemen.

Anatoli had chosen the location for their meeting. On the weekends, Izmailovo Park, five times the size of New York's

Central Park, was the site of a massive market, hundreds of vendors trading goods for rubles and hard currency, goods that had only been dealt with underground a year ago. Caviar, hubcaps, army uniforms, dirty books, automobile parts. The Capones roamed the park on weekends picking up protection money, selling what they had stolen.

Now, though it was not the weekend, Anatoli sat where people would be sure to see him and the two huge bodyguards behind him, young men wearing sunglasses in spite of the overcast day and cold air, one with blue hair, the other with black-black hair. Anatoli himself wore jeans and a pullover long-sleeved soccer shirt of red and green that had the word "Italy" embossed on it in white letters.

Babushkas with strollers, old men carrying sacks and chess boxes, bundled children running for the playground or home passed behind them on the path. Karpo and Tkach had their backs to the path but Anatoli watched the passing parade as he carried on the conversation. Occasionally he would smile as if something seemed amusing.

"He is in Cuba," Karpo confirmed. "We are authorized in his name to ask your assistance."

"To do what?"

"Help us catch the man who killed Iliana Ivanovna," said Karpo.

"Her name was Yellow Angel," Anatoli said.

"Yellow Angel," Karpo conceded.

Tkach sniffled, wiped his nose, and sneezed.

"What has he got?" Anatoli asked, pointing at Tkach. "If he has something, I want him to stay away from me. AIDS, something like that."

It had been reported but not confirmed that Anatoli required that all Capones be periodically tested for AIDS. It had also been reported that anyone found to have the virus would be expelled from the gang. It had also been reported that a carrier who concealed his disease was actually beaten to death and thrown in the Moscow River.

"I have a cold," said Sasha. "A cold. That's all."

"Because if you have . . ." Anatoli began.

"It's a damn cold," Sasha shouted, taking a step toward the bench.

Anatoli didn't move. His bodyguards reached back to where, both Karpo and Tkach were sure, they had weapons in their belts.

Karpo held up his right hand and motioned for Tkach to step back. Tkach wiped his nose again, pocketed the rumpled handkerchief, and stepped back reluctantly.

"I don't like sick people," said Anatoli. "We've got our own doctor. I don't like sick people."

"The person who killed Yellow Angel is sick," said Karpo.

"I didn't like him even when I thought he wasn't sick," said Anatoli. "What do you want?"

Karpo told him.

"And what do I get for this?"

"The killer of the girl is caught. Your people are safe from him."

"And," said Anatoli, "your bosses owe me. You owe me."

"No," said Karpo emphatically. "We owe you nothing. My superiors will not even be told of your assistance."

Anatoli laughed and looked back at his two bodyguards. They did not laugh.

It struck Tkach that the strutting little animal before them was imitating someone, a movie star or a television actor, but the imitation was so bad that he couldn't tell who it was.

"You could have lied to me," Anatoli said to Karpo.

"No, I could not," replied Karpo.

"All right," said Anatoli. "You're honest with me. I'm honest with you. We do this and you owe us. Maybe one favor. Maybe two."

"None," said Karpo.

It was Sasha's turn to smile at Anatoli, who met his eyes with hatred. These two policemen were fools. They should have known better than to turn him down in front of his bodyguards. Anatoli had a reputation. The problem was that he wanted to get *Tahpor*. He wanted to have the man in front of him begging for his life. He wanted to kill him before a gathering of Capones.

"We'll do it," he said. "What do you need and when?"

Karpo outlined his plan and was greeted with nods of approval.

"Then we are agreed," said Karpo.

"We'll use two-way radios," said Anatoli.

"We do not have radios which can be assigned to you," Karpo said.

"We have our own," said Anatoli with a smile. "And ours are better than yours. Japanese."

"No two-way radios," said Karpo. "He would notice. I expect him to check very carefully before he acts. I want him led to Sasha Tkach and only to Sasha Tkach."

Anatoli nodded.

"We use telephones," he agreed. "Your number?"

Karpo stepped forward and handed Anatoli a card on which he had written the number of the Metro station phone where he would be stationed. Anatoli glanced at the card and put it in his shirt pocket.

"We'll lead him to your friend," said Anatoli. He rose and looked at Tkach. "It's our duty as good citizens."

He suddenly leaped over the bench and walked between the two bodyguards, who kept their eyes on Karpo and Tkach as they backed away. When the trio had disappeared into the bushes, Tkach said, "Now we make deals with killers. One killer becomes better than the other. Then we find another better killer to kill this one."

Karpo nodded and walked past Tkach to the path. There
was no denying what Tkach had said, but Karpo believed that
what they had just done was no different from what Colonel
Snitkonoy had done the day before. The colonel had made a
pact with the killers of the foreign minister of an allied
country.

Expediency, he thought.

Tkach, his voice weak with congestion, repeated, "Expediency?"

Karpo had been unaware that he had spoken aloud. The
revelation troubled him.

"Now we justify ourselves by saying we can deal with murderers because it is expedient?" rasped Tkach.

"It appears so," said Karpo. As they walked, people parted in
front of them to avoid the gaunt specter and the obviously ill
young man.

"We have four hours. I'm taking you to see a doctor."

Tkach grew suddenly angry, but he also felt something rattle
in his chest and a surge of bile rise to his mouth. He said nothing more and followed Karpo toward the long night.

Porfiry Petrovich and Elena Timofeyeva ate a late breakfast in
the main-floor restaurant of the El Presidente. The breakfast
consisted of oranges, warm rolls, something that tasted like
butter, almost black coffee, and silence. They were the only cus-
tomers. Others had eaten and departed long ago. On a few
white-tableclothed tables rested dirty plates and crumbs.

Rostnikov told her about his encounters of the night before
and then asked her for her report. She shook her head as if to
clear away annoying hair and then told him. Her account ended
with the statement that she had been driven back to the hotel
and had gone to bed.

"If you do not mind, Inspector," she said when it was clear

that they were finished, "I'd like to remain here and prepare my notes."

Rostnikov, who had partly risen from his chair, looked at her. She made an effort to meet his eyes.

"I may need you, Elena Timofeyeva," he said. "I don't want anyone speaking Spanish in front of me today, at least not speaking it in the belief that I do not understand through you."

"Yes," she said.

"Elena, is there something you wish to tell me?"

"No, why?"

He shrugged and said nothing. Together they walked out of the restaurant and into the lobby. There among others were the haggard KGB shadow and the little journalist Antonio Rodriguez.

Rostnikov guided Elena to the door as the little man with the thick glasses leaped forward to intercept them.

"What happened to you?" the man said as Rostnikov continued to the door and opened it. "I mean last night."

"Nothing," said Rostnikov. "I drank too much."

"Yes, yes," said the man, "but there is much you should know about. I told you I would help you."

They were out on the stone deck in front of the hotel now and the man continued to buzz around them.

"You need a ride? My car is right there, see? Not much, the Packard, but it runs. I'll take you anywhere."

"One condition," said Rostnikov.

"Yes?" asked the little man eagerly.

"You do not speak. Inspector Timofeyeva is suffering a malady from her experiences last night."

"But," he said, "she seemed well when Major Sanchez took her back to the hotel. Maybe it was too much vodka."

"The condition," Rostnikov said.

"As you wish," the man said. He looked at Elena with something that might have been concern. "I'll be silent."

And he was silent as he drove them to the police station where Major Sanchez could be seen looking out at them from his office window.

"Thank you," said Rostnikov, holding the door open for Elena Timofeyeva, who looked decidedly pale.

"I'll wait," said Rodriguez.

"I don't think that will be necessary," said Rostnikov. "I'm sure the major will see to it that we are driven back to the hotel."

"But," the little man said, moving close to Rostnikov, "there are things I want to show you."

"Another time, perhaps," said Rostnikov, walking toward the station.

Though his leg continued to feel better, Rostnikov did not move swiftly, but Elena Timofeyeva was moving even more slowly. Then, decisively, she moved forward ahead of him and held the door open as he joined her.

When they entered Major Sanchez's office, he greeted them with an offer of coffee, which both Rostnikov and Elena accepted.

Sanchez was wearing a neatly pressed uniform. He smiled, pointed to open seats in front of his desk, and said, "And now, Inspector Rostnikov?"

"We close the case." The moment Rostnikov spoke a familiar pain shot through his leg.

"Close it? How?" asked Sanchez, looking at the two Russians expectantly.

"The *Santería*, of course," said Rostnikov. "Shemenkov and Maria Fernandez made the mistake of offending an important *Santería*. He had Maria murdered and made it look as if Shemenkov did it. And the woman in prison, Victoria Oliveras, they bribed or threatened her."

"All very simple," said Sanchez with a shake of his head. "A word here, a conclusion there, and your Russian is innocent."

"We have gathered evidence and depositions," said Rost-nikov.

"And you are both satisfied that this is the case? You have enough evidence to clear your countryman?"

"We are satisfied," said Rostnikov before Elena could answer.

"And you expect us to simply let your Russian free on your statement?" Sanchez asked.

"Inspector Timofeyeva will prepare a report," Rostnikov said. "The report will be sent to you from Moscow. Evidence at the house of the Carerras, scratches, a ladder, all this should help to convince you."

Sanchez held up both hands and said, "I am not convinced, but I will need the report. I will also need to reexamine the murder site. It is possible our investigators were a little less than zealous in their efforts because a Russian was accused. I'll admit, just in this room, of course, that some members of this department might have been a bit too willing to think the worst of a Russian. But those are small possibilities. If your report is confirmed, and I doubt that it will be, Shemenkov will be freed when my superiors are convinced of his innocence. I assume you will now be returning to Moscow."

"As quickly as possible," said Rostnikov. "I would prefer to complete my report in Moscow."

"As you wish. You have been difficult but in many ways I shall miss you." Sanchez looked at Elena, who looked at Rost-nikov.

"You have no more questions?" asked Rostnikov.

"At the moment, none," said Sanchez. "Should I?"

Rostnikov shrugged.

"Well," said Sanchez, "we await the report of your investigation and its conclusions."

Rostnikov grunted.

"If there is anything . . ." Sanchez began.

"I would like to see Igor Shemenkov before we go," said Rostnikov.

"Of course," said Sanchez. He put down his coffee and picked up the phone.

"Shemenkov aquí immediamente," he said, and hung up.

"Thank you," said Rostnikov. "And if you don't mind, I would like to see him alone."

Sanchez rose, bowed his head slightly, and moved to the door.

"Perhaps Inspector Timofeyeva would like to step outside with me and continue our interesting conversation of this morning. I mean last night."

"No," said Elena. She glanced at Rostnikov, who was occupied with the darkness of the liquid in his coffee cup.

Sanchez shrugged and left the room, closing the door behind him.

Rostnikov avoided looking at Elena, though he was sure her eyes were now moist. The door opened and Igor Shemenkov lumbered in.

The door closed behind him and he stood there looking at his two fellow Russians. There was hope in his sunken eyes. He had shaved badly; he had cut himself just below the nose.

"We will file a report from Moscow," said Rostnikov. "The report will provide evidence and reasonable speculation that you are innocent of the murder of Maria Fernandez. Major Sanchez has said that he believes the evidence will not be accepted. We shall see. Meanwhile, you will remain in the custody of the Cuban police."

"I will be free?" Shemenkov said, looking first at Rostnikov and then at Elena.

"If the Cuban government is convinced by our evidence," said Rostnikov. "And I believe they have reason to be convinced."

Shemenkov looked stunned, but a broad smile came to his face. He moved heavily forward with arms open, perhaps to embrace Rostnikov with gratitude, but before Shemenkov could reach them, Rostnikov slapped the Russian twice. As Shemenkov staggered backward, Rostnikov took Elena Timofeyeva by the arm and led her out of the office and toward the street.

FIFTEEN

"I want that one," the man said, pointing at Yevgeny Odom.

He was talking to a thin woman with wild prematurely gray hair and the pinched face of one whose suffering is greater than your own. The woman wore a worn but clean white smock and a determined attitude as she tried to guide the old man into a chair across the room.

Yevgeny did not look up from the fat girl from whom he was drawing two vials of blood. The fat girl looked up at him in gratitude.

"They say he doesn't hurt," said the old man as he reluctantly sat down in the wooden chair to which the gray-haired woman had guided him.

Once in the chair, the old man dutifully removed his hat and looked up at the woman who was preparing her vial and needle.

"Look," said the old man, "the girl is smiling."

"It's her birthday," said the pinched-face woman. "Hold out your arm. Make a fist."

"What has her birthday got to—"

He stopped as the needle went into a bulging vein in his forearm.

"Let's see. Is it bleeding?" Yevgeny asked, examining the fat girl's arm as he removed the needle. "No. Go. You are free."

And the girl wobbled through the open door to her waiting mother in the other room.

Yevgeny stood up and turned to face the old man and the woman who was drawing his blood.

"I'm going," Yevgeny said. "I'm due at work in twenty minutes."

The old man grimaced as the needle was withdrawn.

"My arm will be black. Look, it's bleeding," the old man complained.

"You will survive," said the woman. She put the hypodermic carefully on a towel.

The old man rose, looked at Yevgeny, and left the room.

"How many more out there?" Yevgeny asked, removing his white smock.

"He was the last," she said. She turned to Yevgeny and folded her arms. "You look tired."

"I did not sleep well last night," Yevgeny admitted.

"You work too hard. The Metro, here. May I ask you something?"

"No," he said, rolling down his sleeves and buttoning his shirt.

"Why do you do it?" she asked, reaching into her pocket for a package of cigarettes.

"Do . . . ?"

"Work so hard," she said. "You live alone. You have only yourself to support. But you're always running. It's a killing pace."

Yevgeny removed the Metro motorman's jacket from the peg behind the door and put it on. The woman lit her cigarette and watched him.

"I'm a restless person," he said. "It is a combination of my genes and the hell of life in Moscow. I run to stay ahead of the two-headed monsters who pursue me. I run so I can find a place I can hide and then leap upon the back of the monster and ride him till he breaks."

"And then what happens?" the woman said with a smirk.

"Well, then," said Yevgeny, adjusting his Metro line cap, "I become the monster."

"Odom," she said, inhaling deeply, "I think you may be a little bit mad."

"In a city of madness, with whom do you compare me to make such a judgment?" he asked.

"You're going to kill yourself at this pace."

"I think there is a good chance that you are right." He headed for the door. "I think there is a good chance that I will die this very night."

"In Moscow, that is always possible," she said, looking around the room, deciding that there was much to clean up before she could head home, wondering if her husband was out drunk or had actually spent time in some food line so that there might be something for her to eat at home besides stale bread and pasty tasteless yogurt.

He left her standing in the middle of the room, whose alcohol odor always remained with Yevgeny for hours after he left the clinic. He wondered for the first time if he smelled of alcohol and whether those he found for Kola thought perhaps that he was drunk.

He moved slowly through the halls of the clinic. The place was almost empty.

In the small lobby of peeling linoleum a woman had set up a table to sell small baked biscuits. Now she was packing up what she had not been able to sell.

"Wait," said Yevgeny. "What have you left?"

The dry, sagging woman turned with the pain of an arthritic, a pain Yevgeny's own mother had suffered as long as he could remember.

"Three left," the woman said. "Twenty rubles."

He dug in his pocket for the money and handed it to her. She took the money and looked at him as she reached into her cloth sack.

"They are a little dry," she said.

"That doesn't matter," said Yevgeny.

"And," she said, handing the small biscuits to him in her knotted hand, "they may have lost some of their taste. Flour is—"

"It doesn't matter," said Yevgeny. "It will fill my stomach. The sky is dark early tonight. Go carefully and be safe."

Yevgeny ate the first biscuit in two bites as he stepped onto the street. The night was heavy and the air moist. He breathed deeply and considered the possibility of returning to the clinic, letting Kola murder both the biscuit seller and Lana, who thought her pain was so great. He had to clasp the nails of his left hand into his fisted palm to keep from trembling at the release it would give him to let Kola bring them to their knees and then tear their self-pitying faces.

A pair of young lovers, both with long hair and wearing identical black jackets, watched him as he forced the molecules of his body to stop vibrating. He imagined himself breaking up into molecules—not exploding but simply breaking up and joining with the air and the bricks of buildings.

He walked along briskly past the Peking Hotel and across the intersection toward the Metro station.

"Soon," he said. He was unaware that he had spoken aloud, and unaware that a well-dressed man carrying a newspaper under his arm had heard him and automatically cut around him and down the stairs, a maneuver most Muscovites had perfected over years of encounters with an increasingly mad population that talked frequently to invisible gods and demons.

Yevgeny checked his watch and hurried down the steps, past a pair of begging Gypsies—mother and sleeping child—to whom he handed the last of his biscuits. The woman accepted the food, looked at the hurrying man in uniform, and crossed herself over the sleeping child.

A pair of boys, one with green hair and the other with scarlet, jostled past him, taking the steps down two, three at a time.

Yevgeny Odom followed them into the hole of the earth, toward the sounds of roaring metal beasts that swallowed the wailing somnambulists of Moscow's living dead.

Sasha Tkach was riding the Metro and trying not to blow his nose. He pretended to read a book about welding and watched passengers come and go. From time to time at a station, he would get off, find the phone, check with Karpo, and resume his aimless riding.

A peddler of viruses and promises, he thought. He thought of Pulcharia, blowing her nose with the help of Lydia, who muttered about the way children had been cared for better when she was a young mother.

Sasha smiled.

There was little to do and much time to think. Other Metro engineers had been lulled by the routine; some had been known to fall asleep, others to write poetry. At least four that Yevgeny Odom knew of had gone mad, overridden the controls, and sent their trains smashing into waiting trains in stations ahead of them.

Stop. Ease forward. Switch. Open. Roar. Sway. Hush. Lulling lights. Burst. Ease. Doors open.

It took Yevgeny five stops to notice the pairs and trios of young people with wild rainbows of hair. They were roaming the stations, riding the trains, laughing, looking while trying not to look. There were always some of these in the Metro. More all the time. It was not their number that Yevgeny noticed but how evenly dispersed they seemed to be. They were, in fact, at every station, VDNKh, Rizhskaya, Prospekt Mira, Kolkhoznaya.

It was something to think about while he searched for Kola's prey. Was this some new game? A mass robbery of passengers at a given time? The passenger load was light at this hour. What could they be up to? Could it be a bizarre coincidence? Were they all heading for some site where a ritual would take place?

He thought of other things too. When he ended his shift, he would ride, blending in among the neon and the sleepy, one of many late-night uniforms, until he spotted a lone victim lounging, waiting, just getting off of a train at an empty station.

After the first hour, he could not deny the presence of this army of pale, rainbow-haired, animal youths.

Halfway through his shift, Yevgeny Odom developed a theory, perhaps a fantasy. They were looking for him. Somehow, Karpo, the policeman with the flat voice, had wormed into his brain, torn open his plan with his teeth, and enlisted an army of the damned that now lay in wait for him. No, it could not be. The police had their own armies.

Something else struck Yevgeny as the train pulled out. Where were the Metro police—the nonuniformed men who dealt with thieves, muggers, and pickpockets? He knew them all by sight and had seen none tonight.

Yevgeny Odom decided that he would not change his plans. Kola might have to kill more quickly than in the past, but he would do what he had planned. It was the only way to quiet Kola.

Then, suddenly, he saw one of those Kola had killed, pack on his back, hair in his eyes, slouching. The young man looked miserable. He sneezed, blew his nose with a much-used hand-kerchief, and got on the train.

Process. Sound of doors sliding closed. Computer silent. Lurch. Forward into tunnel semidarkness.

Yevgeny was sure Kola had killed this one recently. But when? A few days ago? Last week? A year? He needed his notes, his board, to be sure. They all looked somewhat alike, that was true, all the young men, all the young women. He had been careful to seek out variety, but he knew now that he had also chosen the same. He knew that he had always known.

The collar of his uniform was tight. Its frayed edges prickled the rough edges of the hair at the back of his neck.

It was not the young man Kola had killed. This one looked a little older, more solid, angrier.

A choked voice within Yevgeny wanted to tell him who his victims had been, but he wouldn't hear it.

"I want to tell you," the voice said to the soothing rhythm of metal wheels against metal track. "I want to tell you."

He could not escape the melody. "I want to tell you."

He recited a poem he had memorized as a child. He remembered his mother prompting, his sister smirking.

When a forest of night hid shadows of our heroes
standing alone as the enemy advanced . . .

"I want to tell you," the singsong voice insisted playfully like a small child.

The spirit of those who had fallen laid hands
upon their brows and shielded them from fear.

A station. An orange-haired boy. A blue-and-white-haired girl. They got on.

Doors closed.

"I want to tell you."

And as they stepped from shadow into moonlight
To stand armed with Lenin's courage and Stalin's power,
the enemy grew pale . . .

"I want to tell you. It is you, you, you, you, you."

the enemy grew pale . . .

"I want to tell you. It is you you hate and kill. You. You as boy.
You as girl. You alone."

the enemy grew pale . . .

"You."
    "No," said Yevgeny as the train pulled into the next stop.
"No." He spoke to the distorted image of a tall, pale man in
black, a vampire from nightmares and childhood memories who
looked at him and looked away. "No."

> the enemy grew pale knowing they could but slay men and
> not the Revolution which would rise in many bodies, with
> many faces till each pale enemy was crushed to dust and
> forgotten.

Anatoli Xeromen sat on a bench next to one of the red marble
columns on the Mayakovskaya platform. His eyes rose and examined the cartoon mosaics or scanned the arriving and departing passengers. He sat patiently as reports were brought to
him by his sunglassed soldiers, though his stomach strangled
with the wish to act. After two hours he considered ordering
the Capones to rob everyone they could see and then head back

to the Gray Blocks. Anatoli had a Moscow apartment with a bath, a CD player, a television, and a VCR with movies about rich Americans, monsters from space, gangsters with ancient guns, and his own secret favorites, the sad ones with Barbara Stanwyck, Joan Crawford, and Bette Davis that made him weep. But he would go home to the Gray Blocks if there was no action today.

Anatoli hated the subway, though he told no one. He hated the deep feeling of the damp grave. He feared that some lunatic's bomb would send millions of pounds of rock and dirt down on him, burying him forever.

But he waited and he was calm. He had his reputation. Sooner or later one of the Capones, possibly Dmitri, or Leonid, or Lev, would step forward and dare to ask how long they were going to keep it up. Anatoli knew just how he would smile and wave his hand to show that he could wait a week, a month, forever, that no one who had ever lived had the patience of Anatoli Xeromen.

But that moment never came. After four hours had passed a girl hurried toward him like one who had urgent news.

As soon as Yevgeny had finished his shift, he checked out with the night duty officer and got back on the Green line carrying his night bag.

There were very few people on the train, and he stayed as far from them as he could until fortune offered him his prey. He had seen the victim earlier—an angry lost lover, a wandering student, or possibly even a police decoy sent to trap him.

The enemy grew pale, he thought, and when a dozing woman looked up at him he knew that once again he had spoken aloud.

He watched the victim take out a handkerchief. He was willing to take a chance tonight to still Kola and to laugh at the policeman named Karpo. He would call him tomorrow and taunt him, but now, now . . .

Inside his night pack were a folded pair of socks, a book, and a short, black, very heavy hammer with a flat, shiny head and a sharpened claw.

The train stopped. The woman who had looked at Yevgeny got off without looking at him. Then his prey rose and stepped to the door. No one else got up. The victim looked around, then got out. There was no one on the platform. Yevgeny hurried off the train. He was twenty feet behind his prey.

The rush of air and the grinding of the departing train covered Yevgeny's first ten feet.

Ten feet more.

Each pale enemy was crushed to dust and forgotten, he recited, looking up through the past at the beaming reflection of his mother in the mirror.

His hand went into the bag. His fingers circled the handle. He looked around. No one. Even if the victim turned, there would be no reason to fear a uniformed Metro man.

He had to decide quickly. Claw or hammer. Claw or hammer. Kola roared. Yevgeny could not control him. The pale enemy heard or sensed someone behind and began to turn. The claw, Kola decided, and he struck.

"Pack," said Rostnikov, "and meet me back here in the lobby. Twenty minutes. I'll arrange for the flight to Moscow."

They had found a taxi waiting in front of the station when they came out. Elena doubted it was a coincidence. Rostnikov had gotten in and looked out the window. Elena had given the driver the name of the hotel.

Rostnikov had not spoken and she had not been willing to speak. At one point, when they passed a block of stained ancient buildings, Rostnikov had muttered something. She thought he said "Atlantis," but she was not sure.

Only when they had reached the hotel and gotten out of the taxi did he speak and that was only to tell her to pack. When she got to her room, the bed had been made and her bag had been packed for her.

She did not want to look at the bed or wait in the room. She was back in the lobby five minutes after Porfiry Petrovich had left her. She stood, too nervous to sit, and watched the thin KGB agent, who sat in the middle of a sofa near the bar, looking at her and her bag.

Ten minutes later Rostnikov emerged from the elevator carrying his bag. His limp was more pronounced now than it had been since they had arrived in Havana. Elena wanted to ask about his pain, about why he had slapped Shemenkov, about why they were hurrying, possibly even about Sanchez. She wanted to know and she wanted to confess at the same time, but Rostnikov's face was distant.

"Your bag was packed?" he asked.

She nodded.

"Mine too. Get a cab. I've arranged for a flight."

Elena nodded and headed for the door, her bag in hand. She looked back to see Rostnikov, who had dropped his suitcase, walking directly toward the KGB agent.

Elena found a cab, told the driver to open his trunk, and waited for Rostnikov. She got in the cab and then got out again. On the curb across the street a child with short dark hair played with a tiny black-and-white dog that looked seriously ill.

The dogs of Moscow still looked cared for. Elena wondered how long it would be before they looked like the dogs of Havana.

Rostnikov came out of the hotel. Without looking around he came down the steps, dropped his suitcase in the open trunk of the taxi, and joined Elena in the back seat.

"Tell him to hurry," he said, and Elena did so.

The driver nodded, looked over his shoulder, and backed into the street, where he almost collided with a rusted green Chevrolet. Then he made a right turn on the Avenue of the Presidents and headed for the airport.

"Inspector," Elena began.

"There is an Aeroflot flight in one hour," Rostnikov said as they passed a park where men and women were building colorful wooden booths.

"I . . ." she said, but he held up a hand.

"On the plane," he said.

Elena sat back wishing she had used the bathroom at the hotel.

She was jolted forward suddenly; her head hit the roof of the cab. She almost toppled over the front seat but was pulled back by a powerful grip.

Elena brushed the hair from her face, looked out the windshield of the cab, and saw a large, black car directly in front of them. A similar car was beside them, pressing the taxi to the curb.

The taxi driver looked back at his passengers, closed his eyes, and crossed himself.

Elena looked at Rostnikov.

"Are you all right?" he said.

Men were getting out of the two cars that had them trapped. Rostnikov did not seem to notice.

"Yes," she said.

"Good," he said. He touched her arm and whispered, "Do your best not to show them you are frightened. Can you do that?"

"Yes," she said.

"Good," said Rostnikov, opening his door.

Elena slid across the seat and followed him out. On the sidewalk, people hurried away, not wanting to see what would happen next.

There were five large men, all wearing suits. None of them carried a weapon. As the men advanced, Rostnikov went to meet them, Elena at his side.

One of the men came over to take Elena's arm. Rostnikov reached across her and removed the man's hand.

"Tell them we will cause no trouble," Rostnikov said in Russian.

Elena was afraid her voice would crack, but before she could speak, one of the men spoke in Russian.

"We do not expect any trouble. That car."

The man pointed to the second car and Elena and Rostnikov walked to it and entered the darkness of the back seat.

SIXTEEN

Anatoli was up before Ginka reached him. There had been a mistake, she reported breathlessly. Teddi at the Arabatskaya Station had gone to the toilet. When he came back to his position, he had found . . .

"Phone," he said. "Tell the others. Everyone to Arabatskaya."

Arabatskaya Station was on one of the six lines of the Metro system that crossed each other at the center of Moscow. A circle line, the Koltsevaya, circled the intersecting lines. Arabatskaya was on the red line not far from the center of Moscow.

Again. Again. Again. Again. Anatoli thought. He could wait for a train or take the car parked above. He was at Kirovskaya, four stops away on the red line. The train might be faster but he could not wait. He ran to the end of the station and up the escalator, shouting words that echoed back to those who followed him with fear but without question.

Karpo had received the call from a boy who did not identify himself.

"Arabatskaya Station," the boy had said as a train pulled in. "A mistake. Another dead."

Karpo was two stops from Arabatskaya on the Studencheskaya platform. He dropped the phone and got through the doors as they were closing. As the train pulled out, he stood rigid, next to the door, willing himself not to imagine. Imagination had never come easily to Emil Karpo and he did not welcome it now.

He focused on a small screw on the door before him. The only other passengers on the car, three men in work clothes, stopped talking.

When the train pulled into Arabatskaya, Karpo got off and looked down the platform at a small crowd gathered in a rough circle. As he hurried forward he could see that three of the people were Capones. One person was a Metro motorman. There was a great deal of blood on the platform, and just beyond the gathering was something he recognized. Sasha Tkach's bag, lying on its side, open, a book half out.

"Shit," cried a girl.

Karpo pushed his way past the uniformed motorman and looked down at Sasha Tkach.

Tkach was on one knee, trying to find life in the body whose dress made it clear it was a girl but whose head was a bloody meaningless mass.

A girl wept. A boy with pink hair wailed.

"Sasha," said Karpo.

Tkach, covered in blood, looked up and shook his head.

"Witnesses," asked Karpo, looking around the crowd.

A woman, three Capones, the motorman. All looked blank and frightened.

All shook their heads.

"No one came up the stairs," said a boy. "I had to take a

leak, but it was quick. No one came up. I think I heard her, but . . . I don't know." The boy shrugged. "Anatoli will kill me," he said.

Karpo turned to the Metro man.

"Did you see . . . ?"

Then, after five years and now forty-two deaths, it was over.

"Nothing," said the Metro man. "I got off the train with these people and—"

He stopped.

Karpo was looking at him unblinking. He was certain he recognized the voice.

"Your bag," Karpo said. "Hand it to me."

"My bag?"

Sasha was at Karpo's side now, and the woman who was standing next to Odom began to move away. The boy, anxious to redeem himself, stepped toward Yevgeny Odom with a shout and slipped in the blood of the murdered girl. He fell backward as Yevgeny, bag in hand, leaped down onto the track and began running.

"Call ahead, next station," said Karpo. "Tell them to be ready."

Karpo ran to the edge of the platform and jumped down.

"What if a train . . . ?" Sasha called, but Karpo had already plunged into the darkness beyond the edge of the station.

Ahead of him, Karpo could hear the running footsteps of Yevgeny Odom, but Karpo did not run. In the dim guide lights of the tunnel he could see a shape moving away with nowhere to go.

From somewhere distant, the grinding of a train touched Karpo's senses. Behind him, on the platform of the station he had just left, there was a new rush of voices, noise, curses.

Karpo stopped. He was breathing heavily.

"There is no place to go," he said, and his voice echoed through the tunnel, repeating "Go. Go."

"We've called ahead to the next station. They'll be waiting for you."

The footsteps raced on for a dozen yards. The dim figure swayed and then stopped.

As Karpo moved toward the figure he thought he heard a new presence behind him in the tunnel.

"Walk toward me," Karpo called out. "Hold your hands up."

"You will kill me, Karpo. I know you will kill me."

The man did not sound frightened, though he was breathing heavily.

"I will not kill you," Karpo said.

"Maybe, maybe not. I have to think."

"There is no time."

"No time," came the voice from the darkness. "I've done what I had to do. If I didn't help Kola, he would have torn through my chest. You understand?"

"There is no time," Karpo repeated, still moving forward slowly.

"It's always been like that. Don't you see? Always. You should understand. I could tell it in your voice. You're like me. You have a Kola inside you."

"I am nothing like you," said Karpo, whose head suddenly went mad with the explosion of a migraine. Always he had warning. Always he had an hour, or at least minutes.

The beating in his head had never come like this. Karpo's eyes closed with the pain. He was twenty yards from the man now and—yes, maybe it was the sudden headache—the figure before him was a mirror image.

"We must leave," said Karpo. "We must find a safe place before a train comes."

"There is no place safe on earth, or in heaven or hell," said Odom. "And there is no heaven or hell. Perhaps there is not even an earth."

Karpo was within a few yards of the man now.

"Hands out," he said softly. "Turn and hurry to the next station."

The black outline ahead shook its head and stepped toward Karpo. It was only when Odom stepped into the partial glow of a tunnel light that Karpo could see the hammer in his hand, bloody claw up.

"You and I will be the last," said Odom.

Karpo reached back for his weapon, disconcerted by his pounding head. He had his gun in hand and halfway up when he knew that there would not be enough time. He might shoot the man but the hammer would still descend. This was faster than thought. The creature over him in the motorman's uniform was not the man he had followed into the tunnel. This was a wide-eyed caricature moving like a wolf.

Then the shot clattered, followed by another and another, and the hammer did come down, missing Karpo and clanging to the track. Karpo backed against the cool tunnel wall and watched the Metro man's body convulse and roll back. More shots and the body danced in a dim glow. The noise tore through Karpo's head but the detective had his gun up now. He turned and aimed it down the tunnel.

"Stop," he called.

One more defiant shot tore into the dead Yevgeny Odom.

Karpo blinked. Anatoli Xeromen walked forward, an AK-47 in his hand.

"Hand me the weapon," Karpo said. Anatoli threw the gun down as he stepped past Karpo and advanced on the body.

"We've got to leave the tunnel," said Karpo. "I can hear a train."

Anatoli kicked the dead man in the face.

"You hear me?" asked Karpo.

"I hear," Anatoli said. "There's no hurry. One of my gang will stop the train when it gets to the station. He has a gun even bigger than the Ah-Kay."

Karpo picked up the weapon and moved to the body. He was in no condition to move the dead man by himself, and he doubted if he could get Anatoli Xeromen's help.

"Let's go," said Karpo, moving down the track.

"I'll be a hero, you know," said the young man.

"You had an illegal weapon," said Karpo.

"And you are going to turn me in?"

They were walking side by side, their own voices coming back at them.

Karpo didn't answer.

"We're partners," said Anatoli. "Partners and heroes."

Partners echoed through the tunnel.

Heroes echoed through the tunnel.

Emil Karpo heard them and heard them and felt the pain.

The house to which Porfiry Petrovich Rostnikov and Elena Timofeyeva were taken was large. It looked like someone's dream of Old Spain.

It was on a hill between two other houses from the same dream.

The two cars had parked before the house. Three of the men who had taken them stepped out and flanked them as they moved forward to be greeted by two more men and a woman. Just inside the doorway, in a cool anteroom, both Rostnikov and Elena were thoroughly searched.

"This way," said the man who spoke Russian.

They followed him through a door in front of which stood a pair of men in fatigue uniforms. Both men had automatic weapons held at the ready.

"The lady will come with me," said the man.

Elena looked at Rostnikov, who nodded. The door opened. The door closed and Rostnikov was alone in a bright room filled with familiar-looking heavy Russian furniture.

"The previous owner was a Russian general," came a voice in English from across the room near a window.

The window was draped, and Rostnikov could now see the outline of a figure.

"He departed, like so many of you, leaving behind promises and trash to be picked up by the real revolutionaries."

The man who stepped out from behind the curtains held his hands behind his back. He had a full-flowing curly gray beard, and wore a perfectly pressed and slightly faded fatigue uniform.

"Sit," said Fidel Castro. "You have a war wound. Sit."

Castro moved to an overstuffed chair and sat, his hands resting on both arms. There was a similar seat across from him. Rostnikov took it, and Castro immediately stood again and began pacing the room.

"You do not seem surprised to see me," said Castro, his eyes turning suddenly on Rostnikov.

"It was a good entrance," said Rostnikov. "But the fanfare was too loud for it to be anyone but you."

Castro nodded, fidgeted with a large ring on his right hand, and cocked his head to one side like a curious bird trying to decide whether the creature in front of it was edible. Then he paced again, pausing to straighten a picture here, move a vase there.

"Would you like coffee?" he asked.

"I would like to catch a plane to Moscow," Porfiry Petrovich answered.

"One question honestly answered and you may leave," said Castro, stepping quickly in front of Rostnikov and leaning forward as he rubbed his palms together.

"You are the host," said Rostnikov.

"Why are you in such a hurry to leave Cuba?"

"I think you know," said Rostnikov.

Castro nodded and scratched his right ear nervously.

"Yes. Yes. Yes. I know, but let us play a game. Humor me.

There are those who believe I have lost my mind, so treat me like a dangerous madman. I'm beginning to think a man who displays the hostility you are showing me may also be considered a madman by some. So, one madman to another . . ."

Rostnikov hesitated for a moment and then said, "Igor Shemenkov murdered Maria Fernandez. I was brought in to find witnesses and clues that would convince me that he was innocent. I was to discover a *Santería* murder. This would spread fear of the *Santería*. It would also clear Igor Shemenkov and permit him to return to Russia."

Castro played with the curls at the bottom of his beard.

"Who would want that?" he asked.

"I can but guess," said Rostnikov.

Castro folded his arms across his chest and waited.

"He was an agent for your people working in the embassy," said Rostnikov. "He gave you codes, messages. His conviction as a murderer might result in embarrassing things coming to light. As a man exonerated of a crime he did not commit, he can go back to Russia and continue to work for you knowing that if he does not, he will face exposure as a spy. I would guess that there are still friends of Cuba in the Kremlin who were more than willing to go along with your request that a Russian investigator be sent to Havana, an investigator who would discover that Shemenkov was framed by the *Santería*."

"Close," said Castro, sitting in front of Rostnikov and drumming his hands on his knees. "Usually, I do not trouble myself personally with such situations, you understand. But I was informed of what you had done. Why did you hit him? You could have left without our thinking you knew anything."

"I could not stop myself," said Rostnikov. "Igor Shemenkov is a traitor, a murderer, and probably many other things."

"You are always like this?" asked Castro, leaning forward.

"No," said Rostnikov with a sigh. "Usually, I look for a way to survive and do as much of my duty as I can. Maybe I'm not accustomed to tropical weather."

Castro nodded and rubbed his eyes.

"But treason and murder were more than you could stand," said Castro almost to himself.

Rostnikov did not answer.

"What am I to do with you, Russian? You and your assistant could have an accident. I can threaten you, tell you that I can have you killed any time, anywhere, even in Moscow. But you've heard such threats before."

"I have already passed the information on," said Rostnikov.

"Povlevich? The KGB agent?" asked Castro. "We are helping him defect to Colombia. He was cheap. Russians are cheap, Rostnikov."

"Not all," said Porfiry Petrovich. He wanted to rise now because his leg pain had returned, but he did not want to appear defiant.

"And not all Cubans. We were very expensive." Castro laughed. "Billions. Billions. And what did we give you in return? Medical services, useless missile bases, vows of friendship. We used you."

"And now it is over," said Rostnikov.

"Perhaps not. We will survive," said Castro, standing erect, his voice rising as he spoke. "We will survive or die in the streets before we give in to capitalism. Socialism or Death. *Resista. Resista. Resista.* Socialism or Death."

"Perhaps they are the same thing," said Rostnikov.

Castro shook his head and examined Rostnikov.

"You are mad," said Castro.

"I am tired. Perhaps I am also mad."

"Can you be bought, Russian?"

Rostnikov said nothing.

"No," said Castro. "You can't be bought. You can't be persuaded. You can be killed. Anyone can be killed. I see in your eyes what you are thinking. You hide it well but yes, I can be killed too. Many have tried, many, but they are the ones who have died. What will be the outcome of this situation, Russian?"

Rostnikov had to stand. He struggled out of his chair and steadied himself.

"I will return to Moscow and give a full report to my superior."

"Colonel Snitkonoy," said Castro. "Yes."

"A full report confirming the guilt of Igor Shemenkov. The colonel will bring it to the council. The council will consider and then decide to file my report quietly in a drawer. To do otherwise would mean another confrontation with you. You would deny it. We would look like bullies trying to give reasons for separating from what many believe is your inevitable downfall. And Shemenkov will remain here, useless to you."

"There are other scenarios," said Castro.

"I prefer not to consider them."

"One only then," said Castro. "Shemenkov is freed. Our police are convinced by your arguments. Shemenkov returns to Russia believing that he has adequate cover. And then, perhaps, he has an accident."

"Given the information in my report, such an accident might well be expected."

"Then we understand each other," said Castro, stroking his beard.

Now Castro rose, folded his hands, and swayed on his heels.

"Go," he said, looking at his large Russian watch. "I have more important things. You'll be taken to the airport."

Rostnikov said nothing as he walked carefully to the door. Then he took a deep breath and turned.

"One more thing," he said. "The *Santería* are not to be accused of the crime."

Castro nodded.

"It was a poor plan, Russian. Between us and no one else I

tell you. The *Santería* will not be accused. There are too many torn edges in this situation. It is best to be done with them and rid of your Shemenkov."

"*Gracias,*" said Rostnikov.

"*De nada*. It is dangerous to have too many secrets," said Castro. "Sometimes it is the only thing that can keep you alive. Still, it is dangerous. Secrets come to light and are misunderstood. I am too busy now to worry about how I will be viewed by history. I will leave it to journalists and scholars to distort and misjudge what I have done. We have not met."

"We have not met," said Rostnikov.

Castro took a step toward Porfiry Petrovich and looked into his eyes.

"I believe you," he said.

Fidel Castro turned his back, and Porfiry Petrovich Rostnikov went into the hall. He was led back to the street and into the waiting car where Elena was waiting. Someone closed the door behind him and the car took off smoothly.

"What . . . ?" Elena began.

"An official asking a few questions," said Rostnikov. "We are leaving Cuba."

The flight back was not comfortable. Rostnikov sat on the aisle. Elena sat next to him, also on the aisle. The seat belts didn't work properly. The food was some Danish cookies and small ham sandwiches on hard rolls. The coffee was fine. Rostnikov slept briefly, waking in time to coax his leg back to life. Elena both slept and pretended to sleep. When she was awake, she worked on her report. The flight was late and conversation nonexistent until they were a few hundred miles from Moscow.

"Elena Timofeyeva," Rostnikov said, "I require a shave. I will attempt one in the washroom. If I fail to return in ten minutes, you will know I have cut my throat. Please tell them in Moscow that it was an accident, not suicide."

Elena nodded dutifully.

"It was a joke," Rostnikov said.

"Yes, I know."

"You did well," Rostnikov said.

Elena tried a smile.

"We leave Havana behind us," he said. "I would prefer to speak no further of it or those we met outside of our official report. And please, put in the report only what is essential for those in Moscow. Confessions are for the holy in the corners of churches."

"Yes," she said.

He patted her shoulder.

"Good," he said. "I think Iosef will be very happy to see you. Perhaps you can come to dinner tomorrow night."

"I would like that," she said as he made his way swayingly down the aisle toward the toilet.

A little over two hours later, Porfiry Petrovich Rostnikov made his way up the stairs of his apartment building dragging his leg and suitcase behind him. It was late and Sarah would be sleeping, but he would have to wake her because the door was bolted from within.

He put the suitcase down and knocked gently. He was preparing to knock even louder when the bolt slid and the door opened.

She stood there in her robe, lights on behind her.

"I'm home," he said, and took her in his arms, determined not to weep.

ABOUT THE AUTHOR

STUART M. KAMINSKY is the author of the acclaimed Inspector Rostnikov, Toby Peters, and Abe Lieberman mystery series. His previous Rostnikov novels include *Black Knight in Red Square, Death of a Dissident, A Fine Red Rain*, and the Edgar Award–winning *A Cold Red Sunrise*. His Lieberman novels are *Lieberman's Folly, Lieberman's Choice,* and *Lieberman's Day.* Stuart Kaminsky lives in Sarasota, Florida.